CONSTANCE

A Story of Early Plymouth
by Patricia Clapp

The girl standing on the swaying deck of the *Mayflower* in
November 1620 could not share her father's enthusiasm for
the life ahead. Fourteen years old, intelligent, and outspoken,
Constance Hopkins does not hide her apprehension about
what is to come.

In a journal given to her by her stepmother, she records
her observations and feelings from the first dreadful winter
when sickness kills half of the settlers to the time of her marriage
at twenty. Constance relates the important events as well as
the petty details of daily living—her fear and growing understanding of Indians, her first flirtation, her care of younger
brothers and sisters, and her changing relationship with her
stepmother. Like any girl in any age, she worries about her
appearance and a lack of pretty clothes. She confides her many
questions about love and marriage.

Ships from England bring new settlers and news of the
impossible demands of the people who financed the *Mayflower*
venture. Two men seek to undermine the colony's unity, and
many of the Indians do not seem as friendly as they did at first.
But through the years of hardship the settlement of Plymouth
continues to expand until it is self-sufficient and confident
of its future.

CONSTANCE
A Story of Early Plymouth

by Patricia Clapp

Puffin Books

PUFFIN BOOKS
Published by the Penguin Group
Viking Penguin Inc., 40 West 23rd Street, New York, New York 10010, U.S.A.
Penguin Books Ltd, 27 Wrights Lane, London W8 5TZ England
Penguin Books Australia Ltd, Ringwood, Victoria, Australia
Penguin Books Canada Ltd, 2801 John Street, Markham, Ontario, Canada L3R 1B4
Penguin Books (N.Z.) Ltd, 182-190 Wairau Road, Auckland 10, New Zealand

Penguin Books Ltd, Registered Offices: Harmondsworth, Middlesex, England

First published by Lothrop, Lee & Shepard Co. 1968
Published in Puffin Books 1986
10 9 8 7 6 5 4
Copyright © Patricia Clapp, 1968
All rights reserved

Map reprinted from *Pilgrim Times*, a publication of
Plimoth Plantation, Plymouth, Massachusetts

Library of Congress Cataloging in Publication Data
Clapp, Patricia.   Constance.
Summary: A young girl's diary reflects life in Plymouth colony.
[1. Pilgrims (New Plymouth Colony)—Fiction.   2. Massachusetts—History
—New Plymouth, 1620–1691—Fiction]   I. Title.
PZ7.C5294Cn   1986   [Fic]   85-43127   ISBN 0-14-032030-X

Printed in U.S.A.
By R. R. Donnelley & Sons Company, Harrisonburg, Virginia

For those special descendants of Constance Hopkins,
my family

Author's Note

Except for one, all of the people in this story existed just as you find them here. The exception is Minnetuxet, who slipped in quietly and refused to leave.

P. C.

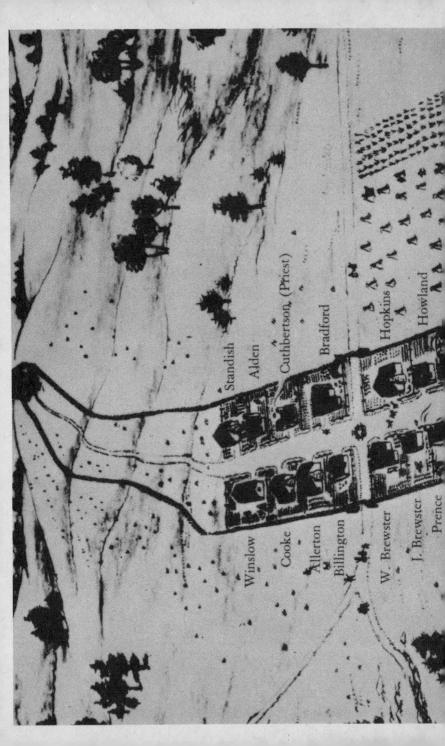

Standish
Alden
Cuthbertson, (Priest)
Bradford
Hopkins
Howland

Winslow
Cooke
Allerton
Billington
W. Brewster
J. Brewster
Prence

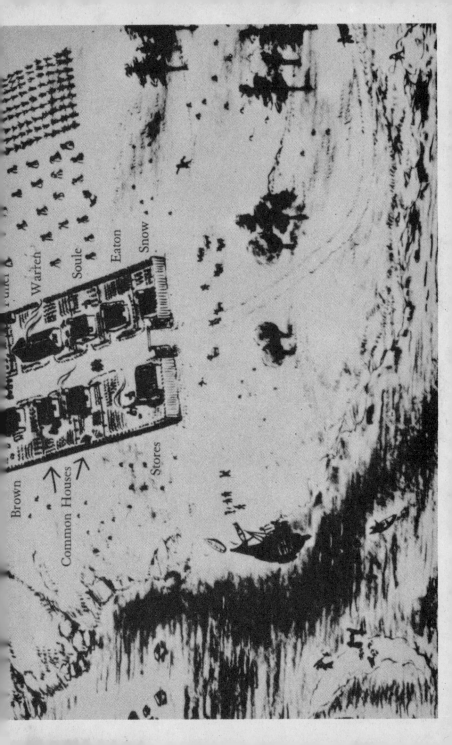

Brown

Common Houses

Stores

Warren

Soule

Eaton

Snow

November 9, 1620

Very well then! I have seen that cold, gray, hard, bleak, unfriendly shore line that everyone is in such a twitch of excitement about. Father hung over the wooden rail gazing at it, his eyes snapping with excitement.

"Come and see, Constance," he roared. " 'Tis America! Come and see it!"

He pushed aside to make room for me, and as I moved close to the railing it seemed a marvel that with so many people leaning there the dreadful little ship did not capsize. With a wide gesture he indicated the line of pale gray sand and scrubby little gray-green trees—all looking like gray ghosts under the gray sky.

"Pish!" I said.

Father glared down at me. "What did you expect, girl? Tropical palms? A city of golden domes and palaces? Use your head, ninny! This is a wilderness! An empty land! We can make of it what we will!"

"Then let us make London of it," I said.

Father looked as though he would like to box my ears, a thing he has not done since Mother died—how long ago? Seven years? It seems like forever, and yet there are times when deep in my memory I can hear her voice singing little rhyming songs to me, or feel her hands tying my bonnet strings beneath my chin. Giles says he hardly remembers her at all, but he was only six. I was eight, and it makes a difference.

"Blast London!" Father exploded. "A tight, cramped, crowded city, filled with underhandedness, bigotry, and the stench of filthy sewage!"

"It could smell no worse than this ship," I said, "and *I* liked it. London is home!"

"London *was* home. No longer. And good riddance, say I! An honest man cannot make a penny in London, only thieves prosper!"

"And how do you propose to make a penny here?" I asked. "And what will you do with a penny if you make one? I see no great array of shops awaiting us."

Father opened his mouth, partially hidden now by the blond beard he has grown since there has been little water to waste in shaving—nor for washing, either, and how we all stink!—and I thought he was about to bellow at me again. I would not have blamed him really, for I know how vexing I can be, and yet I could not hold back the sharp words lest I weep with misery. Because Father and I are much alike, he seems sometimes to know these things, so that now, instead of shouting with impatience, he put one arm roughly across my shoulders and pulled me hard against him.

"I know 'tis all strange, Con," he said, "and mayhap a little frightening. But there is a life here for anyone strong enough to make it. There is land for the taking now, land that will make us rich one day. There is freedom, there is *space!*"

"There must be places in England where there is space, too."

"Mayhap. But this is adventure, girl! Women don't understand that a man needs adventure in his life. To live out one's short span and never *dare* anything . . . I am not like that." He looked down at me and added, "And nor, I think, are you, Con."

"I was content."

"Content! A cabbage is content! Is that what you want to be? A cabbage?"

"I want to be at home in our house in London," I said stubbornly. "I have no wish to be starved to death in this bare place, and eaten by wild animals, and killed by savages—"

" 'Tis unlikely that you will die more than once, and therefore you will escape at least two of those fates. And let me remind you that if the savages can live here, so can we."

"Perhaps you can. Not I. I hate America and I shall always hate it! And at the first opportunity I shall go back to England!" I slipped out from under Father's arm and moved away from him, just as I heard Will Bradford's voice.

"Stephen! Stephen Hopkins! May we speak with you?"

With a glowering look at me Father joined Will and Captain Standish where they stood staring with shining eyes at that ugly hateful coast, and I saw his face light up with the excitement that has filled him all through this hideous voyage. Feeling that I must get away or burst into ridiculous childish tears, I scrambled down the ladder, putting yet another rent in the hem of my gown with my clumsy heel, which only made me smolder the more. Now here I sit, wrapped in my cloak and still shivering, an odd great lump in my gullet, and my eyes stinging with tears!

At least I am alone, for everyone else is gathered on deck. Being alone is a great privilege now. There is rarely a corner of the ship unoccupied, whether it be day or night, and there are times when I feel that I must be by myself for a bit or else become a fit case for Bedlam. I think that perhaps Elizabeth knew that when she gave me this journal and my own quill.

Elizabeth can be very surprising. Although she seems as great-eyed and quiet and slow as a cow, she often understands things that Father does not. For example, she has never urged me to call her Mother, though I know that Father wishes I would. I call her Ma'am generally, but I always think of her as Elizabeth. Giles calls her Mother, and of course 'Maris does, but she *is* 'Maris' mother. And now she is Oceanus' mother, too. What a tiny thing he is! And pale, as Damaris is pale. They look like little goblins, with their huge brown eyes like Elizabeth's.

I wish my eyes were brown; people with brown eyes have always looked more intelligent to me. But instead mine are such a deep blue they are nigh black, I think, and when my hair is clean it is very light, so that hair and eyes seem not to belong to each other. Also my neck is very long and I am far too tall and thin, and although Elizabeth says I will fill out, there will have to be a deal of filling out before I look like aught but a pikestaff. At home I used to look sometimes into the round, polished silver disk that was my own mother's mirror, hoping that by some magic I would wake one day to find a beauty reflected there. Father caught me at it once and roared that he had enough to worry him without preening simpletons in the family, and he thanked God I was plain, since beauty brought nothing but trouble. Elizabeth said very quietly she feared he had thanked God for a peace of mind he would never get, because I was not going to stay plain. How pleasant if she should prove to be correct!

In all events, the little mirror was left behind when we sailed on the "Mayflower," and perchance it is just as well, though I miss it sorely. There has been enough unhappiness on the voyage without the constant reminder that I am but a gawky, moon-eyed wench. With danger, and sickness, and dirt, and hunger—all suffered just so we might reach this dismal America—I needed no other woes.

There has been death, too. First the loudmouthed sailor who took delight in calling us "glib-gabbety puke-stockings" and other names I cannot repeat, and whose death was made more horrible by his shouting and raving profanity, and then —later—poor Will Butten. It was the night Will died that Elizabeth gave me this journal. She found me weeping here in the cabin, and though I feared she would chide me for such weakness, she simply sat beside me and held my hand. She was still weak and tired from having had Oceanus, and I felt like a great booby behaving as I was, but I could not stop.

"It is not that I knew Will so well," I gasped, "but he was so young! Just a little older than I!"

"I know," Elizabeth said, in her soft cow-voice.

"And now he is down there at the bottom of all that dreadful ocean—" My voice did ridiculous things, squeaking and breaking like a bawling babe's. "—and the fishes—"

Elizabeth leaned over the side of the bed and opened the little box she has kept with her ever since we sailed. The cabin is so small that everything is close within reach, and an arm outstretched from the bed can nigh touch either wall. From the box she brought out this book, folded in a brown Holland sheet. She unwrapped it and laid it on my lap, and then used a corner of the sheet to wipe my eyes as though I were no older than Damaris.

"Constance, there are many times when a woman needs someone to talk to, and I hope you will remember I am always here to listen. But there are other times when a woman has thoughts she cannot share with anyone, and yet she must needs rid herself of them, if only to see them more clearly. Perhaps this is one of those times. I brought this journal—it seemed that one of us should keep some account of this . . . this strange adventure. Your father never will,"—she smiled a little—"I doubt he could sit still long enough. My thoughts are not worth the writing, and besides, I can always croon them to the babes, who think they are lullabies. The journal is yours, Constant. May be it will help you."

I have written nothing in the book till now, except on the first page, simply because it was so clean and white and seemed crying for the touch of a quill. There I wrote "Constance Hopkins, Her Book," and underneath I put "1620." It looks very neat, and rather important. Somehow there seemed nothing left to write about poor Will Butten, perhaps because I had said it all to Elizabeth. And since then, though I have held the book often, and smoothed the pages, and looked at that first page that makes it truly mine, I have written nothing more until today.

It is very strange, this being anchored offshore, rather as though we were nowhere at all. Everyone says the voyage is over, for which God be thanked! But where are we? We still must live on this stench-filled, rolling "Mayflower" until those men who already seem to be the leaders—and of course Father is one of them, he could not bear it if he were not—make some decision as to which part of this cold, gray, deadly land will be our home. Home! Oh, London, I miss you!

I want to feel civilized cobbles under my feet, and look out of the diamond-paned window in my little bedroom, and hear the mongers crying their wares. I want to push through the crowds in Petticoat Lane to buy a bit of lace or ribbon, and watch a London wedding—the shy bride and proud groom going into the church, followed by parents and friends and families. I always thought that someday I would be married in the same way, but these psalm-singing folk from Leyden believe that marriage is a civil thing, with no need for churching to make it proper.

If I stay in this fearsome land—and if ever I marry—'tis most likely that old Governor Carver will mumble some few words over me and that will be the end of it. And what matter, after all, since whom would I marry? Gangling John Cooke, no older than I and prone to spots? Handsome John Alden, with eyes for no one but Priscilla Mullins, even though that pallid minx Desire Minter follows him step by step about the ship? Edward Dotey or Edward Leister, Father's two bondsmen, who plague me and tease me and vow they will swoon for love of me? Hardly likely! Father says there will be a stream of ships bringing new settlers. It may be. But it seems to me that any who come here of their own free will are addled in the head, and not such as I would choose for a mate.

Just before we sailed Father gave me a bauble, a pretty bracelet, narrow and gold and with a delicate chasing of ivy round it. "To remember London by," he said.

It rests lightly now on my dirty wrist, and I shall keep it by me always. But even without it, I can never forget London!

November 11, 1620

'Tis two days later, a Monday night, and much has happened. While I was writing last seems all the men in the party gathered together to form a written compact, agreeing on John Carver as our Governor (one of their formalities, since it had in truth been so for some time), and upon a method of government. When that was done a few of them went ashore, and certainly Father was among them. They saw little, and since night was closing in, stayed but a short time. All yesterday, it being the Sabbath, the Leydeners prayed. What a praying lot they are! Father insists we join them for most of their interminable churching, and he roars out the hymns and prayers in a voice that surely can be heard halfway to heaven, casting up his eyes and trying to look holy. He says 'twill do us no harm, and might do much good to follow this group in everything, and I cannot say he is wrong, though I find his saintly attitude most comical.

Today, however, things were somewhat more to my liking. Most of the women gathered together their bundles of dirty clothes and linens, and with much squealing trepidation we clambered down the wavering ladder into the little open shallop and were rowed ashore. Even crowded into the small boat as we were, it took several trips to deliver us all onto the beach, since the children must needs come too, of course, but once there we had a most satisfying surge of laundering in fresh, clear water, cold enough to turn my hands to ice. The sun had come out and there was no wind, and the scrubbing made me so comfortably warm (for the first time in weeks) that, in spite of horrified cautioning from all the women, I washed my hair. What true pleasure it was to sit in the sun, feeling it warm on my cold head, and watching the loose strands of hair shine as they have not for months.

The men had the shallop on shore and had started repairing her so they can sail up and down the coast a bit, searching for the best spot in which to settle, though to me there seems little difference. While they were scraping and hammering—in truth a pleasant sound on a sunny afternoon—and the women draped every shrub and rock and patch of clean sand with their drying clothes, the children found clams and mussels and oysters which we all ate until some were sick from a surfeit of rich food, and of course Giles was one, the glutton! But still the day was a good relief from the crowded, rolling "Mayflower," and I do hope 'twill soon be repeated.

Dorothy Bradford did not come ashore with us, and I know it puzzled Will. She sits by the hour in that dreadful dark, putrid room on the ship, staring straight ahead of her, saying little. I talked with her a bit that day we dropped the anchor and some of the men, her Will and my father among them, came ashore.

"I hope Will is happy now," she said. "He has waited long for this moment—to put his feet on a land he could call free."

Her eyes are as gray as the coastline looks from the "May-flower." Very few people have truly gray eyes.

"You do not share his joy?" I asked.

"I feel nothing, except, perhaps, a small pleasure that he, at least, is content." Her mouth is small and barely moves when she shapes the words, as though speaking were too much an effort for her.

"You miss your son," I said—I don't know why. But Mistress Bradford shook her head a little.

"No, not even that any more. At first I did—for nights I wept, trying not to let Will hear me. But I realize now I shall never see Johnny again. I no longer weep."

"But surely he will join you here—when you have a house, a place to care for him."

"Do you think so?" she asked. "I do not. I have kissed my son for the last time."

"You must not think such things! You *must* not, Mistress Bradford!" I said. "We must all *hope!* I have heard your husband say so."

"Aye, my husband's life is built on hope. But not mine."

"He loves you very much," I ventured. "Many of the women remark on it. They wish their husbands were as gentle and kind."

"Oh, yes, Will loves me. I do not question that. But Will loves many things, Constance. His God, and the freedom in which to worship him; this new land—yes, already he loves it, though he knows it not at all, nor what it may make of him. Will loves his son too, but he could leave him behind."

There was nothing I could say to that. Yet even though I felt no more joy at this new life than she, it seemed I had to lift her spirits if I could.

"You'll see," I said, "once you have a house, and your own small garden, and a fire on the hearth, and meat simmering in the pot, and your son asleep under your roof again, things will be as fair as May!"

She smiled the tiniest bit. "That was my name," she whispered, almost to herself. "Dority May. I was only eleven when I first met Will, and but sixteen when we were married. How long ago it is now! There's a world between then and now."

She rose slowly and pulled her cloak around her—it was a beautiful deep red when we sailed from Plymouth, but now it is streaked and stained and soiled—and then she looked at me, her eyes as cold as the wind.

"I shall never live in this 'free' land, Constance," she said, "never!" And then she walked away.

It distressed me so much to hear Mistress Bradford talk like this that I told Elizabeth of it as we were putting the babies to bed that night.

"She says she will never live in America, ma'am. And she sounded so *sure!*"

Elizabeth gave a gentle little snort. "What would she do then, jump over the side of the ship and swim back to England? I see no other choice."

I supposed she was right, but it did not ease my mind.

December 6, 1620

The days go on and on and here we stay. Sometimes I think the rest of my life will be spent here in this tiny tossing prison. The men have taken the shallop up and down the coast, making trips in weather so cold that the salt spray froze hard on their hair and beards and clothing. They discuss this place and that place—one hill is too steep for hauling supplies; this spot is too open to the weather; that spot too difficult for boats to anchor—and meanwhile we wait. The crew complains bitterly that their food will never last them the trip back to England—oh, if only I were going with them!—and yet Captain Jones must stay until we are somewhat established. It is in his contract.

From time to time many of the women go ashore to wash clothes or hunt for shellfish, and take the children with them so they can run some of their deviltry out. Only yesterday young Francis Billington, who, though he is but eight years old, has mischief enough in him for one thrice his age, came across some gunpowder with which he tried his hand at making squibs in the Great Cabin. He then found a small barrel, half full of powder which, in playing with it, he managed to strew about the room. Feeling very manly, it seems, he chose a fowling piece, fully charged, and proceeded to shoot it off, creating as terrifying a commotion as I have yet seen! Fire started promptly, and there was a great banging of flints and other small metal things flying about the room; and young

Francis screaming; and his father bellowing; and men running with buckets of sea water to douse the flames; and women clutching their babes to their bosoms to protect them; and Captain Jones roaring out that it was bad enough he had to spend his days waiting for his praying passengers to decide where they would settle so he could get back to England before he and his crew all starved to death, but did he have to have his ship blown out from under him into the bargain.

In all this turmoil young Francis managed to escape and hid himself among the barrels in the hold. 'Twas John Alden found him there, it being John's particular task to watch out for the barrels and kegs, and Francis was thence delivered by the seat of his breeks to his father. Punishment took place behind closed doors, so I know it not, but Giles reports that young Francis has not sat down since the doors were opened. Father refers to this episode as the Mayflower Gunpowder Plot, and speaks of Francis as Guy Fawkes.

As though we had not enough children on board, even though most of them are better disciplined than the Billington boys, there is one more child now. Susanna White, who is Dr. Fuller's sister and William White's wife, gave birth to a son she has named Peregrine. The poor woman so lacked for privacy that Elizabeth had her brought into our space. I don't know why it is that we should have a bit of privacy when very few others do, but Father has a way of managing things like this, and I no longer question it. In any case I took little Resolved White out on the deck with Damaris, and showed them how to catch snowflakes on their tongues, and how to see the different shapes when they fell softly on our cloaks. After a while Elizabeth came out and told us a baby boy had been born, strong and lusty and already bellowing. As well he might! Peregrine. The traveler. Methinks most of his travel took place before he knew of it.

Today, December 6, many of the men set out in the shallop again. They say this is to be their last exploration, and that when they return they will have decided where we are to settle. In truth, I hope 'tis soon! Father says 'tis too important a point to solve without careful thinking, but this life on an anchored ship becomes unbearable! The food is better, with fish to eat and wood to cook with, but the air is cold, and the tempers of the crew and of ourselves have become short and triggered. We have all lived here in a heap far too long.

John Cooke has taken to dogging me around—for lack of anything better to occupy him, I suppose—and proves himself a pest. How can a boy with as good a mind as John's act so like a fool? And he does have a clever mind. His great-grandfather was tutor to King Edward VI, and two of his great-uncles were members of Queen Elizabeth's court. Sir Francis Bacon, of whom I have heard Father speak as an excellent writer, is cousin to John's father, Francis Cooke. So with all these great minds in his family 'tis no wonder he is bright and educated, but lately he acts like a true ninny, telling me I have eyes like midnight and wanting to hold my hand. Coming from John I do not find this as exciting as I always thought I would.

December 20, 1620

I was there and did not see it, but I should have!
Even now, trying to write about it—I have put it off for days
—my stomach gripes in knots of guilt and fright and sickness.
It was the day after the men left in the shallop for that last
trip, and since none of us knew how long they would be gone,
there was usually a group standing at the rail, searching the
sea for any trace of their returning. She was there, a little
apart from us as always, her eyes searching too. I moved to
speak to her.

"I doubt they would come back so soon, Mistress Bradford,"
I said. "If this is to be their last trip, as they promised, they
would look thoroughly for the proper place. It may take
days."

"It makes little difference what place they pick," she murmured.

"But they must find good water, and a supply of trees, and
a proper harbor—"

"Oh, yes, I know. Such things are necessary for those who
will live here."

"It will not be much longer now. When our location has
been ·found they will start to build—a Common House first,
Father says, and then houses for each family. Just think, soon
you will be preparing for your son to join you! Does that not
cheer you, Mistress Bradford?"

She was silent for a while, staring out at the sea with her
gray eyes wide and brooding. Then she put her small icy hand
on my arm.

"You are a good child, Constance," she said in that soft, distant voice. "Strong, and brave, and good. Perhaps if I were more like you—" She stopped and pulled her cloak closer around her. "I have been cold so long. It never seemed to be this cold at home. If I could only be warm again—be warm, and sleep!"

She stood a few moments longer, while I tried to think of something to comfort the poor woman, but my tongue found no words. Then she smiled her bleak little smile.

"You will be all right, Constance," she said. "You were made for a land like this. Excuse me, now. I think I shall . . . get out of the wind."

She turned away and moved slowly along the deck to the leeward side. I watched her go—a small lonely figure. And that was all.

It was at least an hour later that we missed her. I think I knew, the moment we realized she was not among us. She was so slight. She would have slipped in with barely a splash.

I don't know who told Will Bradford when the men returned five days later. He shut himself in the Great Cabin, and Giles, who listened at the door, said he never heard such silence. Hours later Will came out again, and joined the men who had been with him in the shallop.

It was then they told us they have settled on the spot for our Colony, here where we have anchored. It is to be called Plymouth.

January 1621

They have actually started building a Common House! We can hear the cold ring of the axes—carried clearly in the winter air—and the thick solid sound of a tree as it hits the earth. Even though the women still have little to do save their usual tasks, there is a feeling of progress that infects us all. The men come back on board at night, so weary they nigh stagger, yet once they have bolted their food they sit for hours talking of their plans.

Father works like a man possessed, as perhaps he is. He lifts great logs the others cannot move, heaving them into place across the sawpit where they are cut into thick planks for building. Elizabeth says all the men will catch most fearful chills do they not take better care of themselves. First heavy work that puts them a-sweating, and then a rest period when they stand in the bitter cold, or gather round a fire—burning their faces and freezing their backs. In truth, Christopher Martin confessed tonight that he felt quite unwell, but there are those who think he may be malingering. Since he was deposed from governorship at the start of the journey by William Brewster's followers he has been at times vexatious, finding great fault with what the others decide to do. Malingering or not, he has a fearful cough!

January 1621 continued

The sailors call it scurvy, and say that they have seen men step from their hammocks announcing that they are in good health, walk a few feet, and fall dead from the disease. Dr. Fuller gives it no name, but does what he can with bloodletting and such remedies as the juice of thyme, which he claims to be excellent for irritations of the chest, and lovage, which is supposed to cure any sort of fever. And yet we are dying! My stomach churns with fear; I flinch at the moaning and gasping, and gag at the dreadful stench.

Those who are taken ill, and there are more each day, are carried from the ship to the Common House, which has at last been built. A few other houses are almost finished, but there is hardly a soul strong enough to work on them. Ours is at least a roof over our heads, although the cruel cold seeps in between the many cracks, and I huddle in it most of the day, staying as far as I can from the loathsome Sickness. Elizabeth, who must give of herself past all understanding, insists on nursing those poor wretches who lie in the Common House, rotting their lives out.

"Someone must do it, Constance," she says, "and it is woman's work."

"Not mine! I will not go near them!"

"Then mind Damaris and Oceanus for me, and feed your father and Giles. I will come back whenever I can."

"And bring that foulness with you that we may all die of it? I will go back on the ship and stay there!"

"There are those with the Sickness on the ship now too, Constance."

"But I thought . . . I thought they were being brought ashore!"

"There is no more room in the Common House. The floor is already filled with pallets, without a spare inch to lay another, save when someone dies. Rose Standish died this morning."

"*Rose?* But . . . but I *saw* her just a day or two ago! She was talking to Mistress Mullins!"

"Mistress Mullins is dead too. And her husband lies ill—" Elizabeth bit her lip hard. "I cannot stand here idle, Constance. Look out for the babes for me." And with that she left the house and walked down the hard-packed dirt path, disappearing into the Common House. I saw the door close behind her.

Father helped Captain Standish bury Rose that night. They dare dig no graves in daylight lest the Indians see, and realize how few we have become. Should they attack us now . . . and yet, if they did, it might be best. It would be an end to all this suffering and filth and cold and fear, for certainly we could not resist them. I said as much to Father when he returned to the house, standing his spade against the wall, where the crumbs of earth from Rose Standish's grave fell softly to the dirt floor.

"What sort of puling, weak-mouthed woman are you?" Father roared at me. "As long as there is one creature alive amongst us to fight, we will fight! We will fight sickness or Indians, it makes no matter which! Now let me hear no more whimpering from you!"

I set my mouth tight and went to the hearth where I filled his trencher with hot boiled fish, silently handing it to him.

"No, Con. I want nothing to eat," he said, and lay down on the bed without even taking off his boots.

I stood watching him in amazement. For Father to refuse his food was unbelievable!

"Are you well, Father? Is there aught wrong?" But already he lay drowned in sleep and did not answer.

Sometime deep in the night I heard the thick, choking sound of his breathing, and forced myself to get up from the pallet and go to him. In the firelight I could see his face flushed and red, and his head turning restlessly on the pillow. Ted Dotey heard it too, and came creeping down the ladder from the loft where he and Ted Leister sleep. He stood beside me, squat and gnomelike among the half-shadows, and I was grateful for his nearness.

"He's got it, Constance," Ted whispered. "The Sickness. This is the way it starts."

"What shall I do?"

"Rouse Giles, while I wake t'other Ted. We'll carry him to the Common House."

"But there is no room there! Elizabeth said so."

"There must be a place. With so many dying—"

"No! Don't take him there! If you do, he'll die too! I know he will! Leave him be. I'll care for him."

"It's a filthy task, Con. 'Twill turn your stomach! Let us take him."

I whirled on him and knew that my eyes were blazing. Sounding to myself just like Father, I shouted, "You will do as I say! Leave him be! Now help me get his boots and clothes off. He must be made more comfortable. And get more wood for the fire! I will not have him chilled!"

"Aye, miss," Ted mumbled, and did as he was bid.

My voice had wakened Giles, although Father had not opened his eyes at all, and he came shuffling sleepily to the bedside.

"What is it?" he asked, yawning. "Is something wrong with Father?"

"He has the Sickness," I said crisply.

"What are you going to do, Con?" My brother's eyes were wide with fear.

"Make him well! Fetch me some cool water and a cloth and then go back to sleep!"

"Water? What shall I bring it in?" Giles asked, gaping at me.

"Bring it in your open mouth, you booby," I snapped, tugging at Father's boot, "or in your shoe, for all I care! But bring it!"

A moment later the water was there beside me in one of Elizabeth's wooden tankards, but Giles did not go back to sleep. Instead we sat the night there, one on each side of the great bed. I knew little of what to do for Father, save to bathe him with cool water when his fever rose, and cover him with an extra rug when the shivering took him. When he retched and then spewed, we cleansed his face again and emptied the vile slops. Once he opened his eyes, fixing them hard on me, as though trying to see through thick mists.

"Leave me be, Con, leave me be," he said. His voice was so weak I could hardly believe it to be Father's. "Let someone help me to the Common House—away from you and the babies."

"You will stay here," I told him.

"Thunder, Con, you will do as I say!"

"No, Father. You will do as *I* say! Hush now. You are only wasting strength."

The faintest sort of smile touched the corners of his mouth. " 'Tis a sad thing when a man cannot command his own daughter," he murmured, and then, closing his eyes, he lapsed back into the Sickness.

Giles wanted to take him to the Common House. "Dr. Fuller is there, Con. He may have medicines—he knows better what to do."

"Giles, if he goes there, he will die. I know it! I will not have him moved!"

"What will Mother say?"

"Elizabeth has enough to take care of without Father," I told him, and then noticed Father's body start its retching and straining again. "Oh, Heaven help us, Giles, get the basin and hold it and stop yammering, or else get out!"

My brother looked at me as he shoved the basin under Father's chin, giving me one of his long straight glances with mischief dancing way deep in his eyes.

"I pity the man ye marry, Con," he said. "You're as stubborn as Father, and ye fight just as hard. But I'm not leaving."

And that was how the night passed.

In the morning I fed 'Maris and Oceanus, spooning gruel into the baby whilst Damaris fed herself and Giles fed Father. Elizabeth has had to stop nursing the boy, but he seems to take the pap with no trouble. Sometime late in the morning Elizabeth came back from the Common House, her eyes dull and shadowed with weariness. When she saw Father she gave a little moan, and knelt beside the bed.

"You should have called for me, Constance," she said, her hands smoothing his forehead, feeling how hot it might be.

"I knew you were busy. We have done all right. Giles has helped me."

"But 'tis such an unclean thing for you to tend—you wanted no part of it, I know. Nor do I blame you."

"Stop fretting, ma'am. There is gruel still hot. Best you have some, and then sleep a while."

"Have you slept, Constance?"

"I am not tired." I filled a bowl and handed it to her with a wooden spoon. "Here. 'Twill do you good."

Elizabeth ate, her eyes on Father. "He does not seem as ill as some of them," she said.

"He is better this morning. The little food we gave him has stayed in his belly."

She took a few more spoonfuls and then gave the bowl back to me. "I can eat no more, child." She bowed her head into her hands, and when she spoke again her voice was muffled and thick with tears.

"In spite of all we can do for them, they die. Christopher Martin was the first, and since him—Rose Standish, and both Priscilla's parents; her little brother, Joseph, lies there now, with no more strength in him than a kitten. Elizabeth Winslow is dead too, and Will White—"

"Baby Peregrine's father?"

"Yes. And both Anne and Edward Tilley sicken more each hour; they lie side by side, their hands clasped . . ."

I wanted to comfort Elizabeth, to touch her, to soothe her somehow, but I could not. Elizabeth and I—well, I know she is most fond of me, and she is always kind and patient and good to me. But somehow I seem to hold her off. I do not want her to be my mother! I seem not to be able to let her love me, or to let myself love her. I do not understand this, I only know that I scorn myself for acting so, and yet I cannot change. I knew at that moment I could have eased her grief with a touch, or a word of sympathy—and I could not give them. I could only pull my pallet out from under the big bed, and lay a rug beside it.

"Rest now," I told her. "You must rest. Father sleeps, and I will watch him."

Poor Elizabeth. She was so tired she could not protest, but fell onto the pallet like a child, and slept.

February 1621

Father recovered, I know not how, but he is one of the few who have. A week after he was taken ill he was able to leave his bed and walk about the room a bit, and then I left him to care for himself and went to the Common House to work with Elizabeth and the others.

Prissy Mullins' brother has died, and the poor girl is stricken with grief and loneliness, but she has put herself to caring for the small children whose mothers are either dead, or dying. 'Tis strange how few of the children are stricken—I know not why this is. Bess Tilley and Mary Chilton help Prissy, and so, without 'Maris and Oceanus to look after, I have been free to help with the nursing.

Were there time to think about it perhaps I might wonder why, after my horror of the awful Sickness, I was willing to assist. It may be that after tending Father and finding myself still uncontaminated, my fears were eased, or it may be simply that every hand is needed and I could not, in all pride, be the one to shirk. Or—perhaps—this is all a part of growing up. In any case, I went.

When I first walked into the Common House I could not believe what I saw. The floor was covered with mats and pallets, with barely room to step between them, and on each lay some miserable creature, blazing with fever, shaking with chills, or spewing a life out. There was a strange hush in the room, with a constant low sound of weeping, soft moaning, or whispered voices. The great fire, which the men keep blazing, threw a fearsome flickering light over everything, making a weak hand, raised in suffering, become a skeleton shadow on the wall. For a moment I stood in the doorway, doubting whether I could force myself to enter. The nauseous stench, the sounds of agony, the nightmare look of the place, made me want to turn and run. Then I saw Captain Standish, kneeling beside some poor wretch, bathing a face drawn with pain. Looking up, he saw me too, and smiled.

"Another pair of hands, Constant?" he said. "God bless you! Here, empty this basin, girl, and rinse it well. The water is there in the cask beside the door."

And that was it. As I carried the cleansed basin back to Myles, I saw John Cooke and his father lifting Edward Fuller from the floor in the corner of the room. As they carried him past me I saw that he was dead. Dr. Fuller held the door open for them, and as he watched his brother being taken from the house his face was wiped clean of all expression. I had just handed the basin back to the Captain when I felt a touch on my ankle and looked down. It was Ann Fuller.

"That was my husband?" she whispered. In the wavering

light from the pine knots and the fire her face seemed all bones, with great black holes for eyes. "That was Edward?"

I knelt beside her. I could not answer—I just nodded.

"Sam—my little Sam—is he—"

"Samuel is well," I told her. "He is with the other children. Priscilla is tending them."

She grasped my hand; her own was scorching hot, the while she shivered. "Watch over him, Constance. Little Sam —see he is taken care of. Please!"

"I will. I promise. Try to sleep now, ma'am."

She turned her head away from me, and there were slow tears seeping from her closed eyes. The next night she was buried beside her husband.

Somehow, I know not how, I was going from one to another, emptying their terrible slops, sponging their faces, spooning gruel into the mouths of those with enough strength left to swallow. There was no time to bathe the dead, nor prepare them properly for burial; we must needs tend the living. Day and night were much the same, save that we removed the dead by night. Sometimes Elizabeth would be working with me, and Desire Minter—no time now to gaze after John Alden—and Mistress Brewster, the only one who took time to breathe a prayer over each corpse as it was carried out. Several times I saw John Cooke, his face tight with disgust at the chores to be done, helping with a gentle tenderness that did not seem strange to me.

It went on for weeks, and days and time meant nothing. There was little talking—no one had the strength to spare for unnecessary words. There was a certain order to our work; there were those who cooked and those who tended the chil-

dren, whom we kept away from the sick ones as much as we
could; there were those who dug the graves and buried the
dead; there were those who bore most of the nursing; and
there were those who—in spite of everything—continued to
build houses! And still they died.

And then one night I saw Father come into the Common
House, carrying little 'Maris. He handed the child to Elizabeth,
and together they stood gazing down at her tiny little face. I
tried to go to them, and something stopped me—they were so
alone with her. Elizabeth sat the night holding the babe, rocking her gently and crooning songs without words. All the
next day Damaris seemed to sleep, though she turned restlessly
from one side to the other, fretting in small unknowing
sounds. Elizabeth went back to nursing the others, stopping
by 'Maris' small pallet each time she passed, kneeling for a
moment, her hand caressing the child's hair and her flushed
face. I sat with her for a while, bathing her with cool water,
trying to ease the fever. Once she opened her great dark eyes
and looked at me and smiled a little, and then started to cry
weakly, so that Elizabeth came back to her.

Sometime in the night I stretched myself on a bench to
sleep briefly, and woke a short time later to see Elizabeth and
Father together before the fire. Father was taking Damaris
from Elizabeth's arms. As he walked slowly out of the Common House, carrying his tiny daughter, I saw the tears that
streamed from his eyes and heard the dreadful sound of a
man sobbing. Elizabeth stood watching them go, one hand
against her throat. She made no noise, not even when I went
to her and held her in both my arms.

And the days and the nights go on, and the sick are brought

in, and the dead are carried out. Mary Allerton died, too weak after bearing a stillborn son to withstand the Sickness. And the whole Tinker family died, and Degory Priest died, and Mary Chilton's parents died, and John Goodman and Thomas Rogers and Richard Gardiner died, and Francis Eaton's wife Sarah died, and John Crackston and John Rigdale and Thomas Williams died, and Anne and Edward Tilley died, and John and Bridget Tilley died, and Jasper Moore and his sister Ellen died, and John Hooke and Robert Carter died . . .

Dr. Fuller said today he thinks the Sickness is ebbing, that fewer people are falling ill. A few or many—what does it matter? Soon there will be none of us left.

And who will bury the gravediggers?

March 1621

And then one morning, just last week, I opened the door of the Common House to look at the day, and it was spring. The air was warm and soft, but with the salty smell that is always here, and I could hear a thousand birds all talking at once in the trees! Priscilla Mullins sat on a rock below me, near the shore, and she was talking to John Alden. He stood like a tall ghost—pasty white and weakened from the Sickness, but standing! He's going to get well, I thought suddenly. He's not going to die!

I looked around as someone touched my shoulder gently, and Will Bradford stood there, one hand against the doorframe to steady himself. "You're up!" I said, like a ninny. "Ought you to be? Are you strong enough?"

He smiled his very slow smile. "I am all right, Constance. Weak, shaky, and badly in need of a shave—but all right."

I looked at him and knew it was true. They were beginning to recover. Those who were left were sitting up, or trying their weak legs in a few shaking steps—but they were getting well! Elizabeth came and stood beside me, breathing in the freshness of the morning.

"They're getting well," I said. "I don't think any more are going to die!"

"I have felt the same thing. Pray God we are right!"

Father came toward the Common House, his feet stepping with their old strength on the dirt path. He stopped in front of us, and stood looking at his wife. Elizabeth's sleeves were rolled up, her hair was an uncombed sight, her dress was reeking with filth. Her face was smudged and drawn and shadowed, and yet her eyes held a peace, a look of ease I had not seen in weeks. Father stared at her, seeing all I saw, and then he grinned.

"Elizabeth!" he said solemnly. "My beautiful Elizabeth!" And then, like fools, the two of them stood and laughed. Father put his arm about her shoulders and pulled her against him and kissed her, a great smacking kiss, and then he slapped her bottom.

"Come home, lass," he roared at her. "There's no one needs you now as much as I do."

And with his arm still around her, they walked down the short lane from the Common House and up the hill. I watched them go, and Will Bradford, still standing beside me, watched them too. From somewhere we heard the sound of hammers and the pull of a saw through wood.

"Plymouth is a-building, Constance," Will said. "Its people are getting well, and houses are rearing their walls, and the spring is come. God is still with us."

But of the one hundred and two people who sailed from England, fifty-one are dead.

March 1621 continued

*My bracelet, my precious golden bangle that Fa*ther gave me before we sailed, is gone! I thought I would keep it always as a part of home, but 'twas my own doing that I have it no longer, and I have no one to blame but myself, and the silly impulses that at odd times beset me. But before I set down here why I no longer have my keepsake (Elizabeth says people *do* forget things, and I never want to forget this), I had best mention how the days have gone.

After the Sickness was over I thought I should never get enough sleep, nor feel myself truly clean again. But after two long nights of uninterrupted rest (I even slept through Father's fearsome snoring) and nigh a dozen washings, I appear to be as before.

Our house is now quite finished, thanks to Ted Dotey and Ted Leister, whom Father calls his Two Teds, but compared to the house we left in London, this one is a poor place. There is but one room, of fair size, its walls of closely fitted boards, the first dirt floor now covered with thick planks. A smooth-

cut beam runs flat around the walls about as high as my
shoulder, holding the boards tight and acting as a shelf for
our trenchers and few platters, our tankards and our various
small implements. The chimney place in the back wall is large
and built of stones, and it gives us a good blaze. Father says
the danger of fire from sparks lighting on the thatched roof is
great, but for the present thatch makes the quickest and easiest
roofing. The three small windows, one beside the door which
opens south upon the Street, and one each in the east and west
walls, have nothing better than oiled paper in them, which
lets in a murky light when the sliding shutters are open. A
ladder runs up the wall to the loft above where the Two Teds
sleep.

The furniture is little more than the few pieces Father and
Elizabeth brought with them—their bedstead, a cradle for
Oceanus, the big chair Father always sits in, a great carved
chest, and Elizabeth's small box. Other than that there are just
the pallets for Giles and the Two Teds and me, stools for each
of us, a trestle board that the Teds made, and pegs pounded
into the wall for our clothing. In truth, I would be ashamed
of living in such a place were it not that here in Plymouth
there is no house any better. Giles finds it quite acceptable, but
he likes everything about America as much as I hate it all.

I do not like the house. I do not like Plymouth, I do not like
America, and there's an end to it! Who would want to live in
a country where savages watch us covertly from the trees,
never showing themselves save in quick glimpses of heathen-
ish dark skin as they slip away? Who would want to live
where an Indian arrow can strike death from the forest with
no warning sound? Who would want to live in a tiny Colony,

helpless against any determined Indian attack? Before the Sickness there might have been a chance to fight them off, but not now. Even after what has happened, and after what I did with my bracelet, I know that this is true. There are far more Indians here than there are Englishmen!

But I was telling of our house. Most of the others are housed now too, with only a few of the unmarried men living together in the Common House. Since the Sickness there are but four married couples left to be the heads of families: the Brewsters, the Carvers, the Billingtons, and Father and Elizabeth. Of the others, the widowed and the orphaned, some have their own homes, and the rest have been taken into the various households.

The weather has been mild and already the men are beginning to turn the earth for planting, though they must first clear away the rocks and trees. There is much for everyone to do, and Governor Carver watches sternly to see that none avoids his fair share. Father seems to be everywhere at once, hunting and fishing for food, helping to complete the houses, clearing the ground for planting, meeting with the Governor and Will Bradford and Captain Standish and the other leaders to plan for the community, smacking his lips over a glass of the brandy he brought and keeps carefully hidden in the bottom of the great chest, and telling us of the wondrous things he plans to do. To hear him, Father will own half America by the time Giles is grown!

And so it was that a very few days ago, the 16 of March, Father was standing in front of the Common House with Will Bradford when an Indian, wearing not a stitch save a leather apron round his waist, came out of the wood and strode toward the two men, calling out "Welcome, Englishmen!"

It was incredible enough that one lone man should enter our little village by himself—unarmed, and unaccompanied —but that he should also speak English was past believing. Giles, who somehow manages never to miss any bit of excitement, broke away from where he was playing stickball with the Billington boys, and came galloping up to Father, just in time, he says, "to see their mouths gawp open like loonies." When the Indian then extended his right hand toward them, neither Father nor Will could do more than to clasp it with their own.

The Indian announced that his name was Samoset and that he came from Pemaquid—wherever that may be—and he had, it seems, simply come a-calling. Master Bradford felt that some sort of formal gathering should be held, and sent Giles thundering off to find Governor Carver and Captain Standish and Master Winslow and a few of the others. Giles took a moment from his errand to burst into the house where Elizabeth and I were sorting through the packets of seed she had brought, looking for some hollyhock which she was sure she had included, but we could not find it (though it turned up later mixed in with some written instructions for herb teas), and blurted out the news. It threw me into such a panic of fear that I jumped up, spilling the packets across the floor. Running to the door, I slammed it shut and lowered the bar across it.

"What's taken you, sister?" Giles demanded. "There is nothing dangerous in one Indian."

"Don't be a fool," I snapped. "There are hundreds of others close behind him! I know it! They have but sent him on ahead to be sure that we are as weak as . . . as we are!"

Elizabeth started picking up the seeds. "Then let us not do anything to make this one man our enemy," she said calmly. "Constance, do you make a corn pudding, child, and fetch the little butter and cheese that is left."

I stared at her. "What are you thinking of, ma'am? Are you mad?"

Elizabeth picked up the wild duck that Ted Leister had shot that morning and left on the table. " 'Tis a good thing we have this," she said. "Your father will have the Indian here to sup, or my name is not Elizabeth Hopkins."

"Here? He would not dare! Why, the heathen will murder us all!"

Elizabeth looked up from plucking feathers from the duck. "Child, if the Indians choose to murder us they won't spend time in discussing it with your father and Will Bradford first."

"But they are *savages!*"

"Whatever they are, they have had ample opportunity ere now to chop us all into small bits while we slept. The fact that they have not done so would indicate they may not be quite as bloodthirsty as you seem to think. Quickly, Constance, the pudding."

Giles took himself off, leaving the door unbarred and ajar behind him, and it was all I could do not to close it firmly again. But somehow, in the face of Elizabeth's calm, I could not. With my hands shaking, and my teeth chattering so I dared not speak, I mixed the corn pudding. Every moment I expected to hear shrieks and screams as hordes of other heathens surged into the village, but the afternoon spun on quietly. Later, when the duck dripped its rich fat into the pan as it roasted, when the pudding cooked thick and creamy in its pot, when the table was laid with trenchers, Elizabeth's precious pewter spoons, and our great tankard filled with water (for the beer we brought with us is long since gone), Father came striding up the hill from the Common House, the Indian beside him, and Giles tailing behind like a dutiful puppy. They walked in the door, and I stood frozen in the center of the room. Father looked at me quizzically.

"This is my daughter, Constance," he said to the Indian.

I opened my mouth to make some sound lest I annoy the man by my silence, but not a sound would come. I could only nod my head like a muted booby.

"And this is my wife, Mistress Hopkins," Father went on.

One would have thought Elizabeth entertained savages at dinner every day of her life! She simply smiled and nodded to him, as if he might have been Mistress Brewster dropping in for a bit of talk, and then went back to her work at the chimney!

Father seated Samoset in his own big chair—the which the Indian considered very fine—and himself sat on one of the stools, with Giles hanging over his shoulder. I could barely keep my eyes off Samoset! He was surely a fine figure of a man, as tall as Father, but very lean and hard, and his skin a most beautiful coppery brown. His hair, black and as coarse as a horse's tail, was shaved into a sort of comb on his head, and his eyes were brilliantly dark and narrow. He looked clean enough, but there was a ripe odor about him that permeated the house very quickly, in spite of the cooking smells. Giles seemed to breathe it in like rose attar, but it soon nigh stifled me, so that when I was by him, serving the food or in passing, I held my breath till I was near blue. Elizabeth caught me at it, and with one of her little frowns and a shake of her head forbade me to do anything that might cause our guest to look at us with aught but kindness.

I thought at first the meal would never end, but halfway through I began to be so caught up in the stories that were told that I forgot the smell, my deep fear, and all else. Samoset told us of learning English from English fishermen who had been working at this Pemaquid for twenty years, salting down their catch and shipping it home. He taught us the names of some of the tribes of Indians who live in this area, and told us which we might trust and which we should fear. Once he looked at me, and his eyes sent a shivering straight to my backbone.

"Samoset have girl child too," he said.

I knew not what to say—not having had to speak to him before—but then I stammered, "Is she . . . is she . . . pretty?"

His voice seemed to get even deeper as he said, "To Samoset she is morning star."

Giles couldn't stand it having me talk to Samoset when he had been told to be quiet, so he suddenly burst out, "I want to give Samoset a present, Father."

Father beamed at him, pleased. "And what have you to give, Giles?"

Giles reached into his back pocket and in that flash-quick way he does things, pulled out the knife he had traded Love Brewster a jay's nest for. "This," he said, and thrust it out at Samoset, blade first. In truth, the Indian recoiled, and a most frightful look went across his face. Father grasped Giles's wrist, roaring at him.

"Have ye no sense, young jackanapes? What are ye doing?"

Poor Giles dropped the knife, which clattered to the floor, and looked as though he would burst into tears.

"I only wanted to give the knife to Samoset," he whimpered. "What have I done?"

Samoset leaned forward and picked up the knife from the floor. "Young brave move too fast," he said. "To give a knife in friendship, it must be like *this!*" He carefully handed the knife to Giles, handle first, his arm extended. Giles took it slowly.

"But I wanted you to have it," he said.

"In friendship?" the Indian asked.

"In friendship."

"Then give again, as I have show you."

Giles did as he was told, the while Elizabeth and Father watched him carefully. Samoset took the knife, smiled just a little, and said, "In friendship it is taken."

I could see Elizabeth give a great sigh before she turned back to the fire.

When the meal was over Father brought out the brandy, and he and Samoset each had a little, while Elizabeth sat in the corner feeding Oceanus. I was beginning to wonder when our guest would leave, for he showed no desire to take his departure, nor Father to have him, yet by this time the Two Teds had scaled their ladder and were fast asleep, and I was nodding on my stool. At last Samoset stood up and Father rose too, and then the Indian said, "Samoset sleep here by fire. In the morning he go."

I looked at Elizabeth and she at me, but there was naught

to do. I brought an extra rug from the chest, and Samoset calmly wrapped it about him, lay down on the floor and started to snore.

Surely no one ever spent a stranger night! Giles and I put our pallets close together, which was a mistake, because as soon as Father fell asleep and joined his snores with Samoset's, we fell into such a state of giggling that we nigh choked to death on our own mirth. At last Giles fell asleep, and I must have too, for when I next opened my eyes it was pale morning and Samoset was standing in the open doorway gazing at the fresh clear sky. No one else was awake, so I rose quickly and went to him.

"I will give you some breakfast," I said.

"No need. Samoset eat later." He stepped outside into the cool spring air, and I followed him. I did not know quite how to bid him good-bye.

"You must bring your daughter with you when next you come," I told him.

"Indian women stay home," he said. "Much to do. They do not travel with their men."

I felt rebuffed, though his tone was not unkind, and I looked down. My eyes fell on my dear bracelet, and, unthinking, I turned it with my fingers so that the sun's first rays caught it brilliantly. I looked up and saw that Samoset was looking at it too. And this is the part I cannot explain! For I took the bracelet from my arm and gave it to him.

"In friendship," I said. "For your daughter."

Samoset took the bracelet and looked at it carefully. "It is good."

"Yes. It came from England. My father gave it to me. Now I give it to you—for your daughter."

He put his hand on my shoulder and smiled at me. "Samoset take gift to daughter. He tell her that white sister sent it to Indian sister. It is a good thing, for it will make friendship. Samoset says his thanks to you."

And then he simply turned around and off he went!

I tried to explain to Father why I had given away his present to me, but it was difficult, because I was not sure myself. He shook his head, calling me quite daft, saying that he thought I had liked the bracelet—the which I assured him I had—and then adding that if he lived to be a hundred and had a dozen daughters, which he hoped God would spare him, he would never understand the female mind. Elizabeth set the trenchers of steaming porridge on the board and told Father not to fret about understanding the female mind, but to concentrate on the Indian mind, which she felt I understood better than he, and that *she* thought I had done more to bring friendship between the Indians and ourselves than anyone else had managed, and would Father please to bless the food now so we could eat. He did.

April 1621

Today the "Mayflower" left us. I think there was not a soul who was not on the shore to see it go, and not a soul who did not feel his throat tighten when the great anchor broke water, the ship turned slowly, and the sails suddenly filled with wind until—like a bird leaving the ground—the "Mayflower" skimmed out onto the sea, her beak pointing for home.

When I recall how anxious Captain Jones was a few months ago to have us ashore and settled, so he could be rid of us and on his way back, it seems strange that he should have lingered so long. But his crew suffered the dreadful Sickness just as we did, and many of them died—just as we did. The others lay for a long time weak and nigh helpless, and to have put them to the task of sailing a ship in winter storms and blasts would have been foolhardy. So the "Mayflower" has lain at anchor until now, and I had become used to seeing it there, familiar and solid, a link with home.

As she slipped away from us with the sun glinting sharp on her metal, Governor Carver bade us all gather at the Common House to pray for the ship's safe passage. I sat there looking round me at the few who make up this little world—so many less than when we started. Francis Eaton and Isaac Allerton and Will Bradford and Captain Standish and Edward Winslow have all lost their wives since we landed, although Susanna White is the only widow. There are the orphans, dear Priscilla Mullins, and Mary Chilton, little Sam Fuller and Bess Tilley, and there are those many other children with but one parent left to them. A handful of young men and boys—John Alden, John Howland, Father's Two Teds, Giles, John Cooke, a few others—and an even smaller handful of young women. Less than fifty of us now, fifty people to make a life for themselves and for those who will come after.

As we left the Common House, all of us subdued and thoughtful, I walked beside Elizabeth, taking Oceanus from her to carry him home. We could still see the "Mayflower," a tiny dot against the sea and sky. I felt a ninny, but I could not stop the tears that came hot to my eyes as I watched it, tears that would not be dried by the warm spring wind blowing soft against my face. Elizabeth put her hand under my arm and we went up the hill together, neither of us speaking. As we entered our house she said, "Lay Oceanus in his cradle, Constant, and let us try our hand at a plum pudding."

I looked at her, surprised, the tears still sharp in my eyes. "A *plum* pudding?"

"Yes. We may have to make shift with a few things, but you will find a cluster of dried plums in my box. I fancy we can manage."

"Dried plums!" My mouth watered at the thought of a dish that would in any way resemble the plum puddings Elizabeth had made at home. "I did not know you had any such—"

"I have been keeping them for some occasion, and mayhap this is it." She laid her hand against my cheek—a thing she rarely does. "Thou art a good child," she said. "Now dry thy eyes, and let us get to work."

The pudding was monstrous good!

May 1621

And now we have one more widow, and from her state it seems she will not be long amongst us, and one less family, if family it could be called, there being nary a child. Just a few days after the "Mayflower" set sail for England, Governor Carver was working in the fields with the other men. It was a tremendous hot day—the sun shines far warmer here than at home, I think—and the Governor, being unaccustomed to it, was most likely working harder than was wise. Whatever the cause, he came stumbling from the field and fell upon the ground, complaining greatly of pains in his head. He was carried to his house, and Dr. Fuller came, but in a few hours the Governor had fled his senses, and lay without moving or speaking for three days before he died.

Captain Standish took it upon himself to plan the best burial that could be managed, calling upon all those who can use a gun to stand at attention at the grave and fire a volley of shots. Poor Mistress Carver collapsed and had to be supported home, as her husband had been only a few days before, and she has now taken to her bed from whence Dr. Fuller doubts she will rise again.

All the men met at the Common House, and Father told us it took them only a few moments to choose Will Bradford as the new Governor. I had thought Father might be angry that he was not named, but he says Will is the man for the job, and that he is a sober and just man, filled with patience and charity, but very firm. Father says himself that *he* may have a deal of charity but that God knows he is not patient, to which Elizabeth only smiles. Since Will is still weakened somewhat from the Sickness (which takes a long time to depart a body), Isaac Allerton has been named to act as Assistant to him, he being healthy and a good friend to Will.

And so our number is one less, and our leader has changed, but the work of planting and building and living goes on, and the world is fair with spring.

The seed that has been dropped so carefully in our fields already shows green promise, far earlier than any of the men expected it to. Father says this is because of the way Samoset, and another Indian, Squanto, taught our people to plant. The corn was placed in tiny hills, with fish in each hill, head down—although how it can matter which way the head of a dead fish lies I cannot see—and then gently covered. Whatever the reason, even I rejoice to see the tiny shoots break through the ground.

Elizabeth had Giles spade up a space about our house, and here she planted her hollyhocks, as well as some herbs and a few other pretties. Do they prosper, they will make the house look less like a square box rearing straight from the earth.

My fear of the Indians, who now stroll openly through our village, has been somewhat lulled by a treaty which was made between our men and a great chief named Massasoit. A few days following his first visit Samoset returned, and announced that this Massasoit and his men would have words with our people. There were nigh sixty of them, and they would not come into the settlement (praise heaven!) but stayed a short way off, where Edward Winslow was sent to talk with them. This he did, and there was a ceremonious exchange of gifts, and a little brandy and a great deal of food (most of it going from us to them and not t'other way about), and at last an agreement of peace was reached, which allows us all to breathe more freely, although I cannot find it in my heart to trust these savage heathens to the full! I asked Father to teach me to shoot one of his guns, but he roared back he would rather face ten Indians with bows and arrows than one female with a gun and a shaking hand, and he would have no part of it. Sometimes I wish I had been born a man!

May 1621 continued

From watching Priscilla and John casting eyes at each other for the past months I had felt sure they would soon be married, but now Captain Standish calls often upon Priscilla, who has been living with the Brewsters. We all see him march up to the doorway, looking like a small red-bearded rooster, for he grew so enamored of the beard he sprouted on board the "Mayflower" that he has never shaved it off. Most of the others have, including Father, because Elizabeth said she would as soon buss a billy goat as a man in a beard. The little Captain knocks sharply at the door, albeit in this mild weather it is rarely closed until the household sleeps, and then stands his musket neatly against the side of the house and enters for an hour's courting. I could not see what Priscilla could be thinking of, till she and I were set to work together gathering early wild mint for drying, and I asked her straight out how it was with her and John.

"Perhaps I should not pry," I said, "save that everyone has seen how you gaze at each other. It cannot be a secret."

"Except to John," Priscilla said. "I swear to you, Constance, that more than once I have been sure the great dear booby was about to ask me would I wed him, and I am sure, too, that everyone—save John—knows what my answer will be, but he shies away at the last moment like a horse on loose cobbles and mutters that the corn is growing well, or that he has built a new chest for Dr. Fuller, or some other startling item about which I care naught. I am in despair!"

"But Captain Standish—do you consider him?"

"As a husband? Oh, Con, I must consider someone! And the Captain—Myles—has been most courteous and kind."

"But he is so much older than you, Prissy!"

"Not that much. I am close to twenty-one and Myles is but thirty-six."

"Why, that's my father's age! He is too old for you, Pris—and John is just right!"

"That all may be true, but what am I to do if John does not ask me?"

"Has Captain Standish asked you?"

"No, but he will." She sounded very gloomy.

"Mayhap not."

"He will, never fear. And I must marry someone. It is not meet for me to live alone, and I cannot stay with the Brewsters forever—though they are kindness itself to me. Oh, Constance, it is such a puzzle!"

So Captain Standish called upon Priscilla in the evenings, and yet often I saw her walking with John Alden, and on some occasions she would see me, too, and throw me a droll look of helpless fury. And then, with no word to anyone, Edward Winslow and Susanna White presented themselves before Governor Bradford (I find it hard not to call him Will) to be married! It did not seem to me to be a union filled with love and romantic notions as I had always thought 'twould be, but Elizabeth says 'twas a very practical thing, since they were both widowed during the Sickness and Susanna has Resolved and little Peregrine to raise, and she and Master Winslow are of an age and most compatible in mind and thought. But still I think there should be more than that.

In any case this was the first marriage in our settlement, and it must have made Captain Standish feel that if it was not too soon after their bereavement for Master Winslow and Susanna, then it was not too soon for him either. Priscilla has told me what happened then, and I find it comical and yet a little sad, I know not why. Seems that when the brave Captain got right to the point of asking Priscilla's hand he was no better at it than John, though he must have done it before or how could he have married poor Rose?

"So at last he decided to have someone speak for him," Prissy said, "and who should the blind ninny light upon but John! I swear 'tis a wonder we look upon Myles to protect us from the savages, for I doubt he could tell one a span away! But John was his choice, and poor John came to me, washed and brushed and wretched and honorable, and asked would I wed with Myles!"

"What did you say, Pris? Whatever did you say?"

"For a moment I knew not what to say! If I said No, I might die a spinster for all the good it would do with John, and if I said Yes—but somehow I could not say Yes!"

"And so—?"

"And so I gathered my courage together and asked John if he was sure that was what he wanted to say, and he turned those great blue eyes on me like a bewildered child and said that was what he had been *told* to say, and I became so put out with his helplessness that I jabbed my fists onto my hips and stood glaring down at him and asked him why he was too much of a mollycoddle to speak for himself! Oh, Con, I felt like such a brazen wench!"

"And he did? At last?"

"He did. At last! And all as though he was much surprised

that I should care for him, and prefer him to Myles! I swear
to you, Con, 'tis a miracle that men ever catch themselves a
wife!"

"But you are happy now, Prissy?"

"Oh, Constance, I would not think I could be so happy!
John says as soon as his house is finished we will be wed. A
month or two at most."

So there will be another wedding in Plymouth, but I never
realized how hard a lass must work to get the man she sets
her heart on. I wonder will it be the same with me?

June 1621

It is June, and in the continued fair weather which
has been granted us the planted fields show green and promising, and Elizabeth's hollyhocks are fat with buds. I found
clumps of violets in the woods a while ago, some of which I
dug up and brought home, and these we have planted just
within the hollyhocks, where they will bloom again next year.
From Elizabeth's amazing chest came also rosemary and sage
and dill and other seeds, which are now prospering, so that we
will soon be able to cut and hang them to dry beside the
chimney place. In truth, with all the green of spring, and the
planting that other women have done within the small, fenced-
off gardens about their houses, our Street has become very
pleasant to the eye.

Early in the month, the planting being completed and not
requiring as much work from the men as before, Governor

Bradford thought it wise to send some representatives to visit Massasoit, both to tighten the peace and friendship which has existed between the Indians and us (and pray God it may continue!) and to find out more about the other tribes that inhabit this area, even though we have seen little of them. For this task the Governor chose Father and Edward Winslow. Father, of course, was most pleased at the distinction and spent an entire day in cleaning and brightening his boots and clothes so that he might show to advantage and do the settlers honor. I should not have thought that Master Winslow would have been so ready to leave his wife, for he and Susanna have been wed but a month, but Elizabeth tells me that I am filled with female notions about love and marriage, and I suppose she is right, since I know little of either. In any case, Master Winslow seemed as eager as Father—wife or no—so they took themselves off, laden with food and arms and gifts for Indians till I wondered how they could move at all.

Since the Two Teds are busy all the daylight hours, Giles appointed himself the man of the house whilst Father was away, and spent a great deal of time sitting in the open door with Father's oldest fowling piece across his knees. This made both Elizabeth and me so a-quiver, since Giles's aim is not yet up to the standards set by Captain Standish, that Elizabeth at last sent him to go hunting wild strawberries, with the promise that could he find enough she would make him a pie. Giles, being very fond of such a pie, and knowing the vast number of tiny berries he must needs find, took some of the younger boys with him—the Billingtons and the Brewsters—believing, doubtless, that he could have the smaller lads do much of the work, while he took unto himself the proceeds. So off Giles went also, with his train of followers, and Elizabeth and I settled down in peace with Oceanus the only man about the house.

Captain Standish had given Father two gowns that once were Rose's, muttering very gruffly that "mayhap Elizabeth or that young maid Constant might find use of them," and since there was a great deal more of Rose than there is of me, Elizabeth and I set to work to make one over for a proper fit. This is work I do enjoy, and though it may sound too prideful to say aloud, I can write here that I have a truly clever hand with a needle, and even Elizabeth will vouch for that, as well she should, since it was she who taught me. We talked as we worked, and the door stood open with June sun shining in, and Oceanus sat on a rug on the floor trying to catch the beams and making his own sweet gurgling sounds at them, and the afternoon was pleasant. In some manner we got to speaking of Priscilla and her John, who are wed at last, and I told Elizabeth all that Prissy had told me about poor John's courtship and we laughed together at the strange ways of men. Then Elizabeth said to me in that quiet way she has, "Is there any man amongst us who pleases you, Constance?"

I looked at her in surprise. "As husband, you mean, ma'am?"

"Aye, as husband. Thou art not too young to be considering." Elizabeth only says "thou" to me when we are alone together. I thought about the men in the settlement and could not help but smile.

" 'Tis my misfortune, ma'am, that they all seem to be either too young or too old, or else they have already taken wives."

"What of John Cooke?" Elizabeth said.

I wrinkled my nose at her. "John is naught but arms and legs and a voice that still undoes him on occasion. And he is just my age—sixteen—which seems far younger in a man than in a girl. No, ma'am, I fear that John would never do."

"I have watched him look at thee—with more than friendly interest."

"He does?" It seemed quite strange that I had never noticed, and I said so.

"It is difficult to notice when one never looks," Elizabeth remarked. "Hast thou paid any attention at all to John?"

"Not when I could avoid it. His hands are damp."

Elizabeth smiled. "He will outgrow that," she said. "Give the boy time, Constance. He comes of good family, and shows promise of being a handsome man. You could do worse."

"But I hope I can do better," I said. "Are you looking to be rid of me, ma'am?"

Elizabeth leaned forward quickly, stretching her hand across the rosy cloth that filled her lap, and taking my hand in hers. "Never, Constance! Nothing would please me more than to keep thee with me always. But thou must make a life for thyself, and a woman does that only with a man. Take all the time thou needst, my poppet, and be sure in thy own mind when the moment comes. Till then, bide here, for my love for you is great! Now, stand up, child, and let me hold this gown against thee whilst I measure the waist."

The sun's stripes were long and slanting when Mistress Brewster tapped at the doorway and entered. I gathered the cloth up in my arms to clear off the stool on which it had been resting as we sewed, so that she might sit down, and then stood folding it neatly to put by for the evening. Mistress

Brewster has a face that turns down all over—the eyes, the mouth, the lines aside the nose—everything slants downward, giving her a most unhappy look. But she is a good woman, and very kind, if one does not mind a bit of preaching. She sat down now, with a great sigh, and greeted us.

"I came for the boys," she said then. "Heaven alone knows how often I have told them to come straight home from their outings and not to dally, but still in these pleasant afternoons they find a hundred things to keep them. They are here with Giles?"

Elizabeth shook her head. "Giles took them berrying with him—the little Billington lads too—and they have not returned. I had not noted how the day had gone."

"Do you think they are all right?" Mistress Brewster asked, and her voice bore a trace of worry. "William says we have naught to fear from the Indians, but the boys are very young, and if they were to do something foolish—"

"Giles would watch out for them, I am sure," Elizabeth said loyally. I did not feel quite as sure as she did, but I felt it better not to say so. I never fully trust Giles to behave intelligently, but mayhap, as Father says, that is just because he is my brother. He has never really done anything too wrong.

Just then we heard running steps along the hard-packed dirt of the Street, and Giles himself came plunging in the door, followed a few seconds later by Love and Wrastle Brewster and Francis Billington. They all carried baskets of dusty strawberries, and their faces and hands bore the proof of a fruitful afternoon. The Brewster boys went to their mother, and Giles faced Elizabeth, all talking at once. Young Francis Billington, "the young Guy Fawkes," leaned in the doorway.

"We have searched and searched, Mother," Giles was saying, with a distress that is quite unlike him, "and we could find no trace of him. I did not know whether to leave or no —but at last I thought it best to come back here for help."

"You did quite right, Giles," Elizabeth said in her calm voice, seeming to grasp immediately whatever the problem was, though I was still bewildered. "But how was it you let him stray away from you? You are the eldest; little John is but seven years old—"

Giles cast a quick glance at John's brother, Francis, where he still stood, unspeaking, in the door. "John does not always do . . . quite . . . as he is bid," Giles said carefully.

Love Brewster, only ten, but a good and sturdy child, nodded his head in strong agreement. "Giles *told* John not to wander off," he said, "but John said Giles wasn't old enough to tell him what to do."

"Nor is he," muttered Francis sulkily.

Wrastle, just seven himself, marched up to Francis, a year his elder. "Then why did *you* not watch him? You are his brother!"

"How long since you last saw him, Giles?" Elizabeth asked.

"At best an hour or more, Mother. We have been looking and calling all that time, but he never shouted back, and we could find no trace of him. I tried to watch for footprints as Squanto showed me, but the ground there was thick with pine needles—I could see nothing."

"Mayhap he just didn't *want* to answer," Francis said. "You'll see. He will be back safe and sound—and with more berries than anyone!"

"God knows I pray you are right, Francis," Mistress Brewster said, "but I think it better we do not wait. Go and find your father, and I will send William, and—"

"I will go with them," Giles said. "I can best show them where we were."

"If I tell my father he will trounce me," Francis whined.

"And to good purpose," I heard Elizabeth murmur very softly. "Too bad 'twas not done more often ere now." In her usual voice she spoke briskly as she rose. "Mary, if William could go with Master Billington and Giles, that might be best. Stephen is not here, as you know, or of course he would look for John. And best they start soon, before nightfall."

"I shall call Will," Mistress Brewster said, and took her own boys firmly by the hand. At the door she looked down at Francis. His hair was uncombed and matted, his nose was running as it always seems to, and occasional swipes at it with his dirty hands had smeared his face. His arms and legs were scratched by briars and thorns, and his bare feet were filthy. He was not a pleasing child, but Mistress Brewster has a very Christian nature.

"Come, Francis," she said. "I will go with you and tell your father of John's misadventure. He will not trounce you if I am there."

Francis peered up at her suspiciously, sniffed, and wiped his nose with his hand once again. "He will, once you leave," he muttered, but he turned and went with her across the Street and up one house, to the Billingtons'.

Elizabeth made Giles wash his hands and face, and rest long enough to eat some corn bread and cold meat. By that time Master Brewster and Master Billington were ready to leave. Looking at Master Billington I could not but feel for young Francis. It seemed quite sure his father would not only be very ready to trounce him for any misdemeanor, but would take great pleasure in the doing.

Until dark that night, and throughout the next day, and the next, the search continued for John. By this time poor Ellen Billington, whom I like little more than her husband, she being a loud-voiced, shrewish woman, was sure her child was dead and lying somewhere stiff and cold and never to be found. She knew he had been set upon either by wolves or Indians, and in truth it seemed most possible, but John Cooke said to me that he knew Indians were very smart and he had always understood that animals were too, and he doubted whether either one would bother with the Billington lad.

At last Governor Bradford ordered that word be sent to what Indians we knew were friendly as to whether they had seen aught of John. It was Massasoit who replied, telling our Governor that John had wandered into an Indian plantation *twenty miles* south of here—a place called Manamet—and that the Indians there, on their way to Nauset, had taken John with them! This news caused Ellen Billington to moan that her son would be better off dead than raised by the Indians, as would surely be the case, for they would never let him go. John Cooke said they would let him go fast enough once they found what a troublesome child he was, but he only said it to me.

Nauset being far down the coast from here, Master Billington and the Captain and a few others took the shallop and started out. They had been gone only an hour or so when a most horrible storm broke, with thunder and lightning enough to end the world, but they did not turn back. Poor Giles, who had not been allowed to accompany them, was in a fearful state, taking all the fault unto himself, though Elizabeth and the Two Teds and I told him that was not warranted.

And then, after three dreadful long days of waiting, the shallop came sailing into the bay, and there was John, standing jauntily in the bow, decked with beads and feathers, and looking mightily pleased with himself. His mother fell upon him, weeping and sobbing and clutching him close to her, and then stood back and handed him a clout on the ear that knocked the child back into the water. From thence his father plucked him out, curtly thanked Captain Standish and the other men who had manned the shallop, and grasping his wife by the arm and dragging John after him—with Francis bringing up the rear—he strode up the hill to his house, pushed them all inside, and slammed the door.

Upon the heels of this came Father and Edward Winslow, wearier and hungrier than I have ever seen them. They paused briefly to speak to Governor Bradford and put his mind at rest as to the success of their trip, and then each went to his own home. While Giles pulled off Father's boots and I rubbed his sore, raw feet with an unguent, Elizabeth piled his trencher high with a steaming hotchpotch of venison. We told him all concerning John's disappearance and the great disturbance it had caused, and he told us some of the events he and Master Winslow had shared, yawning mightily the while. Elizabeth laid her hand on his shoulder.

"Did you not sleep, Stephen, whilst you were gone?"

Father wiped his mouth with his napkin, swung around in

his chair, and pulled Elizabeth down on his knee.

"Bess," he said, "each night the Indians have been creditable hosts to us. As they slept, so did we."

"Well, then?" Elizabeth said. "What keeps you gaping so?"

"One night we slept in the open field, making a juicy feast for the mosquitoes. Another night we laid upon boards covered with a thin matting. At one end lay the chief and his wife, at the other end lay Edward and I, and among us lay two other chiefs, who deemed it an honor to rest with white men." I saw Elizabeth's lips begin to twitch.

"And the other nights?" she asked, with something close to a giggle.

"The other nights—wherever we were, we were treated to the best bedding our hosts could provide, and in every case they shared it with us."

"Then I do not think you should complain, Stephen. It seems to me you had excellent treatment."

"Bess, every night we slept with Indians! You know how Indians *smell,* but blast it, woman, do you know how Indians put themselves to sleep?"

Elizabeth shook her head, her eyes wide and sparkling, as Father stood up, letting her feet slip to the floor.

"No, Stephen, how do Indians put themselves to sleep?"

With a roar that sent Giles and me into an agony of laughter, Father bellowed; "They *sing!*" Then he added, "I am now going to bed. If anyone dares to raise his voice before noon on the morrow, may he be struck dumb from above!"

And with that Father tumbled into bed, breeches and all, and while Giles and I—aye, and Elizabeth too—gasped with smothered laughter, his loud and ferocious snoring most comfortably filled the room.

September 1621

It is hard to believe that the summer is nigh gone. Now, in September, the nights grow cool and the fire is welcome, though the daytime sun still shines hot.

The men say that the crops have done fairly well, in particular the corn they planted as Squanto had told them. The barley is indifferent good, and the peas by far the poorest. Herbs hang drying now beside our chimney, and they make the house smell wondrous sweet. Many of them Elizabeth raised, and Susanna Winslow planted others, and there were some we found growing wild, so what with a great deal of trading and sharing, every house now has its sweet small bunches. There are seven houses on the Street, and four buildings which we share as storage places for grain and fish and meat that has been smoked, and powder and shot and the like, all of which structures make us feel we are truly a village.

Aside from the growth and prospering of our new Plymouth, it seems that I also grow and prosper, although I am not sure it is just as I would have it. The rosy gown that Elizabeth and I made from one of Mistress Standish's did in truth make a remarkable change in me. Elizabeth says it was because my other gowns were all too small (for that filling out of which she used to speak has taken place). I appear now to be shaped like a woman, and the new dress does make the most of it.

The first time I wore it was to Sabbath meeting (to which we often go, though we are not members of the Plymouth church), and though I should have had my eyes on heaven the whole time, I would have had to be blind had I not noticed how John Cooke stared at me. I do not find this quite as annoying as once I might have, since the hours of working outdoors in the fields and on the houses have made a deal of difference in him. Where there was nothing but gangle, there now are knots of muscle, and his skin has darkened from the sun to so deep a shade that with his brown eyes and dark hair he looks almost like an Indian. Yet he is still bumbling John Cooke, and not one to rouse any female emotions in my newly developed bosom.

When meeting was over I walked out of the Common House with Father and Elizabeth, who was carrying Oceanus, in the fashion of three abreast as we are bid to do, but halfway up the hill Father stopped to speak to John Alden and Elizabeth paused to share words with Priscilla, and I suddenly found John Cooke waiting for me. I greeted him and we walked in silence until John swallowed hard a few times and then murmured something I could not catch.

"Speak up, John," I said. "I cannot hear you when you mumble."

The boy reddened like an apple and blurted out loudly, "I said you look monstrous fine in your new gown, Con!"

There came a snicker from behind us and I looked back to see the Two Teds mincing hand in hand like the ninnies they are, assuming, I suppose, that they were aping John and me, which was not so since *our* hands were not touching. This so provoked me that I could feel myself blushing also and all I wished was to get away from them, so I said to John in what I hoped was a casual fashion, "Shall we walk along the shore for a bit?"

John looked as though I had just offered him a slice of silver moon on a golden trencher, and this set those dreadful Teds to hooting and bawling with mirth.

"Oh, Johnny boy, the lass is leading the way," they shouted, "best follow bravely, for who knows what she may have in mind!"

I could happily have run them both through with Father's sword, but the Sabbath is no time for such thoughts and the best I could do was to turn and walk very quickly back down the hill toward the shore, with John striding to keep up beside me and the twin beasts holding their sides with laughter. I was so angered that I did not watch carefully where I stepped and my foot slipped on a stone and I would have fallen had John not caught my arm, a move which brought forth one last bellow of glee from Masters Dotey and Leister. They did not follow us, however, having had enough sport, I suppose, and John and I came down onto the shore alone.

The wind was strong here, though pleasantly warm, and it flattened my new gown against me in such a truly brazen fashion that I began to wish we had not come. What with trying to keep my dress from blowing immodestly, and endeavoring to step where my shoes would not be filled with sand, the walk was not as pleasant as I had hoped, so that I was relieved when John found a curve where rocks formed a little shelter. Taking off the jacket that he wears to meeting (which has become too tight for him across the shoulders) he spread it on the beach.

"Come, Con, sit down and stop fighting the wind," he said. "We can talk here."

I sat, and we looked out over the water, very blue, with the sun sparkling on the gentle waves and bouncing back into our eyes. The air was fresh with salt and pine trees and the good smell of warm sand, and the rocks behind us held a pleasant heat. My eyes squinted in the sun and I looked as far out on the sea as I could.

"Somewhere across there is England," I said.

"And Leyden," said John.

"Were you never in England?"

"No. I have heard much of it from my father, but I was born in Leyden. I have never seen aught else but this."

"An Englishman who has never seen his country," I mused. "It seems odd."

John smiled. "My mother says the same. 'A fine English-born-Dutchman,' she calls me. It makes her laugh."

"Will she ever come here, do you think? Your mother?"

"For sure she will. With Jane, and Jacob, and little Hester. You will like them all, Con."

"I am sure I shall."

"And they will like you." There was a pause and then he added, "Father hopes to have a cow sent us, too."

Rather puzzled, I said, "Oh?"

"And some of the other men talk of a bull, and then . . . you see . . ." He stopped, looking embarrassed.

"You mean there would be calves," I said.

He looked relieved. "But not only that, Con. One of the calves would be mine—Father has said so—and I could breed that, and then there would be more, and soon I will have the start of a herd, and then, with some land of my own . . . well . . ." Again he stopped, and sat looking at me hopefully.

"It will put you in very good state," I said politely.

"Indeed it would. I should be able to take a wife!"

There must be some small demon in me, for without truly meaning to, I found myself looking up at John in a sidewise manner from beneath my lashes. I have seen Priscilla look at John that way, but my lashes must be longer or thicker than Prissy's because I could not see very well, so I had to open my eyes wider. John was gazing at me like a puppy hoping for a bone.

"Have you someone in mind?" I asked. "Bess Tilley perhaps, or Mary Chilton? Or mayhap you wait until new settlers arrive?"

"I have no need to wait," John said, his voice quiet but husky. "My mind has long been made up. And 'tis neither Bess nor Mary, as you well know!"

Truly my wits left me, and I could think of nothing to say except, "Oh."

John leaned a little toward me, and I felt his hand close over mine. Elizabeth was right. His hands are not damp any more. He must have outgrown it. Suddenly I felt it was well past time to be home and having supper, and I got to my feet as quickly as I could. John, surprised, rose too.

"What is it, Con?"

"I . . . I think we had best get home," I said. "The sun has fallen low."

"Constance," John said, "wouldst thou mind if I kissed thee?"

This so startled and undid me that I knew not what to say! Father has always told us to be truthful, and in truth I was curious as to what it was like to be kissed by a male to whom I was not related—though neither Giles nor Father are much for kissing me—and yet Elizabeth has said maidens should never be forward, so I was sore perplexed. But 'twas John who had asked *me,* and not I him, so perhaps I could not be called forward, and it would be wrong to disobey Father and be untruthful, so at last I said, "I do not think so."

I watched his face come very close until I got cross-eyed, and then I saw only a dark blur and felt his lips touch mine as gently as I touch little Oceanus with my own lips, and then his head moved back to where I could see it and I did not feel any different at all.

"Thank you, Con," John said.

Then we walked back up the hill and I went home and we had a roast wild turkey for our meal. I do like turkey!

November 1621

I think I shall never eat another bite of food! For three wondrous days there has been naught but feasting and games and laughter and sport and talk, and now the turkey that I did like so well I could not face were I to starve! Father says in two days I will have changed my mind, and Elizabeth says it might be just as well did I *not* eat more for a bit, since the seams of my rosy gown are close to bursting, but how monstrous good it was to have my belly *full!*

The crops and the fishing and the hunting had all done so well that Governor Bradford ordered a day of thanksgiving and feasting. This being the first sort of pleasurable festivity since we landed a year ago, everyone on the Street relished the prospect and set to work to make the day memorable. Such a to-do of cooking, and hunting, and cleaning, and preparation this little village has never seen! To walk the length of the Street was to smell such promising odors as to make the mouth wet in anticipation. Corn puddings, and pasties filled with berries, steaming hotchpotches and roasted fowl, fish in every guise and great piles of mussels and clams—it was un-believable! Giles was never so eager to help about the house as when Elizabeth and I were cooking, and he went from chore to chore in an open-mouthed daze of expectancy.

Governor Bradford invited Massasoit, thinking to renew the friendship we have with him, which has in truth made our first summer here one of peace, wholly free from worry of at-tack by those we once called savages. On the appointed day, as the older boys were taking the trestle tables from every home and setting them up in a field, Massasoit came striding along, closely followed by some ninety braves! Poor Governor Brad-ford stared at this unexpected company, and then held a hur-ried conference with Father and Master Winslow and some of the women. Having looked for one Indian and being pre-sented with ninety—a number far greater than the people in our own community—máde our great store of food appear much smaller. At last the Governor spoke with Massasoit, tell-ing him, in the ceremonial terms they use to each other, of our embarrassment. Massasoit immediately turned to some of his men and ordered them into the woods that surround us, with instructions to bring back additional provender.

It seemed little more than an hour later that they returned with five deer, which they quickly prepared and then hung over the fires they built in pits dug in the ground, where the smell of their cooking filled the air.

And thus everyone ate plentifully! During the day, as appetites were sated, the Indians showed off their skill with bow and arrow, causing Captain Standish to gather his best trained men to prove *their* skill with firearms. There was a great deal of drink made from the wild grapes that grow in profusion all about us, and as this took hold, there were matches of physical strength between the men—Indians and white alike—and foot races in which none of our people could outdistance Massasoit's, and there was lusty singing and a certain amount of trading of small articles between the Indians and us. When these various things roused appetites again, back we all went to the boards for more food.

I do not know whether it was the grape wine, or my well-fitting gown, or just what the reason, but the Two Teds spent much time in showing off whenever I was about, and when I was not, they sought me out. Nothing would do but I watch them wrestle, or watch them race, or watch them do absurd tricks, such as standing on their heads or walking on their hands or some other nonsense. Ted Dotey is a small man, not so tall as I, with bandy legs and a hot temper. Ted Leister is taller and dark and dour and brooding. They are both hard workers, and Father chose well when he chose them as bondsmen to bring to America, but although they are generally close friends and do well together, there are also times when they become bitter rivals and enemies.

I thought all their carrying on in front of me was most comical, and laughed at them, saying one was the winner, or the other—not caring which, nor thinking they cared. But presently Ted Dotey became angry when I called Ted Leister the better runner.

" 'Tis not true," he shouted. "He cheated! He started afore I did!"

"Liar!" Ted Leister raged. "With your legs a tortoise could outrun you—and going backwards at that!"

"What's wrong with my legs?"

"They look like halves of barrel staves!"

"Better that than to have a face as ugly as the bottom of the barrel!"

The next minute they were fighting, and this time not in play, and since I thought the whole affair ridiculous I walked away and joined another group.

By nightfall the Indians who had come with Massasoit showed no inclination to leave us, a characteristic of Indians which I have noted before, so the fires were heaped high, and the singing and the storytelling and such like continued throughout the night, with those who found themselves over-come by sleep taking short naps. The moon hung large and bright and clear, and the great fires kept us warm, and it was a most pleasant and exciting time. The Indians started some sort of rhythmic chanting, with a clapping of their hands to accent it, and I sat a little apart at one of the fires listening. It was a strange sound that somehow sent my blood pulsing more quickly and made me wish I could stand up and dance round and round the fire, but this I knew would not be fit-ting. Of a sudden I was aware of someone beside me, and turning, saw Ted Leister easing himself down to the ground. I thought it best to say nothing of the disagreement he and t'other Ted had had, so I spoke of the singing.

"It nigh makes me giddy," I said. " 'Tis not at all like English singing."

"If it makes you giddy, lie back and close your eyes," Ted Leister told me. " 'Twill soon pass."

I did as he suggested, and I could feel the very earth under me throbbing from the beat and beat and beat of the voices and hands. My eyes were closed, but the dizziness got no better and I moved to sit up when I felt Ted's hand push me gently back again, and then he kissed me. This so astounded me that my eyes flew open and I would have bolted upright had not his hand held me down. I lay quietly for a moment, and discovered that Ted's kiss was far more interesting than John Cooke's had been, and when he took his lips away I could not but smile at him.

"Pretty Con," he murmured, and in truth I felt quite dazzled!

"Am I pretty?" I asked.

"Pretty and sweet and ripe," he said, and leaned down to kiss me again. I could smell the wine on his lips, and it is odd that wine never smells as pleasant after it has been drunk as before, but I let him kiss me once more just because I found it quite enjoyable. However, the ground began to feel chill and hard and I moved to rise, turning my head away.

"Don't go, Con," Ted said softly. "Don't go."

"I am cold."

"I will warm you. Don't go." His hand lay heavily on my shoulder.

"No, I am tired of kissing. Let me up."

Slowly he drew his hand away and I sat up, smoothing my rosy dress.

"Do you like me, Con?" Ted asked.

"Of course."

"Truly?"

"Of course," I repeated impatiently. "Why should I not like you?"

"You are a most—most *fetching* wench, Con! I dream of you at night."

I looked at him, quite pleased. "In truth? It puzzles me why you should. What do you dream?"

"I'll tell you sometime. Not now."

I tried looking at him the same sidewise way that I had looked at John, and Ted must have thought it inviting, for he bent his head for another kiss, but I jumped up, and laughed when he fell forward a little.

"I am hungry," I said. "Let us see what food there is left."

Ted got to his feet slowly. "Come for a walk with me instead."

"No! I am hungry! If you do not choose to come with me —stay here. It matters not to me." And so I left him standing there, glowering after me.

As I neared one of the tables I saw Ted Dotey standing by it, a turkey leg in one hand and a tankard of wine in the other.

"That's what I want," I said. "Is there another turkey leg, Ted?"

He turned to look at me. "Where have you been?"

"Over by one of the fires, listening to the Indians singing. Why?"

"Who was with you?"

"T'other Ted. Find me a turkey leg."

"What were you doing?"

I whirled on him, quite vexed by all his questions. "What business is it of yours?" I snapped. "Will you find me a turkey leg or shall I fetch one for myself?"

He pulled one from a great roasted bird and handed it to me. "Be careful of yon Ted, Constance," he said. "The man is not to be trusted."

"Pish! All he did was kiss me."

Little Ted Dotey nigh hopped from the ground in a quick spurt of rage. "*Kissed* you! You should not have let him!"

"Why not?" I asked, and took a bite of turkey. "There is a deal of kissing going on here and there tonight." Then I flicked one of my eyelash glances at him. "Or would you rather it had been you?"

He blushed so crimson that even in the pale moonlight and the flickering firelight I could see it plain. I laughed.

"Hah! I am right! You *would* rather it had been you! You are jealous!" He looked so put out that I felt sorry for him, and yet I was in a teasing mood. Heaven knows why this fit came over me—the excitement, perhaps, or the moon, or the singing. I made my voice soft and purring, and laid my hand gently on his arm. "Do you want a kiss too, little Ted? You have only to ask."

His pale blue eyes grew large, almost popping from his reddened face. "Not here, lass—not like this—gnawing on a turkey leg! Come, walk with me! We will go into the wood —it is quieter there!"

I laughed. "What great walkers you are, you and t'other Ted!"

"What do you mean?"

"Oh, he wished to go walking into the trees too. What is there in the trees? 'Tis far too dark to see anything."

Ted Dotey threw the clean legbone over his shoulder and lifting his tankard, drained it. Thumping it onto the table he grasped my wrist.

"Come, lass!"

I fast twisted my arm away from him in a way that Giles once taught me. "Catch me, then," I laughed at him, and started running. I could hear little Bandy-Legs pounding after me, but I love to run, and it was not difficult to stay ahead of him. I knew exactly where I was going, and before Ted Dotey knew in which direction we were headed, I had ducked under Father's arm and was standing close beside him in a little circle of men. Captain Standish was there, and Will Bradford, and Edward Winslow, and Francis Cooke—all talking some sort of dull business about debts and payments.

"Well!" Father said. "Where do you come from, lass?"

I looked up at him, wide-eyed. "I had not seen you in some time. I wondered whether all was well with you."

Father snorted. "A likely tale! You've been up to some mischief, I'll be bound!" He turned to the Governor. "At times I think Constance should have been a boy," he said. "She has more spirit than a girl is safe with."

The Governor looked at me, with the smile he keeps deep in his eyes. "I can think of no one less like a boy, Stephen. Spirit she may have, but it is purely female, believe me!"

I glanced over my shoulder to see Ted Dotey some distance off. He was glaring at me, but he dared not take me to task with Father there. Soon after that I went back to our house with Elizabeth and Oceanus, and we slept through the rest of the night. I do not know whether the Teds came in or not.

All that was the night afore last. It is now the end of the third day of festivity, and Massasoit and his ninety well-fed followers have taken their departure. The boards are empty of food, the casks of drink are drained dry, the children are tired and cross, the field is littered with ashes and gnawed bones, and surely every receptacle that little Plymouth owns is in need of scouring. Father and Giles have fallen into bed, where Father's snoring seems louder than ever, and Giles, every few moments, belches in his sleep. The Two Teds have climbed their ladder to the loft, scowling at me and not speaking to each other. I think Elizabeth noted the scowl, but we are all so weary that she has not pursued it. She and I stood for a while, looking at the confusion and turmoil about us, and then decided that since it would most surely still be here on the morrow, it could stay unwashed for tonight. I do not look forward to the morrow.

November 1621 continued

The first I knew of aught out of the way was when I saw Squanto running past our house and up the Street. Squanto rarely runs now, feeling it beneath his dignity in his new position as adviser and constant help to Plymouth, but when he chooses—as at the races during our feast days—he covers ground with his long easy lope at an unbelievable speed. I was sitting just inside the open doorway, the day being bright and mild for November, sewing on a little coat for Oceanus, who—now that he can walk—can no longer wear swaddling clothes. (And what we should have done for clothing without the garments left by those who died during the Sickness, I do not know!) Looking up, I saw Squanto pass our house, and though I did in truth wonder a bit at his hurry, I thought little more of it until of a sudden there came the terrifying sound of one of the sakers being shot off from in front of the Common House. This is something we have heard only once or twice before, and in every case it is enough to shoot me full of quaking fear! Even Elizabeth left off sifting ashes to add to the fat she was making into soap, and came to the doorway to peer out over my shoulder.

"Oh, ma'am," I stammered, "is it finally Indians, do you think?"

"I see no sign of them," Elizabeth said, leaning out to look up and down the Street.

"Squanto just ran by—he looked to be in a vast hurry."

"Leave your work, Constance. Go and see what is brewing."

I fled out the door, just as others did the same from all the houses along the Street, while still others came running up from the shore and in from the woods and from wherever else they had been on their various chores, all summoned by the roar of the little cannon.

"What is it? Is it Indians?" I kept asking, but no one seemed to know.

At last I saw Father, coming up the hill from the Common House. He was half running, and I ran beside him to keep up.

"Father! Stop, please! What is it? What is happening?"

He did not stop, just said, "It's a ship making for our har-

bor. Squanto brought word. We know not what she may be—
Captain Standish wants every man armed and ready."

"Might it be pirates?" I gasped, clutching at his arm.

"It might be anything. Out of my way, girl!" He went into
the house, while I turned and stood looking down toward the
water. On every side of me men, buckling on their belts over
their jackets, and carrying their odd assortment of firearms,
were hurrying down the Street toward the beach. Behind
them came the boys who were too young to be counted as de-
fenders of our little town, but who could not bear to miss the
excitement, and behind them came the women and small children. Father brushed by me again, holding his gun in the
crook of his arm while he fastened his sword belt.

"Best stay where you are, Con, until we see how things are."

I stood in the Street outside our gate, and now I could see
the ship, still far out in the water, but putting in for our harbor. The very air seemed filled with a dreadful tension. Below
me the men of Plymouth stood drawn up in what we all felt
was a battle formation. The sun shafted off their guns and
buckles, and while they seemed pitifully few in number, I
could not help but be proud of the fearless way they waited,
Captain Standish and Governor Bradford standing just ahead
of them.

From beside me I heard a hushed voice whisper, "She's going to show her colors!"

I looked to see Susanna Winslow, clutching little Peregrine
by the hand, and then I turned quickly back. In truth, we
could see a flag being hauled up, and I felt my breath tight in
my chest. Then a sharp gust of wind caught the distant cloth
and lifted it, whipping it straight out until everyone could see

the white ensign with the red cross of England, and a great sigh went up from all of Plymouth. A moment later the men broke into cheers and howls of joy, some of the women wept openly, and the little children, too young to understand, kept saying, "What is it? What is it?"

Nothing held us back now. Houses were deserted, the doors left open, while everyone ran down the hill to join the men on the shore. With the wind behind her the ship came in quickly, and we could see the decks lined with people waving at us, and below them, painted jauntily on the prow, the golden word "Fortune."

And then they came ashore! As the small boats unloaded on the beach I thought I had never seen so many strong young men, all half-afraid themselves at what they might find in this strange place, and relieved at the sight of a gathering of sturdy, healthy Englishmen, with only Squanto and Samoset to fill the threat of "the savage land" to which they had come. There were a few women among the passengers, and a handful of children. One poor soul was rowed ashore, her three small children gathered close to her, looking so far gone with a fourth that I marveled she did not bear it in the boat between the ship and the beach. Someone told me she was the Widow Ford, and that her husband had died on the voyage, a sorry circumstance indeed.

But such rejoicing as there was! Master Brewster's son, Jonathan, a sober-looking man much like his father, was among them, and Edward Winslow's brother John. Deacon Cushman and his son Thomas were warmly welcomed by the Governor, and indeed the entire occasion was a joyous one. Presently the Governor bid us all to the Common House, and the women hastened to their houses to fetch whatever they could in the way of food and drink for the newcomers.

There were hours of talk—news from home, and word of what was going on in the world, and questions about our village and our life in this new country, and introductions of one to another. In the midst of all this the Goodwife Ford, she who was great with child, excused herself from the company, and together with Mistress Brewster and Ellen Billington went to the Brewsters' house, where, with no further ado, she brought forth a fine son.

At last the Governor and Master Allerton, by a sort of lottery, apportioned most of the new arrivals out to the seven households, the remainder agreeing to sleep in the Common House "or anywhere save on that weaving ship," until such time as they might build homes of their own. With so many strong young arms it should not take long!

So finally, in the chill fresh moonlight, I went home with Elizabeth and Oceanus, to help prepare our loft room for a young man named Stephen Deane, and another named Thomas Prence, and still another named William Hilton. Of these I know little, save that Stephen Deane (to my thinking) is *most* well-favored!

December 1621

It is Christmas Day, 1621. Outside, the snow has drifted high against the houses, although the Street is packed down hard from the traffic of many feet. There is no Christmas celebration here such as I remember from London. These people take no special recognition of Christmas, saying that nowhere in the Bible is there mention of the day of Christ's birth, and also that the sort of rowdy holiday which England celebrates on Christmas is not meet for New Plymouth. Even did they not feel so, there would be little gaiety about, since it is very hard to be gay on an empty stomach.

After the "Fortune" arrived, leaving us with thirty-five eager, ambitious, but desperately ill-provisioned settlers, the Governor and Isaac Allerton and a few others took stock of the food we had gathered and stored away in the Common Storehouse, only to find that with the extra mouths to feed, our supplies were alarmingly low. Everyone's ration of food has been cut to half, and there seems never enough to eat. We go about with growling bellies, and when I think of the mounds of food that disappeared during our feast days I could weep!

As if being hungry were not enough, we received an odd threat from an Indian tribe called the Narragansetts, who seem not to feel as friendly toward us as the Wampanoag, Massasoit's people. Soon after the "Fortune" departed, Father was called by Governor Bradford. A strange Indian had come into the town and had asked for Squanto, but Squanto was away for a few days, trying to find game in the woods. Then the Indian left a bundle of arrows tied in a snakeskin, and would have taken himself off save that the Governor, mistrusting him, ordered him held. Father and Captain Standish and Master Winslow questioned him in the hope of learning more particulars, but could find out little, so they presently sent him packing, keeping the ugly snakeskin and its contents.

When Squanto returned (with very little that could be eaten), he said the snakeskin was a challenge, whereupon the Governor removed the arrows, filled the skin with bullets, and sent it back again. The sachem of the Narragansetts, a man named Canonicus, was so terrified when the skin was delivered to him that he would neither touch the skin nor have it near his place, and so at last—unopened—it was sent back to us. Nothing more has come of this, but the men have decided that we had best build a Fort atop the hill, and enclose our village with a high fence. It is to go along Town Brook, around the new Fort, down the far side of the clearing, and along the high bank above the beach to the brook again. This is nigh a mile around, Stephen Deane says, and seems a great undertaking.

Captain Standish has taken all the men in the community and divided them into four companies, with Father, Master Allerton, Edward Winslow, and the Governor as commanders. These are to guard each of the four walls of our stockade in case of danger. A sentry will be kept at all times to warn us of any attack, and so far the only result of all this is to increase my fears by the very number of precautions being taken.

But there are good times, too. In the evenings, at our meager supper board, Stephen Deane and Tom Prence and Will Hilton, eating with Elizabeth and Father and Giles and the Two Teds and me, add greatly to the pleasure of conversation and jollity. Master Hilton is married and has two small children, and his wife waits only for him to become established, when she will join him. He speaks kindly of her, and is a quiet, pleasant man.

Stephen and Tom, both of them nineteen years old, are very

different. Different from Master Hilton and different from each other. Tom is an intelligent person, with a quick wit and a deal of sureness about him. Elizabeth says he will prove himself an asset to Plymouth does he stay, and Father says the way things are at present, anyone with two hands and a small stomach is an asset to Plymouth. Tom is of medium height and well built, with a strong face, but I doubt he would ever be deemed handsome.

And Stephen—Stephen has the brightest red hair ever I saw, redder far than Captain Standish's, and his eyes are flame blue. He is as tall as Father, and lean, with great hands that could, I am sure, easily span my waist, should they ever try. He laughs! At himself, at us, at the world, at Plymouth, at life, at everything! Never have I known a man with so much joy in living, and so little worry. He comes from Southwark, where his father is a miller.

"And that will be my trade, too," Stephen said. "You have a mill?"

"None yet," Father told him.

"Then I shall build one! There be not a town that should not have a mill as the heart of it, and I am a good miller. At least as honest as most."

"The statement leaves a deal of margin," Father remarked drily, but Stephen only laughed.

"A man must look out for himself," he said, "for who else will do it for him?"

Elizabeth glanced at Father and murmured, "There are those who say a wife can be of use."

Father grinned back at her and added, "And I am one of them."

"Oh, I shall take a wife," Stephen said. "But she must be the prettiest lass in town!" He looked at me and winked one blue eye wickedly. "And mayhap she's not far away!"

At this the heads of the Two Teds jerked up from their trenchers and they looked first at Stephen Deane and then at me, Ted Leister with his eyes narrowed and his jaw thrust out fiercely, and Ted Dotey with his eyes popping and his face growing flushed. I could not help throwing each of them a most demure look from under my lashes, a trick I have been practicing in private, and though in truth they did look most amusing, I rather hoped that Stephen Deane would note their concern. Certainly the Two Teds mean nothing to me, save as they are Father's property until their seven years are done. If I have teased with them at all 'tis but in fun. It does a girl much good to find that she can beguile a man, and what harm can there be in a little pleasant coquetting?

But Father, perhaps, thinks differently, for with all the winking and glaring and glancing going on he cleared his throat roughly and said to Stephen, "Whoever you choose for wife, best you first make a place for yourself and have something to offer a wench besides your good humor. It takes more than an easy laugh and a few promises to provide for a family."

"Aye," Stephen agreed. "That it does. And what it takes, I shall have when the time comes. For now, I shall look most carefully, lest I miss some pretty face by being hasty."

This made me smile, for in all of Plymouth the only unwed women are the Widow Ford, in whom Peter Browne already shows great interest, Humility Cooper who is but fourteen, Bess Tilley, Mary Chilton, Desire Minter, and me. Poor Desire is so thoroughly lacking in all feminine graces that even kind-

hearted John Cooke avoids her; Bess and Mary are dutiful
girls, and not plain, and with so many unmarried men they
will have no hard time finding husbands, but so far they have
attracted little attention. I will let Master Deane learn these
things for himself. In the meantime he is excellent company,
and brings much laughter and gaiety to our home, although
he has little patience nor respect for authority.

This morning, when most of the men went to work on
building the palisade that will surround us, there were some,
mainly from the "Fortune," who claimed that this being
Christmas Day it went against their consciences to work. Stephen was spokesman for the group, and the Governor looked
at him squarely and said, "Very well. If it is a matter of
conscience with you, I shall excuse you till you are better
informed."

But only a short while after the Governor and his workers
had left the Street, these great men of conscience sallied forth
and enjoyed themselves mightily, playing at stoolball, and
pitching the bar, and racing, and suchlike sports. So deep were
they in their antics that they did not see the Governor coming
home for dinner, and he caught them quite unaware when he
took their playthings from them, glowering blackly the while.
I was watching, and could not help but find amusement in
their surprised faces when Will Bradford spoke to them.

"Ye told me 'twas against your conscience to work on
Christmas Day," he said firmly, "and for that you were excused. But 'tis equally against *my* conscience that you should
play while others work. If you choose to make the day one of
devotion, then keep to your houses, but there will be no gam-
ing nor reveling in the streets."

And with that he continued to his house, carrying their

balls and bars, and leaving them all standing openmouthed and somewhat shamefaced in the snowy Street. I do think 'twas good for Stephen!

February 1622

How innocent teasing can get a maid so embroiled in trouble I do not know! I certainly meant no harm, but those two witless knaves must have taken seriously all I meant only in jest. Often when I gave one Ted or the other a soft smile, or fluttered glances from under my lashes upon them, 'twas done that Stephen Deane might see how other men found me inviting. And Ted Leister kissed me but that once, and Ted Dotey never at all, and even that would not have happened had it not been for the Indians chanting and the moon and the wine and all the rest, but they would not have it so!

More and more they became enemies, and jealous of each other, and would not work in harmony, until Father berated them, saying they were not worth the meals he fed them, which in truth have been so sparing as to make little difference whether we eat or no. Each of them would scheme to find me alone somewhere, and then make such silly calf-eyes, and protest so much of the love they bore me, that I grew quite out of patience with them both. The only speech they shared was when they argued as to which of them I liked the better—though none of this where Father might overhear—or to mutter most dreadful threats of what they would do to each other so that only one would remain.

I knew they did these things, but I never thought they were in earnest! How could they have imagined that a smile, or a soft word, or a warm glance could have any deeper meaning? Yet early this morning, while all the household slept, Ted Dotey and Ted Leister crept out the door and made their way to the beach.

They must have stalked silently down the hill, the light just beginning to break in the winter sky. Surely they could not have talked together, not even to dissent or argue. Of what were they thinking? Of me? They must have been! I could weep when I think of their foolishness! Could they not *see* 'twas only in sport? That I had meant nothing by my lightness and my teasing? If I had heard them go out, I could have stopped them—save that I never would have guessed their intent! But I knew nothing at all until I was awakened by Father leaping from bed, bellowing and cursing, and racing to the door. Outside there were the voices of other men, and heavy footsteps running down the Street. Father threw the door open, calling to someone.

"What is it? What's afoot?"

"On the shore," a voice shouted back. "Two men fighting, I know not who."

As he pulled his breeches tight about his waist Father went to the foot of the ladder.

"You Teds! Come down here! There is trouble!"

Stephen's red head poked into the opening at the top of the ladder. "They are not here, sir. Their beds are empty."

"Zounds!" Father roared. "I might have known!" He whirled around, facing me as I sat up on my pallet, half-asleep. "If this is your doing, miss, 'twill be a day you'll remember!"

"My doing?" I asked. In truth, I could not think what he meant.

"Yes, yours! You and your sweetsop ways! Oh, why could I not have ten sons and be spared one such daughter!" And with that he was out of the house and on his way to the shore. I was so bewildered I knew not what to do. Giles and Stephen both went after Father, and I was of a mind to follow till Elizabeth stopped me.

"Best you stay here, Constance. It may be that you have caused enough trouble already."

"But what have I *done?*"

"You have roused such jealousy between those two as takes a fight to stop it, would be my guess," she said.

"But I never *meant—*"

"It matters not what you meant, Constance! I have seen it coming, but I hoped 'twould all blow over like a summer storm. I did not think they could be such fools as to battle over you!"

I sat there, the covers wrapped around me, hunched and shivering, deathly afraid. Supposing it was true? Supposing the Two Teds were truly fighting over me—what if one of them was badly hurt? Or . . . killed? What would be done to me? I was in such a state I could do naught but whimper. When at last Giles came bursting in the door I stared at him, too terrified to ask any of the questions my head was filled with.

"What fools!" Giles said. "To fight over a girl!"

"So they *were!*" Elizabeth muttered.

"Indeed they were. With sword in one hand and dagger in t'other! They *are* a bloody sight, believe me!"

"Oh, no!" I screamed, and jammed my hands over my ears. "I don't want to hear!"

"You are going to hear plenty," Giles said with satisfaction. "You might as well hear some of it from me. They nigh slew each other, and would have, had the Captain not disarmed them both at his own sword's point."

"The Captain," I gasped, "but how did he get there?"

"He heard them raging at each other—he must have an ear tuned to such sounds. And he was in a fine froth himself! He said that with Indians all about us no one had a right to risk his life, much less to murder another! He also had a monstrous lot to say concerning his opinion of any man who would be addlepated enough to fight over a wench."

"Oh, heaven," I sobbed. "What am I to do?"

Elizabeth is more practical than I. "Are they badly hurt?" she asked Giles.

"Leister has a great gap in his leg—here, above the knee," Giles told her, laying his hand on his thigh, "and Dotey's sword hand will be of little use for weeks. They were evenly matched, it seems."

"Where are they now? What has been done to them?"

"Father and the Captain have taken them to Governor Bradford's. I know not what his decision will be."

Still all of a tremble, I managed to get up and splash cold water on my face, and, with my hands shaking, I was helping Elizabeth with the small servings of breakfast porridge when Father returned. He walked in the door, followed by Stephen Deane, and without even looking at me, took his place at the head of the board and bowed his head for the blessing.

I thought he would never be through! All of the things I

expected him to say to me he roared aloud to God during the prayer.

". . . and make this flirtatious chit fully understand the dangers—the sins—the pitfalls—of overweening vanity, Lord! Turn her mind to the modest thoughts that befit a woman, and bring Your great wrath upon her in her moments of evil weakness. And save *me*, Lord, from the perils of my own anger against her—let me not lay my hand upon her, lest I do her more harm than I intend! And Lord, if Your all-seeing eye should find her again engaged in such trouble-brewing fripperous behavior, let it not be with the two men who are here for the one purpose of working for me, for Thou knowest, Lord, that I have gotten not a tuppence worth of labor from either one for weeks past, and an honest man is hard put when he can count neither on his bond servants nor on his daughter for aught save worry. For Thou knowest I am a patient man, Lord, and do not complain unduly, but there is a limit to human endurance, and I swear to You up there in heaven that between these two fools with but one thought between them, and this minx who put that thought in their empty heads, I am a most unfortunate man among men! And now, Lord, we are about to eat what You have seen fit to give us, and though there is little of it, God knows, bless it for us, and do not let Constance open her mouth until I am fed, lest I speak to her as ill befits a father. In Thy name I ask it! Amen!"

"Amen," Stephen Deane echoed, and there was something in his voice that sounded like the hint of laughter, but I did not dare raise my eyes to see his face. I think perhaps he knew what a state I was in, for after he had eaten a few mouthfuls he said, "How long think you the Governor will keep the pair tied thus together, head and heel?"

"Long enough, I trust, for them to cool off," Father answered between his teeth.

I shuddered at the thought of them, bound back to back, bleeding, hurt, raging, saying who could know what dreadful things of me. Would they bleed to death? Were they in fearful pain?

" 'Twas Christian of the Governor to have Dr. Fuller bind their wounds," Stephen remarked, and this time I did look up quickly, to find his eyes full on mine.

"The Governor is a very Christian man," Father said. "More so than I would be."

We were not finished with our meal, and never have I had less appetite, when we could hear two voices raised in the most piteous cries for mercy. This so distressed me that I could not swallow another bite, and sat at table, my head lowered, the tears pouring from my eyes. No one mentioned the anguished howls that came from farther up the Street, but at last, with the sort of oath Father rarely uses, he pushed back his chair, rose from the table, jammed his hat on his head, and stomped out the door. Stephen leaped from his stool, murmured an apology to Elizabeth, and took after him. The door had no sooner closed than I could control myself no longer, and burst into such a torrent of tears, sobs, and gasps as made Giles throw up his hands in despair at the vagaries of females, and he, too, departed.

"Oh, ma'am," I wailed to Elizabeth, "how can I ever face them?"

"Thee might have thought of that before," Elizabeth said,

and though her voice was crisp, it was not unkind. She moved
from her place to sit beside me. "Thou hast made a mountain
of trouble by thy whimsies, child, and it is not unfair that you
should suffer for them. This duel between the Teds—it might
have ended in death, you know."

"I know! How well I know! I was feared to the marrow!"

"Then keep some trace of that fear with thee always. Mayhap it will help thee when thou'rt tempted to engage in more
'innocent flirtation.'"

"I never will again, ma'am! Never! I will never *look* at any
man again!"

"I trust thee will, and often. 'Tis meet you should. Looking
at a man does little harm. But curb thine own mischief, child,
and do not test thy strength against a man's emotions. 'Tis a
most dangerous game to play."

"Oh, yes, it is! It *is!*"

"Be more honest with thyself and them. When thou lovest,
say so. But when thee wishes only to amuse thyself, find other
ways!" I nodded, unable to speak. "Now dry thy eyes, Constance, and cleanse the trenchers for me. The chores are
waiting."

With a little pat on my shoulder Elizabeth rose, picked up
the broom, and started sweeping vigorously. I washed my face
again, and was hard at work scouring the breakfast trenchers
when Father came back, the Two Teds walking silently behind him. Ted Leister's breeks were blood-stained and torn,
but his leg bore a clean bandage. Ted Dotey's hand was also
wrapped, and he cradled it in his other arm. Neither one
looked at me nor spoke to me. Helping each other as gently as
two women, they climbed the ladder to the loft.

"At most, an hour of rest!" Father told them. "You understand?"

"Yes, sir. An hour only."

"And then you are to meet me in the Common House. If you are good for nothing else, you can at least check the stores!"

"Yes, sir," they repeated, almost in unison. I heard them walk across the floor, heard the soft crunch of the pallets as they lay down, listened to muted indistinguishable voices for a few seconds, and then there was naught but silence. Father started out the door again, then he turned to me.

"Constance," he said.

My voice was barely a whisper. "Yes, Father?"

He pointed to the loft. "Those two. You! I—" He could not finish, just stared at me, shook his head, spread his hands helplessly, shrugged, and went out.

I rubbed the back of my hand across my eyes and went back to work. Oh, what a fool I've been!

April 1622

At times it is of great wonder to me how the world ever came to pass. How was London built? How did its people exist in the beginning? Here we are, trying to build what Father always calls 'our new world,' and it does seem that for each step forward we manage to take, there are two steps back.

For example, the men continue to build. The high fence

that surrounds us is completed (but whether it makes me feel secure I do not know). New houses are continually being raised to accommodate those who came on the "Fortune," and a lean-to was added to the Common House for further storage. All this work (and the men are always hungry since our food supply is low, so that they seem to need twice the effort to accomplish these things), and then came a fire which started next to the Common House and flattened four of our dwellings! 'Twas a dreadful thing to watch, first just thick smoke, and then great arrows of fire that whipped high in the air. Every living soul helped—the women soaking rugs, blankets, cloths, in water and the men throwing them over the flames. There was shouting of orders from one man to another, and the sharp cracking of the fire, and then the screams of women as they saw their houses caught by the sparks. Captain Standish and the Governor directed the work, and they did well, for although we lost the dwellings, they kept the Common House wherein lie all our stores. Had that been burned, it certainly would have wiped out New Plymouth.

To make our nights yet more sleepless, there has again been trouble with the Indians. Squanto lives with us all the time, considering Governor Bradford as his "adopter." But a short time back came another named Hobomok, whom Captain Standish supports. While each is friendly to us, there is great rivalry one against the other, each Indian thinking he is of more importance to us, and trying to oust his fellow from the village. It was, no doubt, due to this enmity between two who should be friend to each other as well as to us, that Squanto slyly managed a rumor saying that Massasoit (who is a better friend to Hobomok than to Squanto himself) was planning to war against us. This put everyone into a monstrous frenzy! We have heard, only too often, and in too much detail, of the massacres at Jamestown. The savages come screeching and howling into the villages, thrusting firebrands into every building, dragging the people into the open and there killing them in terrifying fashion, or—even worse—keeping them to torture. My fear is so great that even to write of it makes my flesh crawl on my bones! Some of the doomed settlers have their scalps hacked from their heads, and these the Indians keep as proof of prowess. I cannot bear to think of it! The screaming, the blood, the licking flames—the thought makes my hand shake so I can barely bring quill to paper! Could this happen to us? Father says he believes Massasoit to be our friend, but is he right? Can these creatures be trusted? Or are they like animals who will turn unexpectedly and kill without warning? Between this terror and the constant hunger I am in sore state!

May 1622

There has been so much fear in me I have felt like an apple riddled with worms. At any sudden sound I jumped. Did I see an Indian, even at a distance, my heart clogged my throat. Nor have I been alone! Priscilla said she would not step outside the palisade for aught, and but barely dared to step outside her door! The whole settlement has lived in unrest, waiting for—we knew not what!

A few mornings ago I was emptying the water from the

bucking tub after Elizabeth and I had washed all the sheets.
Standing in front of the house and holding the tipped vat so
that the water would run into the flower garden, I looked up
to see a procession of savages coming up the Street from the
shore. Their faces were painted and grim, and they moved so
silently and with such purpose that I was engulfed in fear! My
hands could no longer hold the tub, my breath caught and left
me gasping. I could feel my scalp prickling as though a toma-
hawk were within inches of it! My knees shook so I could
barely move, but somehow I dropped the tub, and pushing
open the door, I ran back into the house, dropping the great
bar in place, and fell on the big bed in a spasm of weeping.
Elizabeth came quickly, sitting beside me, her hand warm on
my head, making little soothing sounds in her soft voice.

"What are we doing here?" I sobbed. "We should be safe in
London—where there are no Indians—and no dangers we
cannot overcome."

Elizabeth patted my head. "There, poppet, there," she
soothed. " 'Twill be all right. You will see."

" 'Twill *not* be all right! There are Indians walking
through the Street *now!* They'll kill us all! Oh, I want to go
home! I want to go back to London!"

"London is not the safest place in the world, either," Elizabeth said. "There is plague, and dreadful fires, and lawlessness
even in London."

"But there are no Indians! I want to be where there are no
Indians!"

"Come, child. You would not want one of those Indians to
hear your sobbing and know that you are afraid. Here, wipe
your eyes." She offered me a corner of her apron, and I sat up

sniffling and rubbed it across my eyes. "Much of our strength is in *seeming* strong, Constance. Whatever befalls us here, and I do *not* think there will be trouble, we must always remember we are English and we are brave."

"I may be English," I gulped, "but I am not brave!"

Elizabeth smiled. "Perhaps not, but you can appear so." She rose from beside me and unbarred the door, opening it wide. "I always like a door that stands open," she remarked easily. "It gives a feeling of friendliness and welcome."

"Besides, it will keep the Indians from having to break it down when they come in to scalp us," I muttered.

I slid off the bed, splashed a little cold water on my face, and went to the door. Peering out cautiously, I could see the last of the Indians filing into the Fort, where the Captain stood at the door, his face as set as those that passed him. I did not need to be told that the Governor would be inside, with Father and Edward Winslow and whatever other of the settlement leaders were available. I forced myself to step outside, fetch the tub, and bring it back in.

For the next hour I hovered by our doorway, my eyes tight on the Fort. When at last the heavy door opened, the Indians came out first and walked down the Street as silently as they had climbed it before. I could tell nothing from their expressions, though I watched them as they went through the palisade's East Gate at the foot of the Street. They strode across the beach to where their boats waited. Even when I saw Father step out of the Fort, I was not sure. I saw him shake Will Bradford's hand and nod in approval at something Will said, and then he started down the hill. I could not wait. I ran to meet him.

"What was it, Father? What did they come for? What did they want?"

"They wanted Squanto."

"Squanto! Whatever for?"

"Massasoit feels the mischief-maker should be punished for his spreading of such a false rumor, and in truth he should."

"Then the rumor *was* false? Massasoit intends us no harm?"

"Not a whit! Massasoit is no fool. He knows he will be in better fortune if he stays friendly with Plymouth. Our trading alone has been most profitable to him."

"But they did not take Squanto with them—I watched."

"No. The Governor would not give him up."

"But if he deserves punishment—"

"Indian punishment is not a pretty thing, Con. 'Twill be better for us to spare him that and put him in our debt. Squanto has been, and can be, of great service to us."

"And Massasoit is not angry with us for keeping Squanto? We are still at peace with him?"

"There were a few bad moments, but between Will's firmness and Ed Winslow's smooth tongue things stay well with us." He stopped just outside our gate and looked at me keenly. "Do not tell me you have been fretting, child!"

"Oh, no! I . . . only wondered how it was. Now come. It must be time for supper."

"Supper!" Father opened the gate to let us through. "A royal feast of roast leg of mouse, I fancy. Believe me, Con, my belly and my backbone are become close friends!"

I feared that Elizabeth would tell Father of my weakness and fright, but she did not mention it. I am beginning to learn that the things one fears rarely come to pass. Danger and trouble are generally from unexpected sources. I cannot decide whether this comforts me or not.

June 1622

Shortly after that silly terror of mine, for which I have felt great shame since, I was in our little garden, pulling the weeds from the herb patch. I heard no approaching steps, but of a sudden a shadow fell across me and I looked up quickly to see two Indian figures black against the sun. For an instant I felt my belly plunge in fear, and then I saw it was Samoset and a young girl of about my own age. Nigh the first thing I noticed was my bracelet—the one Father had bought me in London—on her dark wrist. I rose and stood gazing at her, and she stared back and then she smiled. It was a small smile, and shy, but still a smile, so I answered it with one of my own. It was Samoset who spoke first. He said something to the girl that I could not understand, and then he spoke to me.

"This is daughter I told you about," he said. "She wear your bracelet with pride and happiness."

"I am glad," I said. "I give her greeting, and you too, Samoset."

"She has brought you gift."

He spoke again to the girl, and from behind her back she brought forth a pair of white slippers of the kind the Indians wear, and held them out to me.

"Take them," Samoset ordered. "She has made them for you."

I took the slippers from her hand. They were most wonder-
fully soft, and decorated with some sort of stiff quill, brightly
colored. Without thinking I lifted one and rubbed it gently
across my cheek to feel the smoothness of the leather. The girl
giggled and shook her head. Then she pointed to my feet. For
a moment I did not understand, and then I laughed too.

"I know they are for my feet," I said. "It is just that they are
so soft—never did I know leather could feel as velvet-soft as
this!"

Samoset told the girl what I had said, and she giggled again
with pleasure. Then he spoke to me once more.

"Samoset visit with Governor for a small time. Daughter
will visit with white girl."

Turning, he started up the Street toward Governor Bradford's house, leaving me with my guest. I was at a loss, but I
gestured toward the door.

"Will you come in?" I asked. She looked at me, her eyes as
large and dark as a doe's, and then she moved hesitantly toward the door while I walked beside her. Giles was off on
pursuits of his own, Elizabeth had taken Oceanus to Dr. Fuller's to ask for some syrup for his constant coughing, and Father and the Teds, of course, are rarely about the house save to
eat and sleep—so there we were alone. I pulled out two stools
and sat down, indicating that she should sit on the other. For
a few moments we sat staring at each other, neither of us
knowing what to say. Then I leaned down and pulled one of
the slippers on my bare foot, where it nestled as gently and
firmly as a well-fitting glove.

"Shoe beautiful," I said, waggling my foot.

"Moccasin," the girl replied.

"Moccasin?"

She bent forward and touched the slipper with her slim finger. "Moccasin."

"Oh. Not shoe—moccasin," I repeated. She nodded with delight. I put the second moccasin on and held up two fingers. "*Two* moccasins," I said.

"Two moccasin," she repeated after me, giggling.

I pointed to myself. "I Constance."

The girl's smile widened. "I Constance," she said, pointing to herself.

I tried again. "*My* name Constance," I told her.

She looked puzzled, and her voice held a rising note of question. "I Constance?"

Feeling rather a ninny, but, in truth, enjoying myself too, I shook my head, pointed to myself once more and said firmly, "Constance." Then I pointed to her and raised my brows in query.

For a moment she stared at me, and then with another giggle she pointed to me and said, "Constance," and then to herself and said, "Minnetuxet." I said it after her.

"Minnetuxet?"

She nodded happily. Then I held out my hand and said it again, smiling at her. After a moment she laid her hand in mine, and said "Constance," and we sat there, our hands clasped, smiling broadly at each other. Presently I put my foot out to admire the moccasin again, and wondering about the bright decorations, I pointed to them.

"What are these?" I asked.

Minnetuxet knitted her smooth brow in an effort to answer me. Then to my delight she crouched on her knees on the floor, and pulling herself into a tight ball, thrust splayed fin-

gers out from her sides. It was as vivid a picture of a porcu-
pine as I could have wished for and I threw back my head in
laughter. Pleased with her success in making me understand,
Minnetuxet sat back on her heels and laughed too, her teeth
sharp white against her lovely dark skin.

When Elizabeth returned a few moments later she found us
walking hand in hand about the house, pointing to one thing
after another, with me saying the English word and Minnetuxet saying it after me. I told Elizabeth who she was, and
then tried to think how to explain a stepmother to Minnetuxet, but I might better not have bothered. She laid her finger
gently on Oceanus' cheek, so flushed and feverish from his
cough, and said, "Papoose." Then she placed her arms as
though she were cradling a baby and repeated the word again.
"Papoose."

I said it after her, and turning to Elizabeth, explained,
"Papoose means baby." Then I pointed to Elizabeth and
added, "Papoose *mother.*"

Minnetuxet looked at Elizabeth, who smiled at her encour-
agingly, and the Indian girl said softly, "Papoose *mother.*"
Then she looked from Elizabeth to me and asked, "Constance
mother?"

I glanced at Elizabeth, and then shrugged a little and nodded. "Yes," I said. "Constance' mother, too."

I heard Elizabeth catch her breath, and looked at her
quickly. Two bright tears were in the corners of her eyes, but
she was smiling at me as she went and laid Oceanus in his
cradle. Minnetuxet and I stepped outdoors to meet Samoset
who was coming back down the Street.

June 1622 continued

Oceanus lay sick all that week. He coughed and coughed, and neither Dr. Fuller's syrup nor anything that Elizabeth could concoct seemed to help him. He ate barely a mouthful, and his little belly growled with hunger, though it rounded grotesquely.

"If only there were some milk for him, I could warm it, and drop an egg in it—if there were any eggs."

Elizabeth rocked a little to and fro, her arms folded hard across her breast as she sat beside the big bed where Oceanus lay. His dark eyes were closed and there were great shadows beneath them, and his hair was in flat brown whorls from the sweat.

I picked up the damp cloth she had been using as a sugar-tit, and smeared it again with the last of the wild honey. "Try this," I said. "Mayhap he will suck a little of it."

She took it from me, but shook her head the while. "Poor baby," she murmured, "poor little boy." She touched her son's dry lips gently with the honied cloth, but the child only whimpered and turned his head away.

"There's some porridge left from breakfast," I said. "I could add some hot water to soften it for him—"

"He cannot keep it down." Elizabeth's voice broke, and then, as though she spat the word from her mouth, she said, "Corn!"

"But 'tis all we have," I began, and was interrupted by a storm of words, the like of which I had never heard from my stepmother before.

"I am sick to death of corn! I wish I had never to look at it, nor taste it, nor touch it, nor speak of it again! I want white bread for my baby, and milk, and eggs, and sugar, and good English beef, and a rasher of bacon, and a fresh fowl—not these wild birds with their scent and taste of wildness! I want fresh apples from which to make cider, and clear brown ale —and a leg of mutton! My mouth waters for mutton! Oceanus could eat it—his teeth are strong enough—but corn, corn, *corn!* My baby is *dying* from corn! Oh, Constance, what can I do for him?"

And suddenly Elizabeth put her head down on the bed and cried until I thought she would tear herself apart with the great racking sobs. Never had I heard her cry before—not even when little 'Maris died. Never! And this was as though all the tears and sadness and hopelessness of her whole life had suddenly burst out in a torrent of grief. To see Elizabeth cry—Elizabeth, who was so strong, so unshakable, so calm, who always dried the tears of others and never shed them herself—if ever a heart has broken for someone else, mine did then, for her. I dropped to my knees on the floor beside her and put my arms around her.

"Don't, Mother," I said. "Mother, please don't cry!"

I held her like that, rocking a little back and forth as she had rocked before, and realizing that for the first time in my life I had truly called her Mother. Yet somehow I felt that I was the mother, and that I held in my arms Elizabeth, the child. The sobs went on, a little softer, but choking her so that I could feel her whole body shake.

"Hush," I whispered. "Mother, hush thy tears. Thou wilt fright the babe."

Instinctively her hand went out toward Oceanus, resting

gently against his tiny wrist. Then I felt her stiffen, and the weeping ceased on an indrawn breath. Slowly she drew away from my arms, leaning toward her son, her eyes wide and tear-washed, her face streaked. She sat gazing at him, her hand moving, trembling, from his wrist to his little chest, until it lay softly across his lips.

And then, in a voice I could barely hear, but one that was cleared of all weeping, she said, "Nothing can fright the babe now, Constance. The babe is dead."

John Alden made his little coffin, and Father and Giles brought a great flat stone they had found, heaving and sweating with the weight of it, and laid it gently atop the tiny grave. Afterwards Father and Elizabeth walked slowly home again, and I started to follow.

"Con, walk with me a bit," Giles said.

I looked at him in surprise. "Of course."

We walked slowly down the Street, Giles scuffing up little clouds of dust as he went. His head drooped, and the long front lock of his blond hair that never stays in place moved softly up and down against his forehead with every step. The Lower Gate in the palisade stood open, and Stephen Deane was on guard duty.

"You buried the child?" he asked.

I nodded. "May we walk down to the water?"

"Go. There is no reason why you should not."

Giles and I went through the gate, and as I passed him Stephen laid his hand on my arm, so that I looked up at him, his red hair flaming in the sun.

"I'm sorry," he said. "He was a bonny lad."

Not quite trusting my voice, I managed a small smile and nodded at him again, and Giles and I went on down the path to the beach.

We walked for a while, neither of us saying anything, and then we came to the spot where John Cooke and I had sat that day—the day he kissed me.

"Let's sit here a while," I said to Giles.

He dropped down beside me on the sand, resting his chin on his drawn-up knees and staring out at the water. I watched him, noting with sudden wonder how he had grown. His eyes, deep blue like mine, and with the same long thick lashes that often hide our eyes, gazed unblinkingly into the distance. Presently he spoke, his voice husky and nigh as deep as a man's.

"I thought the new world would be a great adventure, Con."

"It is," I answered. "There should be enough adventure here to do you all your life."

"But it is not as I had imagined. I saw myself accomplishing great things—fighting battles singlehanded against tribes of Indians, though I did not even know what an Indian looked like; discovering gold and mayhap even precious stones that would make me as rich as the King; building a home that would be finer and bigger and greater than anything I had ever seen . . ."

He paused, not lifting his eyes from the rhythmic movement of the sea.

"I hope you will never have to fight Indians," I said, "but you might well do the other things. In a land as great as this there must surely be gold, aye, and jewels too. Mayhap you will find them someday."

"No, Con. There will be no chance for that. All our days must be spent in simply making a land that others can live in with more comfort."

"Is it Oceanus who made you feel thus?"

"In part. Oh, I grant you he might have died in London, too. There are many who do. But our mother is right—if he could have been cosseted a bit, fed the things he should have had—"

"No one else has them either. It is not only Oceanus."

"But they must. There must be cattle sent to us, and chickens, and other animals. We must plant more crops, and raise more—surely there is something that will grow here beside corn! We must build better houses, raise sheep for wool so that we may have clothes that are not a mass of holes and mending, start orchards that there may be apples, and plums, and pears and peaches—"

"But while we must all plant and tend crops for the common good, to put them in a common store, there seems little desire to work," I said. "Father says each man feels he is working as hard for his neighbor as for himself. There is no incentive."

"Then somehow we must work for ourselves! Do we go on like this—" He shrugged. "No, this is not the way. I must talk to Father."

I could not help smiling at him. "You sound like a man, Giles."

"I am all but fifteen. Had you forgotten?"

We sat quietly for a few moments, watching the waves slide in and break against the sand. My eyes traveled far out across the water.

"We will never go back to England, will we, Giles?"

"I doubt we do." He paused, and then, not looking at me, "Do you mind very much, Con?"

I thought carefully before I answered. "Not so much," I said slowly. "It seems different somehow, with both 'Maris and Oceanus . . . staying here. We could not all go home to-gether—not any more."

"But you still call it 'home.'"

"Aye, I did, didn't I? Perhaps 'home' can be where one comes from, as well as where one lives."

"Or mayhap it is where things—events—'happen' to us. The place where our lives wind through each day, building some-thing strong from every joy, and every little victory, from every trouble—even from death. It may be that these are what make 'home.'" As though embarrassed at his own seriousness he cleared his throat, and then got to his feet, offering me his hand to help me up. "We had best go back now. I think to put the cradle in the loft where our mother need not see it all the time."

Elizabeth was just serving the small portions of supper into the trenchers when we entered, and Father made us come to the board. I saw Giles glance at the cradle, and Elizabeth, as she so often does, must have seen him, too, and read his thoughts.

"You were going to move it?" she asked. Giles just nodded. She patted his shoulder, already higher than her own. "Better to leave it," she said. "There will be another baby very early in the spring."

Father cleared his throat, and took his place at the head of the board. As he bowed his head and began the blessing I saw him reach out and take Elizabeth's hand in his, and they stood thus until we sat down to eat our meal.

September 1622

I think I am in love!

At night I lie in my own room (for Father and the Teds have built two small rooms on the back of our house, one for stores and one for me), and I dream of that flaming red head. A dozen times a day I start from what I am doing when I imagine I hear his voice. In the midst of my work I fall to thinking of his hands on my waist—they *can* span it, with ease! I find myself wanting to walk where I think I shall see him, and then when I do, I am tongue-tied and can bare speak a word.

The time I was first aware of how I felt was a night of rain so heavy that it lashed in sheets against the house, running in rivers down the Street, some drops splatting down the chimney to hiss in the fire. Our evening meal, made tastier by the addition of two rabbits Stephen had trapped, had been shared by the hunter himself, and by the Two Teds (who, ever since that fearsome duel, find great comfort in each other's company, and treat me with grave formality). When we had done eating, Father brought out the last of his precious brandy—he even gave a small portion to Giles—and we all sat by the fire, talking of England, and of the way life used to be. Father was telling of the merry-making on May Day and on Christmas, and suddenly Ted Dotey jumped from his stool and clambered up the ladder to the loft, two rungs at a time. We heard him scrambling about up there, and a moment later there came the thin, sweet notes of a flute piping the gayest tune ever I heard! Down the ladder he came again, one hand holding the flute to his lips, his eyes filled with glee. Elizabeth's face lighted with pleasure, and she clapped her hands almost like a child.

"Oh, Ted!" she cried. "You have a flute! You never showed us before."

"There has seemed little time for amusement, ma'am," he said. "I had forgot I had it."

"Oh, play for us," Elizabeth begged. "Play something happy."

Ted needed no coaxing. He sat on the floor by the fire, leaning his back against the chimney piece, and played his flute. It was like magic! My toes started tapping of their own volition, and the first thing I knew Stephen was on his feet, pulling me to mine.

"Come, lass, dance with me!"

"But . . . but . . . I know not how," I stammered.

"Can't dance? What kind of an English girl are you?" He looked at me in mock despair.

"I . . . I was never taught," I said, and I could feel myself blushing at being found so stupid in his eyes.

"Then I shall teach you! Come, put your hands thus—now, simply do as I do!"

Before I knew what was happening I was skipping about the room, Stephen's big hands holding me and guiding me so well I could not miss a step. Father and Giles moved the board close against the wall to give us room, Ted Leister clapped his hands in time to the merry tune, and suddenly Elizabeth rose and grasped Father's hands, and then they were dancing too. I had never seen Elizabeth dance, and I wanted to watch, but I was so busy keeping my own feet moving, there was little time to spare observing hers. I did note that she moved as lightly and easily as a girl, even though the new child has already thickened her waist. Her eyes were shining, and little wisps of her brown hair bounced from her cap, curling softly against her reddened cheeks. Giles took up the clapping, and we danced and danced until we were all gasping, when we threw ourselves back on our stools.

I felt more excited than I ever had in my life! Stephen's eyes, so clear blue they are close to green, kept sparkling at me, making me want to laugh. He started singing, then, in a voice I consider exceeding fine—bold songs, in some of which Father joined him, both of them roaring out the flighty words at the top of their lungs. Father filled their tankards again, and the songs got louder, with Ted Dotey leading the air with his pipe—and of a sudden there came a knock on the door so thunderous we were all startled into silence. Father opened it, and there stood the Governor, rain pouring from his hat, his cloak soaked black.

"Good evening, Will," Father said pleasantly, while behind him Ted Dotey slipped the flute inside his shirt.

"Good evening, Stephen," the Governor replied.

"Won't you come in?" Governor Bradford stepped inside the door, his face long and serious. "Have a nip of brandy, Will. 'Twill dry out the rain."

The Governor looked at the bottle longingly, but shook his head. "It grieves me to say this, Stephen," he said, "but you well know there are laws against a master and his servants drinking and idling together."

"But on such a night, Will," Father protested. "Surely there is no harm—"

"There are better things to do with our time. I feel certain

there are some worth-while chores to which your men can put
their efforts. It is not meet for hired men to have idle hands."

Father just looked at the Governor, knowing from experience that no words he might say would be of help.

"As you say, Will," he murmured. He replaced the top on
the bottle of brandy with a little sigh. "There shall be no more
tonight."

"Isaac and I will determine what your fine is to be," the
Governor said as he turned to the door. Then, as though he
had forgotten something, he turned back and added politely,
"I trust you are in good health, Elizabeth?"

"Quite, thank you," Elizabeth said demurely, her hands
folded quietly in her lap.

With a little nod at the rest of us the Governor departed,
ducking his head against the driving rain. Father closed the
door. I felt shocked—I had never known my father to be fined
for anything, nor even openly reproached. It seemed a dreadful embarrassment! A tiny sound made me look quickly at
Elizabeth, who was sitting with her hands covering her
mouth, trying to stifle—of all things!—a surge of giggling!

"Oh, Stephen," she gasped, her eyes sparkling, "suppose he
had come a few moments sooner? Whatever would have happened had he seen us dancing?"

Father stood looking down at her, and then he grinned.
"What could he have done, Lizzie? Did he take but one look
at you, he would have asked you to be his partner!"

It cost Father forty shillings, but he said it was worth it. As
for me, all I can think of now is Stephen!

October 1622

There have been times this year when I have felt that the most important thing in the world would be to have my fill of eating. Our diet goes in a tiresome circle of corn, fish, a little venison or wild duck or goose, then back to corn again. In the summer there are berries and a kind of wild plum that is moist and sweet—and then corn. Corn bread, corn pudding, corn porridge, dried corn, boiled corn—but always corn! Each one's ration from the general stores has been cut, until any meal is but a great deal of blessing and the smallest portion of food. And yet—except for little Oceanus —we live. But now I find there are others near us who are not so fortunate.

A few days ago I was standing by the open door—the morning being mild for early fall—combing my hair. I bethought myself it needed washing, but there were chores awaiting me, and no time to do it then. Just as I laid down the comb and began to twist my hair in the coils that I fasten with wooden pins and cover with my cap, John Cooke walked by. Seeing me, he paused, we exchanged a morning greeting, and he approached the door, smiling shyly.

"Your hair looks like corn silk," he said.

I was holding a pin between my teeth, ready to secure my hair with it, which made speech a little difficult, but I *had* to answer him.

"Corn silk!" I blurted. "Belike it *is* corn silk! When there is naught on the diet but corn 'tis wonder we don't have corn teeth, corn eyes—" I stopped to take the pin from my mouth and plunge it into my hair.

"Even ears of corn," John said, grinning. Then he sobered. "Still, think of the men at Wessagusset, Con. They would welcome corn more than gold."

I knew that Thomas Weston, who had helped to finance the "Mayflower's" voyage, and who was now causing our Governor and his aides much worry by his importunate demands, had sent some seventy Englishmen to form a new settlement twenty or so miles north of here, on the Massachusetts Bay. I had heard Father speak of this place, called Wessagusset, but with the unfriendly feeling between Plymouth and Mister Weston, there had been little visiting back and forth, and I had nigh forgot the colony was there. This I told John.

"They are even hungrier than we," he said. "They came ill-provisioned, and have had no time to raise any sort of crop. What they did bring, and the further food that they traded the Indians for, they have long since eaten. Now they have nothing left with which to trade, and until Weston sends another ship they are virtually without food, save what they can catch."

"Let them come here. I will gladly give them my share of corn," I said.

"Governor Bradford has given them a little—we have none to spare ourselves—and that was soon gone."

"But what do they do now?" I asked, sitting down in the doorway, where the morning sun was warm on the Street.

John sat down beside me. "Some of them have become servants to the Indians," he said. "They carry water and firewood for the Indians in exchange for a handful of corn. They have given up their blankets, most of their clothes, whatever the Indians will take."

"But that is dreadful," I said, shocked through. "They are Englishmen! How can they lower themselves that way?"

"For hunger men will do many things. Just a few days ago there was one of them digging for a few clams, and he was so weakened from lack of food that, sticking badly in the mud, he could not move."

"What happened to him?"

"He died there."

"Like *that?* In the *mud?*"

"Yes."

I shuddered. "What will become of them?"

"I know not."

"Are there women among them? Children?" I thought of Oceanus.

"No. Naught but men."

"Thank God for that," I breathed.

John looked at me with the trace of a smile. "You think so poorly of men, Con?"

"It isn't that—"

"I know. I was but teasing." John leaned forward, picking up a small pebble from the ground, tossing it lightly up and down in his hand. After a moment of silence he said, "You are much with Stephen Deane, Con."

I widened my eyes at him. "He shared our roof. He is a friend to all of us."

"Will Hilton and Tom Prence shared the same roof, but I do not see you making such friends of them."

"Will Hilton is married," I said primly. "He but waits for his wife. In any case—"

"In any case they no longer live with you," John interrupted. "They have their own quarters in the Common House with others of the wifeless men."

"That is *not* what I was going to say! I was about to point out that I find it no business of yours who my friends are, and I regard Master Deane's company as most pleasant!"

"You did not need to tell me that," John said gloomily. Then he looked straight at me, his long dark face solemn. "Do ye plan to wed with him?"

I rose quickly to my feet, giving my skirt a little twitch. "In truth, John, I cannot see that it is your affair," I said indignantly. And then, because I could not help but be curious, I added, "Why do you ask?"

John rose too, his head level with mine, since he is not as tall as Stephen. "He is not right for you, Con, that is all. He is a boisterous rogue, and you deserve better!"

"Like you, I suppose?"

"I have little to offer any girl—yet, but I have . . . great fondness for you, Con."

To my surprise I found myself giving him what can only be called a coquettish glance, though I have promised myself never to behave lightly again.

"La, sir," I said, with what I trust was an airy laugh. "You do me honor!"

John frowned. "Stop behaving like Desire Minter. It does not suit you."

His quick remark shook the silliness out of me. "You seem to be very sure just what and who is right for me," I flung at him. "With such keenness of perception 'tis wonder you do not also see that whoever it may be, it will *not* be you!" And then I flounced into the house and closed the door.

Going about my chores, my mind kept harking back to things that John had said. Was Stephen really a rogue, or was it but jealousy on the part of Master Cooke? Stephen is in truth a spirited man, with little regard for authority, but not since Governor Bradford berated him and the others at Christmas have I seen him do anything worse than drink a bit too much, so that he becomes loud and roughened in his speech, but never belligerent. Stephen works hard, being strong and ambitious for himself, and I do believe he will make his mark in Plymouth.

Then I bethought how John had spoken of my hair, and I wondered what Stephen would say of it, were he to see it long and loose, which he has never done. I suddenly had the immodest thought to wash it and sit in the sun to let it dry when he would be coming by on his way to supper. I know that to draw attention to oneself is not meet, but that same devil urged me on, so that as the afternoon began to fade I was gathering herbs in the garden by the front of the house, my hair falling long and damp and straight and shining around my shoulders and to my waist.

I kept one eye on the Street, and at last saw him coming in the South Gate that breaks the palisade between the Brewster and Billington houses, directly across from ours. His jacket was thrown across one shoulder, his stride was slowed by weariness. Pretending I noticed him not, I rose with my herbs and shook the hair back from my face. Stephen stopped in front of our house.

"Well, look at this!" he said. "I thought there was no horse in Plymouth, but there's a yellow mare's tail if ever I saw one!"

A mare's tail indeed! I looked up in anger, my poor attempts at coquetry completely dashed. "Had I known your sensibilities might be offended I would have covered the 'mare's tail' with my cap," I said.

Stephen moved closer to the little fence that surrounds the garden and the house, leaning against it, and reaching out until he grasped a thick handful of hair. He pulled me gently toward him.

"You knew full well I would be coming by, Con," he said. "Do not try your fancy tricks on me." I tried to toss my hair free, but he held it tight. "And mare's tail or no," he went on, looking very straight into my eyes with his bright green-blue ones, "I should like to see this hair spread on my pillow."

I was aghast! How *dared* he speak to me like that? As though I were some common strumpet!

"Before that ever comes to pass, your hair and mine will both be white," I snapped, and tried again to pull away from him. "Let me go!"

He loosed my hair gently, and smoothed it back from my face with his big hand. "Aye, go," he murmured. "And best you hide this shining mop beneath your cap when I am by, lest I forget myself." And with that he kissed me very quickly on the top of my head and marched on down the Street to supper!

In a fine taking I ran into the house, threw the herbs on the board, and coiled my hair as quickly as I could, pushing the pins in so hard they nigh went through my scalp, and settling my cap securely. By the time Elizabeth came in a few minutes later with some wild onions she had found near Town Brook, I was busy at the fire, so that she took no notice of my flushed cheeks.

Will I *never* learn to behave in a meek and modest manner? Mayhap Stephen is justified when he speaks to me as to a common woman. Yet, I want him to notice me, and he will not if I walk always with downcast eyes, saying nothing. Is it better to be demure and unnoticed, or brazen enough to rouse a spark in a man's eye? Oh, me! If only there were a hornbook to guide a growing maid as there is to teach the youngest child!

December 1622

It is hard for me to believe that we have been here more than two years! The days and weeks and months go by in constant work and constant hunger. The clothes of many are ragged and few of us have cloth or other clothes which can be remade. My rosy dress, once my pride and most becoming in its color, is now a sad thing, worn and faded. The second gown that Captain Standish gave us has been used by Elizabeth to cover her expanding belly, since the new child comes soon.

Giles did truly talk with Father on many occasions about the unwillingness of our people to work in the fields for the common good, and others must have felt the same, for Governor Bradford met with Father and the others whom he considers his advisers, and they have ordained that each man may plant and reap for himself in goodly plots of ground apportioned by the Governor. Ours is on the bank of Town Brook, and Father and Giles go each day to gaze proudly on the hard, snowy earth and plan the planting of it. There seems now to be a feeling of hope among our men, hope that they will be able to raise a crop to stave off the threat of starvation. Father says 'tis only to be expected, since any man will work harder for himself than for his neighbor, and that ownership gives him pride and a will to work. God knows I hope this is true, for constant hunger is a fearsome thing! It can drive men to degrading and abominable deeds, and it is surely responsible for the end of Wessagusset.

I do not understand all of what has taken place, but from what I have heard Father saying, it does seem that one John Sanders, a second governor of Wessagusset, proposed to take corn from the Indians by force, since Weston's men no longer had anything with which to trade or buy. Master Sanders sent word to Governor Bradford of what he meant to do, and we sent word back that it was most ill-advised and could only result in sad trouble, not only for the Weston colony, but for Plymouth too. Even though Master Sanders at last agreed not to pursue his plan, the Massachusetts tribe, who like us not, had wind of it, and spread the word of the proposed treachery to other Indian tribes.

Thus, when Captain Standish went out in the shallop to bring back some supplies for which our Governor had bargained in friendly fashion with the Indians, he was met with what he felt was suspicion and enmity. Now that it is all over, Father says that the Captain may have imagined such treatment. Father says "a small chimney is quickly fired," and in truth Myles Standish is a small man, whom some of the boys call Captain Shrimp. In addition, this continual gnawing at our vitals makes us unlike ourselves in many ways. In any case, whether he was truly treated ungraciously or whether it was in his mind, he took great offense, and determined to dispose of those whom he considered enemies.

By now there was great unrest on every hand, with all the tribes hereabouts suspicious of the white men, whether they were of Wessagusset or Plymouth, and all the white men suspicious of the Indians, not knowing whom to trust nor believe. At last Captain Standish took Hobomok and eight men, heavily armed (of whom, to my surprise, Father was not one, and this by his own choice, and not from cowardice, I know), and sailed to Wessagusset. There, with the connivance of Master Sanders and others of Weston's ungodly crew, he lured some of the leaders of the Massachusetts into a building by promise of a feast—and how they could have been unwitting enough to have faith in such an invitation, I cannot see!—and there set upon and killed them all!

There are those in Plymouth who say that it had to be done, lest we be the victims instead of the Indians, but there are others who find it hard to condone such behavior. For my part, I know not what to think. To know that any man could kill in such cold blood—not in an open battle, but by a ruse—makes me greatly disturbed. And yet in truth the Massachusetts are a devious and crafty tribe, and mayhap it was the only way. The sad remainder of Weston's men, those who somehow have not died from hunger, have left Wessagusset in fear, lest the Indians revenge themselves upon them, and have sailed in their little ship, the "Swan," to a safer (they trust) harbor, and thence, in time, to England. And so Wessagusset is empty, and our palisade has a heavier guard, and I find it hard to agree with those who think our Captain is a hero. From what I have seen of the Indians in these parts they are but men of a different color than we, but at heart they are the same. I recall how terrified I was of them at first, and what great fear I knew when Samoset came to our house, and how that fear was eased by his behavior. I feel the softness of Minnetuxet's moccasins on my feet, and I know that these people are not our enemies. I think of Squanto too, who, but a month ago, was stricken with a raging fever which none of our most careful dosing could ease, and who died, leaving his few treasured possessions to the Governor, and asking that he be prayed for that he might go to our English God in heaven—and I know that Squanto was our friend and constant aid the while he lived with us. Surely we need not have feared people such as these, and surely what Captain Standish did need not have been done.

But 'tis done now, with no way to alter it. It makes my heart heavy.

February 1623

Tonight, as I sit writing by the flickering light of a pine knot (and oh, for some proper tallow so we could dip candles!), there is a new, and strange, and welcome sound in the house—the lusty crying of a babe. Elizabeth's son, Caleb, was born this afternoon. He is a sturdy child, and though Elizabeth now lies weak and tired, she smiles to hear him. 'Twould seem all is well with them both, though with the little food we have had (now there is rarely even corn, and I could bite my tongue out for the way I spoke of it, since at the very least it helped to fill our bellies) I know not how she had the strength to bear him, nor how he emerged into this hungry world so healthy. But let me go back to the start of the day.

I sat in Priscilla Alden's house this morning, helping her to adjust a dress that was her mother's so that it would fit Prissy's new girth, for she, too, is with child. As we carefully ripped the old seams and sewed the new, we talked. I admired the furniture and household goods that John has built for them, working, Prissy says, long hours into the night.

"There may not be food," she said, "but 'tis sure there is an abundance of wood, and this John takes as a personal blessing. You should see him hold a board, Con! He turns and rubs and fingers it, looking for just the way to use it so that the grain will show to its best advantage. I swear he becomes as enamored of wood as of me!"

"Who are anything but wooden," I teased her, as I held the widened garment across her stomach to ascertain the fit.

"The Governor has commissioned John to make him a great bedstead," Prissy said.

"Well, 'tis right that he should have things in his house that reflect his position," I murmured, absorbed in how to gain another two inches to fit Prissy's swelling waist.

"If you are right, then I believe his position is about to change."

I looked up quickly to catch a smug expression on Prissy's face. "What do you mean?"

"John says if ever he saw a marriage bed, this is one."

"Marriage! To whom?"

"I know not. But to no one here, I think."

"Then . . ." I was confused. "You mean . . . others are expected?"

Prissy leaned forward slightly, her hand on my knee, her eyes sparkling with her bit of gossip. "They say that Will Bradford sent letters back on the 'Fortune,' and with Weston's men on the 'Swan,' though when *those* will reach England is a question."

"But of course he would have sent letters back," I said. "That means nothing."

"To a Mistress Southworth?"

I refused to be convinced. "La, it could be his sister, for all that!"

"But it isn't. I know whose sister it *is,* though . . ." She paused in the most exasperating manner.

I put the dress firmly aside. "Prissy," I said, "if you are going to tell me, then tell me and leave off the teasing! If you are not—then finish your gown yourself!"

Hastily she picked up the gown and laid it back on my lap. "I will tell you! The little I know, I will tell you."

Resuming my sewing, I settled back to listen, pleased as all women are when they have a tiny nut of news to chew on.

"Mistress Southworth was born Alice Carpenter, and she is sister to Mistress William Wright, who came on the 'Fortune,' and to Dr. Fuller's first wife, Agnes. There is another sister also, a Mistress Juliana Morton, but I know little of her save that her husband, George, and the Governor have been friends for many years. The Governor has known Mistress Southworth for a long time, also—some say since before he married poor Dorothy."

"But, Prissy, all this does not mean that he plans to *wed* with her."

"You are right, of course, Con. And yet I do hope he is. He needs a wife. I know a bit more, too."

"What?"

"The Governor is not the only one who has been writing letters to England, addressed to a female."

"Prissy," I said threateningly, starting to lay the dress aside again.

" 'Twas Captain Standish!"

"In truth?" I tried to imagine the small, belligerent, blood-thirsty warrior composing a tender love letter, and gave up in despair. "Are you sure he did not ask John to write it for him?" I asked. " 'Tis hard to think of him being brave enough to propose to a *woman!*"

"You must not tease me about him, Con. I cannot help but admire the little man, even though I could not marry him. And if you are going to talk about that sad affair at Wessagusset," she added quickly, "please don't, as I truly do not know what to think of it."

"Nor I," I admitted.

There was the sound of running feet on the Street outside, and then a great knocking at the door, and I heard Giles's voice.

"Con! Con, are you there?"

Priscilla rose quickly, opening the door. "Yes, she is here, Giles. What is it?"

" 'Tis our mother. She thinks the babe is about to be born, Con."

I had a sudden queasy sensation in my stomach. I had never helped deliver a child and the very thought of it filled me with fear.

"Is there no one else you could call?" I asked Giles.

Giles looked at me just as Father does sometimes, his chin high, his eyes slightly narrowed. "She told me to call you, Con. Are you coming?"

"Yes," I said. "Yes, Giles. I am coming." I followed him out the door.

"Can I be of help?" Priscilla said faintly. "I know little about it, still—"

I could not help laughing at her obvious reluctance. "Two of us who know nothing would be twice as bad. Bide where you are."

She looked mightily relieved as she waved after us.

Giles opened the door of our house, and then stood back to let me enter.

"I . . . I'll split some wood," he said, his voice gruff. "I would be little help."

I agreed with him, but I felt most fearsome as I walked into the house, knowing not what to expect. Elizabeth was spreading some of Oceanus' small clothes on the back of Father's chair, and setting it before the fire so they would warm. There was a beading of sweat on her forehead and her breath was coming quickly, but she managed a smile.

"Poor Constance," she said. "I had not meant to need you." She sat down on the edge of the bed, leaning forward and gasping so that I went to her quickly.

"Tell me what to do."

After a moment she straightened up and took a deep easy breath. "I was going to call for Ellen Billington. She may be a bad-tempered woman, but she is a good midwife."

"I will fetch her!"

"She has gone with her family and the Brewsters way past

Town Brook to hunt for mussels. I think we cannot wait for her return." She looked up at me and gave a little laugh. "Seems 'twill just be you and me, Constance."

I grinned, and I could feel that the grin looked like Father's. "Never you fear," I said. "We'll manage. Now get into bed like a respectable woman, and do what you can to get this over with!"

It was truly remarkably simple. I could feel Elizabeth straining to bear her child, but she never cried out, though at times she gave a deep animal grunt that seemed to relieve her. She had prepared the few things I needed, and guided me with calm, explicit directions—and there, finally, was my tiny half brother, red and wrinkled and slippery, but responding to my hand with a shrill complaining cry.

There was a deal to be done, but somehow, with Elizabeth instructing me, I managed it all, having little time to wonder or to fear. When at last the bed and all the room were clean, and the child, wrapped comfortably in the warmed clothes, was sleeping by his mother, I stood looking down at her. Her eyes had great shadows beneath them and her face was pale, but I knew she was all right. And somehow a great love for Elizabeth filled me, and for this scrap of life which I had helped to enter the world. Leaning, I kissed Elizabeth softly on the cheek.

"Sleep now," I said. "All is well."

"Thank you, Constance." Her voice was sweet in its whispered softness.

I opened the door. The westering sun was dipping behind Fort Hill and the reddened light filled the room, touching the edge of the newly smoothed bed. Stepping outside, I folded my arms and stood breathing in the salty, tangy air, feeling a surge of strength and confidence such as I had never known. I could hear the ring of Giles's axe somewhere behind the house, and thought to go and tell him of the babe, but just then I saw Father coming up the Street from the fields. He turned in at our gate and paused, looking at me.

"Well, daughter," he said. "You stand there with your head high, as though you could conquer the world!"

"I can," I said, and smiled at him. "I just did. Go inside, Father. Your new son is waiting for you."

He looked at me a moment in astonishment, and then burst open the door.

"Elizabeth," he bellowed, and then as I heard him move quietly to the bed, "Bess. Sweet Bess!" And his voice was as soft as a woman's.

Noiselessly I drew the door closed, and went in search of Giles.

May 1623

I do not recall that a London spring was exceptional. In England winter's damp, biting cold gave way to a warmer but still damp atmosphere, bringing with it the fear of plague which only the winter months put an end to. Father says that in the heat the streets, with their load of sewage, smelled worse than in winter, but this I do not recall. The trees, wherever trees had room to grow, sent forth new leaves, and the grass showed greener and the streets got dustier, and the brave little sparrows chirped a little louder—and that was spring.

But here! It seems every bird God ever fashioned tumbles its song out of the thick trees. Beneath them, carpets of pine needles press softly under my feet, and I can find patches of violets, and fragile white flowers shaped like pipes, and others like a delicate slipper for a lady. Ferns uncurl their fingers in the cool shade, and there is the heady smell of wild mint near the Brook. And always, always, there is the fresh, cool, clean salt scent of the sea, mixed with the odor of sun-warmed pines. I never really *knew* spring until this New England.

In our acres by Town Brook, there is reason for joy. Since each family now has its own field, each family works as never before. The ground is kept hoed, the weeds are pulled, the crows and rabbits frighted away, and as a result there are already the proud young green shoots of corn (I welcome it!) and peas and barley, and whatever else each family has found to plant. We have pumpkins, the seeds for which were given me by Minnetuxet on a shy visit just after baby Caleb was born, and turnips and beans, as well as a corner wherein Giles is trying his luck with some wild strawberries he has dug in the woods and planted here, and some raspberry bushes and a few plum trees. We do not know whether these will prosper, but surely we are trying!

The men of Plymouth have formed themselves into little parties of seven or eight each, and take turns sailing out in the shallop to fish. They do not return without a catch, no matter how long it may take them, and this is surely wise, because there is such a scarcity of food that for them to come home empty-handed would cause great grief and disappointment. These fish are divided among all the families, as are the few deer they shoot. We search for groundnuts, and clams and mussels, and there are lobsters to net—so that we do not starve, but surely our daily fare becomes monotonous. But with the promise that our planted acres hold for a crop that will feed us well through next winter, it may be that hunger will no longer be our greatest fear. Stephen Deane says that can we ever get our minds off our bellies long enough, we may turn them to other things that would improve the settlement. I asked him what sort of things he meant.

"We need a mill, Constance, and that will be my work."

"No use a mill until there is enough corn to grind," I said.

"True. But perhaps there will be now. There should be a tavern, too, where men can gather together over good ale and discuss the affairs of the town. From there 'twill be small shops, and—"

"Stephen," I interrupted. "Where does the good ale come from? And the wares to sell in the shops?"

" 'Twill come, Constance. It must come. There will be ships, and each one will bring goods and supplies—"

"As the 'Fortune' did," I murmured with more than a trace of sarcasm. "All it brought was thirty or more hungry mouths, without a spare ship's biscuit between you!"

"It was not our fault," he said. "We were not told."

"Well, you might have *thought!*"

Stephen pursed his lips in disapproval. "Tut, Constance! Shrewishness does not become you!"

Thinking back to the talk I had had with John Cooke the morning he said my hair was like corn silk, I stamped my moccasin in annoyance. " 'Tis a great wonder," I said, "how many people know what is right for me!"

"And just what does that mean?"

"I have been told I must not be coy, and I must not be shrewish, for neither suits me. I have even been told that *you* are not right for me!"

"Have you indeed! And who told you that?"

"What matters it?"

"It matters to me. I would have words with him."

"How do you know it was 'him'?"

" 'Tis not the sort of thing one woman tells another."

"You seem to know a great deal about women."

He smiled with pleasure. "The study is one of my favored pursuits! And one of the things I have learned is that women are evasive. Who said I was not right for you, Con?"

"Someone."

"I could wager a guess. John Cooke."

I looked up at him, startled. "What makes you think of him?"

"My fair Con! He follows you about with his eyes as though they were on stalks, waving after you in whatever direction you tread. His feelings for you are no secret."

"Oh," I said weakly.

With assurance he placed both hands on my shoulders and turned me toward him. "You may have to make up your mind between us one day, Constance. How will you choose?"

I looked down demurely, and then slowly raised my lashes until I could gaze at him fully. Stephen looked as though he were drowning in my eyes.

"Does that time ever come, I assure you I will let you know among the first," I said, and turning with a deliberate whirl of my faded dress, I left him standing there.

July 1623

For weeks there has been such a drought that to walk in our planted acres is to break our hearts. The corn, the beans, the tiny beginnings of pumpkins—all hang brown and wilted on their stalks. The earth is dry and hard, the water in Town Brook gets lower and lower. The prospect of another winter without supplies to feed us seems more than we can bear! The sun rises above the sea each morning, hot and bright in a clear blue sky. It pursues its course through a day of warm, dry, breezy hours, and drops behind Fort Hill at night in a blazing red ball. The only water that falls is the sweat from those who stand gazing at what is almost certain ruin.

Giles saves every drop of water from the house and carries it the whole way to his special corner of our field, pouring it carefully on the transplanted fruits he is trying to grow, but the ground is so hard it but rolls away and is dried by the warm air before it can ever reach down to the thirsting roots.

I find it is better not even to go into the fields. There is little to be done there, and certainly no pleasure to be found in the destruction of our work. If it should rain now, there would still be a chance, but the sky has never been more cloudless, nor the breeze so steady from the south and west.

Minnetuxet came a few days ago on one of her rare and fleeting visits, bringing with her a woven basket filled with wild cherries. Each time she comes she wants to learn more

English words, and always amazes me by remembering all I have taught her before. I was sweeping out the house when she arrived, and not seeing her at first as she came to the door, I nigh swept a great cloud of dust into her face. She stepped back quickly and then laughed—she has a pretty laugh, soft and a little hesitant—and then pointing to the settling dirt puffs, said, "Smoke?"

"No, dust."

"Dust?"

Leaning down, I scooped up a little handful of the dry, crumbling earth, and breaking it with my fingers, let it drift back. She smiled, remembering the word I had told her once before.

"Earth," she said.

I nodded. "Yes, earth. Now earth very dry—no water—dry earth is dust!"

She stood a moment, absorbing this, then nodded vigorously. "Dust! No water—earth dry. Is dust!" Looking up at the clear, brilliant sky she said, "Rain. Earth need rain."

Sadly I agreed, showing her how the poor flowers in the little beds by the house were crisp and brown. "Corn like this," I said. "No corn grow—no food."

"Minnetuxet know. Indian corn same."

"If it would only *rain!*"

"Indians make rain magic," Minnetuxet said. "Dance, sing, but rain not come."

"I fear it takes more than magic," I murmured.

She made her face very solemn and said, all in one word, as she must often have heard it about Plymouth, "Takes Will-ofGod."

I could not help but laugh, she sounded so much like Mistress Brewster or the Governor, for whom the "WillofGod" is a phrase uttered a thousand times a day.

"Oh, Minnetuxet," I said. "I do like to have you visit! I think you are my closest friend!" I knew she would not understand each word, but she caught more than I expected, and looked pleased in her quiet, shy way.

"A friend is good," she said. "Friends laugh. A laugh is good."

I took her hand and squeezed it gently. "In truth, it is," I told her, and then we came inside so that she might play with baby Caleb, whom she loves deeply.

And it *is* good to laugh, for these days, with the fear of a winter famine hanging over us, with our patched, worn clothes, and even those in rags, with the lack of so many things we need—there is often little to laugh at.

John Cooke just came to the door, while I was writing, and said that Elder Brewster has proclaimed tomorrow to be a day of prayer for rain. We are to assemble in the morning, every soul in Plymouth, and spend the day pleading with the Almighty. It is hard to know whether this will be any more effective than Minnetuxet's dancing and singing. Is it, mayhap, the "WillofGod" that there be no crops to gather? But to believe this is to deny the years of hardship and privation that we have already poured into this new world. Surely, somehow, we must survive here! So—tomorrow—we will pray.

July 1623 continued

This morning, the day of prayer, dawned as every morning has for nigh three months, although now, being the very end of July, the weather was hotter and dryer than ever, the sky brazen in its clarity. We gathered in the fields by Town Brook, every sorry soul in Plymouth, and behind us, at some distance, stood Hobomok and Indian friends of his. Their faces wore the aloof, superior, half-amused expression that an Indian knows so well how to assume, and I could not but feel that even though rain was as essential to them as to us, they had more curiosity than faith in the Englishman's magic.

Elder Brewster took his place alone, facing us. In his dusty, patched black clothes his lean frame had a dignity that inspired admiration, and his voice, when he started to pray, rolled out strong and clear across the sere yellow fields.

As the sun rose higher we stood and Elder Brewster prayed. Small children, becoming tired, lay themselves on the dry ground and napped. A few mothers, Elizabeth among them, moved sometimes into the partial cover of the trees and nursed their babes, then returned to join us once again. The sun climbed to its noontime height, pouring down on us in a torrent of heat that dried our clothes on our backs nigh as quickly as they became soaked again with sweat. Poor Prissy swooned from the heat, and John picked her up gently and carried her into the slight shade, coming back at once to take his place among us.

Down the other side of noon the sun began to slip, and still Elder Brewster beseeched his God for help. Once I noticed

that the number of Indians had increased, standing still and
statuelike behind us. Somewhere, late in the afternoon, I felt
the slightest movement beside me, and turned to find Minnetuxet there. She said nothing, nor did I, but our hands
touched for a moment, and we stood together, our faces raised
to the sky.

The blue above us had already changed to the shafted rose
and gold and aquamarine of sunset before Elder Brewster
closed the meeting. Our muscles stiff from hours of being still,
we moved slowly to gather up sleeping babies and to lift tired
children. Going to Elizabeth, I took Caleb from her arms.

"He frets a bit, Constance. He needs to stretch and move.
Would you take him home? I will follow." She spoke softly;
none of us wished to raise our voices after the long day of silence.

"Of course," I said, and with Minnetuxet beside me we
started slowly across the fields to the Street. Behind us most of
the others gathered in little groups for a few last hushed
words before going to their homes. Entering through the East
Gate, we walked up the hill, the dust rising in little puffs
around our feet. Minnnetuxet kept close beside me, her beautiful copper face bent over Caleb, murmuring little sounds of
endearment to him until his sweet toothless mouth opened in
a smile.

At the door of our house we stood for a moment, Minnetuxet stroking the babe's head with one slim finger. Then
she turned away to start back down the Street toward home. I
waited to wave to her as I always do when she leaves, but instead of moving she stood dead still, her head raised, looking
up Fort Hill to the west. Puzzled, I lifted my eyes to follow

hers, and stood transfixed. For there, where but a short time before had been the flamboyant pageantry of sunset, now a thick bank of clouds mounted, one upon another, rolling across the sky like silent thunder. Speechless, with the strangest feeling of awe, I stood clasping Caleb close against me, staring unbelievingly at the darkening heavens. Then Minnetuxet whirled toward me, her black eyes wide, to be sure that I was aware, and seeing that I was, raised both her arms as high as they would reach and let forth the clearest, loudest sound I had ever heard.

"Aaieeee!" she screamed in triumph. And then again, "Aaieeee!"

At the foot of the Street those who were coming home stopped in their tracks, their movement seeming to freeze. Looking up at us, they turned their heads as ours were turned, seeing for themselves the majestic procession of swirling darkness as it moved closer and closer. From some throat, hoarse with long silence, came a shout, and then another and another. The people of Plymouth stood, their faces lifted, and on many were open tears. Praying again, hoping, hardly daring to hope, we watched the world turn a soft gray, felt the shifting wind bring with it a fresh coolness, turning the leaves high above us until their undersides shone silver.

And we stood—and the first drops pattered gently onto the dust of the Street.

Minnetuxet turned back to me, her face exquisite in its joy. "WillofGod," she said. And then, placing one hand softly against my cheek, "WillofGod," she murmured again, and skimmed off down the Street, running soundlessly and fast as she always does. I watched her go, but she did not turn to see me wave. And baby Caleb and I felt the cold rain on our faces.

It came, not in torrents that would have crushed and broken the dry growing things, but in a steady, delicate, penetrating, soaking, quenching shower that now—at bedtime—still goes on. I can hear it on the thatch of the roof, smell it when I stand by the open door, feel it on my face and hands and head when I step outside. If it will only continue. If it will *only* continue.

I thank God.

August 1623

There has been such a pother of excitement these past several days that I hardly know where to start noting it here in my journal! So much has passed, and all of a pleasurable nature, that—but let me try to put it down in orderly fashion!

The morning following the day of prayer I woke in my little room to hear the precious gentle music of the rain, and thought that never before had this homely sound been so sweet nor so welcome.

While alewives cooked over the hot embers on the hearth, Elizabeth was setting a basket of velvet raspberries on the board. These were not from Giles's poor drying bushes, but from others deep in the woods, where roots have gone down so far they can still find water to nourish them. It has been many months since there has been a mouthful of porridge or a piece of bread in our house, and I have missed them sorely, but for some reason the food this morning could not have been sweeter. The whole day appeared to be blessed by rain.

It was later, after I had helped Elizabeth with the chores, that I went down to our field by Town Brook. I made no pretense of wearing shoes (a poor name for the almost soleless things I own), delighting rather in the cool softness of the mud on my bare feet. Mud! It seemed something I had not seen nor felt in years! I wanted to laugh like a child as my toes squeezed into it, and I kirtled the skirt of my poor patched rosy dress a little higher to keep the hem from dragging.

Father and Giles and the Two Teds were standing almost like loonies, with great grins on their faces, as they looked at the corn already seeming greener and straighter, at the pumpkin vines that were regaining a firmness, at the beans, and peas, and barley, at Giles's bushes and little trees, their leaves dripping happily.

"Do it continue, Con, we will be in good stead come winter," Father roared at me as I approached, brushing my way through the rain-wet rows of corn.

" 'Twill continue," I said firmly. "I feel it!" And I truly did!

For some time we worked, loosening the earth around the plants so that the water might better soak in, making sure that none would be washed away by the running of rain from one plant to another. All about us, in the neighboring fields, others were working as we were. Our clothing wet, our feet muddied past the ankles, and yet all of us rejoicing in the feel and smell and promise of the rain. I noted Governor Bradford working not far from us, the rain dripping from the brim of the wide hat that he chooses to wear winter and summer. He wore his oldest clothes, and old they were indeed, with clouts and patches in every part. Captain Standish walked by us, his hoe across his shoulder, his red head bare and little runnels of water dripping from the end of his beard.

"Good rain, eh, Hopkins?" he shouted at Father.

"Good, indeed!"

With a little wave of his hand to Giles and me the Captain marched on through the mud.

It must have been close to the noon hour, or so my stomach told me, when the first cry went up.

"A ship! A ship! There's a ship entering the harbor!" And then, a moment later, "She flies the English flag!"

Hoes were dropped, spades forgotten. From the fields, from the houses, down the Street, came the people of Plymouth, patched, soaked, muddied—and breathless with excitement.

"What ship? Who comes? Is it more of Weston's men? Is it our families? Are they for Virginia or Plymouth?" None could tell. I saw the Governor and the Captain in a hurried conversation, and then they both breasted the tide of those hurrying down the Street, and proceeded to run up it to their homes. I was puzzled and somewhat frightened. Always these two are among the first to greet any visitors, yet now they did not even join us! I spoke of it to Father as we stood watching the ship slowly move into the bay.

"Think you it means trouble?" I asked. "Have they gone to arm themselves?"

Father bit his lip as he sometimes does when he is trying to hide his grin. "If 'tis as I imagine," he said, "it may be trouble, but firearms will be of no help."

I could not understand him, but he would say no more. Giles eeled his way through the gathering crowd standing on the beach, and I pushed after him to a spot where I could see clearly. Just as a little shallop was being lowered from the now-anchored ship, Will Bradford and the Captain shouldered through to the forefront of the people, and I gaped in amazement. The Governor was clean and dressed in the blue suit he keeps for the most state occasions. His broad collar was freshly white, his shoes shone, his hat had been brushed almost dry. Beside him, the little Captain stood in splendor. His breastplate and helmet were polished, his breeches were his most beautiful scarlet ones, his beard had been combed. Together they made a truly impressive sight, putting the rest of us to utter shame! I could not help but wonder what important personages they expected, to have thus arrayed themselves in their rarely worn best apparel. For their sakes I was glad that the rain chose this moment to slacken, so that it fell in only the softest possible misty shower.

The shallop was loaded now, and coming in toward the shore, and suddenly I heard John Cooke's voice shouting, joined a second later by that of Mistress Brewster.

"It's Mother," John bellowed. "Father, Mother has come . . . and . . . yes . . . I see Jacob, and Jane . . . and little Hester."

And then Mistress Brewster's voice, "William, our daughters! Patience and Fear—both of them! Oh, thank the Lord!"

Never have I seen such happy tears, or heard such joyous commotion. Good Dr. Fuller spied his wife in the approaching boat, and then Robert Hicks and William Palmer, both of whom had come on the "Fortune," saw theirs. The men ran to the very edge of the water, reaching out to pull the boat ashore, lifting the women bodily from the shallop and carrying them the few feet to the sandy beach. There was such laughing and crying as affected us all, and the sight of men holding close to them women they must sometimes have feared never to see again was a beautiful thing. The questions rose all about us.

"What ship is she?"

"Is my wife aboard?"

"Are all well?"

"Who else has come?"

The ship was the "Anne," this much I learned. With another, the "Little James," they had left England some weeks before, but since a storm many days back they had seen nothing of the "Little James." In the midst of the joy this brought fear to many, as the newcomers were asked repeatedly who had sailed on which ship. On the faces of some shone relief as they were assured their friends or families were safe on the "Anne"; others turned away in despair, praying for the safety of the "Little James."

As the shallop started back to bring more passengers from the "Anne," I looked at those who had landed, and felt an unexpected shock. Without exception these people were well dressed and well fed. Beside the Plymouth residents, all of whom were thin and drawn from lack of food, and all of whom, with the notable exception of the Governor and Captain Standish, were ragged, patched, and muddied, the newcomers with their sleek skin, their fresh and well fitting clothes, made us look a sorry sight indeed! They saw it too, I know, for Fear and Patience Brewster, both very fair young women, were weeping in their mother's arms with sorrow for the condition in which they found her. I could see that we must look a discouraging sight at best to people who were about to make their lives here!

The little boat was coming back with its second load, and I watched eagerly as the Governor strode to the side of the shallop and extended his hand with the greatest ceremony to a most handsome woman.

"Mistress Southworth," I heard him say as he handed her from the boat and bowed with a gallantry I had not seen in any man since we left London. I glanced quickly around the crowd for Priscilla, and seeing her, she and I smirked at each other with our pleasant secret knowledge. A second woman, greatly resembling the first, was handed out, and then a man who embraced the Governor affectionately. Prissy, by this time, had pushed near enough to me so that we might whisper together.

"That must be George Morton," she said, "and his wife Juliana, who is Mistress Southworth's sister. And see, there are their children, hopping out now."

"Do you think they will truly wed?" I asked softly. "The Governor and Mistress Southworth?"

"Surely she would not have come all this way did she not intend to marry him," Prissy answered. "What a fine-looking woman she is!"

"And note her gown," I murmured. "That soft green becomes her well. And the fit of it!"

"You could sew as well had you something to work with," Prissy said loyally.

"Perhaps they have brought fabrics with them on the ship," I dreamed aloud. "Oh, Pris, I do hope they have!"

As the shallop went back and forth, discharging each load,

and being aided by our own shallop which some of the men took out to speed the landing, I saw Captain Standish move away from the group and walk slowly up the Street toward his house. Something in his dragging step and his drooping head made my heart ache for him. Quite surely, if it were true that he, too, had hoped for a bride, she was not on the "Anne." Whatever his faults of belligerence and hotheadedness, I could not but be sorry for him now.

We gathered in the Fort, which we now use as a meeting place, where Elder Brewster offered a prayer for the safe arrival of so many loved ones, and for the deliverance of the "Little James" from whatever trouble it may have seen. Then the company, so many of them filled with thanksgiving at being reunited with their families, and so many others yearning for news of the second ship, dispersed to the various homes along the Street. There could be no toasts, since there was naught but spring water to drink, and there could be no breaking of bread, for bread we do not have. But of lobsters and other fish there was a plenty, and it would have to do for these new residents of Plymouth as it has done for the old.

September 1623

It seems that all our prayers are being answered! Ten long days after the "Anne" had arrived, the "Little James" came limping into port, bedraggled and battered, and with a captain who bitterly cursed his crew, saying they were but greenhorns who neither knew nor cared which end went forwards. But all aboard are safe, and again there has been great rejoicing amongst us.

We gathered, as we always do, to welcome the ship when she was sighted, and this time with greater joy than ever, since many had feared her lost.

I was watching closely to see whether the bride we suspected Captain Standish of wooing was one of the passengers, and each time the shallop came in to the shore I would scrutinize the women. Several times I saw one I felt might be she for whom he so obviously hoped, but in each case I was mistaken. At last there came a boatload of young men, save for one female who sat well to the front of the little craft, peering eagerly at the shore. She was a sturdy young woman, with a round and rosy face, and from the joking and laughter between her and the young men in the boat, she seemed a jolly soul. As the shallop scraped on the sand she waved off any offer of help and clambered out. Striding a few steps forward, she searched the faces of those who watched, until she saw the Captain's brave red beard.

"Myles!" she shouted in a voice that could certainly be heard over any other. "Myles! Here I am—it's me! Barbara!"

Master Standish took a hesitant step toward her, but without waiting further Barbara clutched her skirts out of the way in two firm hands, and running along the beach to him, proceeded to throw her arms about his neck in a hold that would have done justice to an Indian wrestler. I could see one embarrassed eye peering over her shoulder as the Captain looked to see whether her forward behavior had been observed (as it most certainly had), but Captain Shrimp proved himself a gentleman by taking no further notice of the general amusement. Instead he bussed the girl soundly, lifted her off the ground, and bellowed, "Thank God ye got here safe, wench! Come with me now, we've much to talk about!"

And hand in hand, and nearly of a height and sturdiness, they went with no further ado up the Street and into the Captain's house to talk. Methinks the little Captain has met his match!

William Hilton, he who stayed with us for some weeks after arriving on the "Fortune," found his wife and their two children on board the "Little James," and in his quiet way could barely speak for happiness and relief. Another little cluster of passengers stepped from the shallop after one of its ferrying trips. Father learned from Elder Brewster that the man was a Master John Oldham, with his wife, his daughter Lucretia, and several other friends or family members, eight or nine in all. They kept much to themselves, and seemed to have no ties with Plymouth. I know not what their business may be here, but somehow I have taken a dislike to Master Oldham. And this for no reason, save his nose-in-air attitude as he stood and regarded us all. I must try to curb these unchristian impulses!

September 1623 continued

It is plain that the heaven-sent rain (which lasted to a greater or lesser degree for two weeks after the praying) has done its good work. The corn is full-eared, the pumpkins never so large. Peas, beans, barley—all the crops are fruitful. Giles's carefully tended bushes and fruit trees grew better than even he could have wished, and the late flowers that still adorn the tiny plots around each house are a riot of scent and color.

All along the Street a great building goes on, the air ringing with the sound of saw and hammer. There are many new faces in Plymouth; each day I seem to find one I have not seen before. Some of the newcomers have fitted easily into our lives; others seem intent on crossing us at every turn. Some there are who laugh behind their hands at our sad clothing, complain of the lack of certain foods, or deride our simple dwellings—an attitude which rouses a strange anger in me. Surely I like these things no better than they, yet they have not the right to speak ill of us. We, at least, have built a town to shelter them, with nothing more than great determination as a tool. 'Twould serve them well were they to live through the sickness and death and hunger and fear that we have known! They would not laugh so quickly!

Just this morning, while on my way to Prissy's with a kettle of lobster stew which Elizabeth had made (for Prissy has had her child, a daughter, and though she and the babe do well, we thought to help her with a bit of supper for her and John), I passed a space where a new house is being built. Perched high on a ladder a young man was readying the roof for thatch. His hair, thick and curling, shone butter-yellow in the sun, and his skin was browned almost to walnut color from weeks on the ship and working under a summer sky. As I approached I heard him singing lustily, accenting the words with blows of his hammer. Never had I heard the song before,

and it did make me so filled with anger that I stopped dead in
the Street to listen. He sang:

> *"If flesh meat be wanting to fill up our dish,*
> *We have carrots and pumpkins and turnips and fish.*
> *And when we've a mind for a delicate dish,*
> *We repair to the clam-bank and there we catch fish.*
> *Instead of pottage and puddings and custards and pies,*
> *Our pumpkins and parsnips are common supplies.*
> *We have pumpkin at morning and pumpkin at noon;*
> *If it was not for pumpkin we should be undoon.*
> *If barley be wanting to make into malt*
> *We must be contented, and think it no fault;*
> *For we can make liquor to sweeten our lips*
> *Of pumpkins and parsnips and walnut tree chips."*

I could stand no more!

"Stop that!" I cried up at him.

He paused, looked down at me, and waved jauntily. "Good
morning, mistress! Did you speak to me?"

"I did, indeed! What right have you to sing such words of
us?"

His eyebrows rose. "Right? What right does a man need to
sing when the morning is fair and the work goes well?" He
started slowly down the ladder. "Or is this another of your
Plymouth rules of which there seem to be far more than
enough?" He reached the ground and came toward me, and I
could see that he was most enormous tall.

" 'Tis no 'Plymouth rule,' as you call it," I stormed at him.

" 'Tis only common decency not to deride your very means of existence! Pumpkins, indeed! You should be grateful for every bite of pumpkin you are allowed!"

He stood close to me now, and I was startled to see that his eyes were a deep brown which went most oddly with his yellow hair. His eyebrows went up again in a way I found vastly annoying.

"It might interest the hotheaded young lady to know that, in the first place," said he, bending down an index finger, "none of us poor starving wretches who but recently arrived have eaten any of the food raised by your industrious townsmen; that in the second place"—and another finger went down—"we do not intend to, but will continue to exist on the supplies brought with us until such time as we can raise crops of our own; that in the third place" (another finger!), "the song which so offended your delicate sensibilities was writ not by me, but by a most respected member of your community; and in the fourth place . . ." He smiled in a thoroughly exasperating manner, and added gently, "In the *fourth* place, if I choose to stand on top of your Fort and sing in *Greek,* I cannot see that it would be any of your concern!"

I know it was ridiculous, but I could think of nothing better to snap at him than, "You couldn't sing in Greek!"

"Would you care to hear me?" He put back his head, opened his mouth, and let out one tremendous note before I could say, "No! I have no wish to hear you sing in Greek or English or . . . or *anything!*" I took a deep breath and added, "In fact, the less I have to hear of you in any way, the brighter my day will be!"

He shook his head in mock sorrow. "How sad it is that a

lass so fair should be such a termagant. You must be a great trial to your husband, mistress."

"I have no husband!"

"Ah! *That* I can readily understand! And now, sweet shrew, if you will have the kindness to excuse me—" He bowed like a gentleman, which made me want to kick him in the stomach, turned and climbed up his ladder again. Perched atop it, he looked down, smiled, waved, and opening his mouth started to sing.

> *"We have pumpkin at morning, and pumpkin at noon,*
> *If it was not for pumpkin, we should be undoon!"*

Raging, I hurried up the Street to Prissy's, nigh spilling the stew in my haste. If Plymouth is to be cursed with men such as these, what hope is there for a successful community? I told Priscilla of it as I sat fondling her babe.

"What was his name?" she asked.

"I neither know nor care! He is insufferable!"

"Can you remember any of the song, Con?"

"Oh, 'twas about the monotony of our diet—a silly thing! Something about *'pumpkin at morning and pumpkin at noon—'* "

"If it was not for pumpkin we should be undoon!" Prissy finished. "La, Con, have you not heard that afore? 'Tis said that Master Winslow wrote it, but he will say neither aye or nay. John and I have found it comical."

Thinking of the words again my lip twitched in amusement. "I grant you there is truth in it," I said reluctantly, "and perhaps if one of *us* sang it, I might find it humorous. But for that—that *newcomer*—"

"He seems to have made a deep impression on you, Constant."

"Aye, that he did," I said firmly. "A most unpleasant one! Tall as a tree, and with a great shock of yellow hair—and so pleased with himself!"

"That sounds much like Nicholas Snow," Prissy said. "John thinks very well of him. He has been here once or twice."

"I pity you," I said.

"Has he great brown eyes?"

"Like a stupid cow!"

"And extremely broad shoulders?"

"As I recall."

"And he is well spoken?"

"He assumes airs."

"And he sings most tunefully?"

"In both English and Greek!"

Prissy burst into laughter, though I saw little reason why she should. "Oh, Con," she said, "how good it is to have new people in town! I vow there was little left that we could say of the old!"

On my way home from Priscilla's I was very careful to turn my head in the opposite direction when I reached the spot where Master Snow (if that was truly his name) had been working, but I found that to be a grave error, since he was now on the other side of the Street, in pleasant conversation with Humility Cooper. He bowed politely as I passed. As best I could, I ignored him.

October 1623

The "Anne" has sailed back to England, taking with her Edward Winslow, who is commissioned to do various errands for us, but the "Little James" is to stay here as a fishing and trading vessel. Many feel this will be of great value, allowing for sailing up and down the coast to trade with the Indians for beaver skins which are much wanted in England, and bring a good price. Hundreds of these were sent back on the "Fortune" when it left us, but word came later that the ship was captured by a French privateer and all her cargo confiscated, which was a fearsome blow to those who had hoped the skins and other things, such as timber and wainscoting, would ease our debt to our sponsors.

When we first came to New England I had little interest in such things, and therefore little knowledge. But of late, being older and more responsible, I had a desire to learn all of the story. To this end I asked Father to explain it to me one evening.

"What does a child like you want to understand such things for?" was his first remark.

"I am not a child, Father. I'm close on to eighteen."

"So help me!" he said. "Is that the truth? I must have lost count! But it seems such a short time ago that you were a babe." For the first time in months he really looked at me. It was a long look, and ended with a slow, quiet whistle under his breath. "Yes, you have grown up!" he said. "Well, miss, what is it you want to know?"

"Start at the beginning, Father. This great debt, of which everyone talks constantly. How did it come to be?"

"But surely you know! There had to be money to make the voyage here, and to buy the supplies we would need. Those who were in Leyden then, they who first had the thought of removing to America—Will Bradford, and Isaac, and Will Brewster, and Francis Cooke—well, you know the group as well as I—they attempted various negotiations to finance the voyage, but all of them came to naught until they met up with that rascal Weston. He wasn't so much of a rascal then, for he had dreams of great wealth in this country, and he likely felt he had found just the people who would do the labor for him. He gathered together a group of London merchants who were willing to invest their money in the hope of making much more, and shares were issued, each worth £10. To everyone over sixteen was given one share, and there were ways in which we could gain more, such as by outfitting ourselves with £10 worth of provisions and supplies—things of that nature."

"Did we do that?" I asked. "Buy our own supplies?"

"We did," Father said, "but there were many who could not. Everything save the most personal possessions was to be owned communally by the entire party. We expected to have the debt paid off at the end of seven years, and to that end we agreed to work five days a week for the London company, and two days a week for our own families and properties." Always restless, Father rose from his chair and took a few paces up and down the room.

"That does not seem an impossible plan," I said.

"Nor would it have been. But there was much disagreement just before we sailed from England. Some of the investors had not put up their money, so we must needs sell part of our supplies to make up the difference; the company insisted that we work full seven days a week for them, with no time for ourselves—"

"But how *could* they insist on these things?" I interrupted. "It is as though we were slaves!"

Father paused by my stool and shook his strong finger under my nose. "Con, any man who owes money to another is a slave! And never forget that!" He moved back to his chair. "At all events, we sailed." He paused a moment, then he said, "Con, do you recall that first spring? The sickness, and the dying, and the cold?"

"Always," I said softly, and thought of small 'Maris. "I shall never forget it."

"None of us will. But Weston and his group could not understand how we could send the "Mayflower" back to England without loading her with a valuable shipment that would be the first payment on the debt."

"Valuable shipment," I repeated, "but of what?"

"Beaver skins would have been the best, or dried fish—"

"But when were we supposed to find time to do such things? To trap beaver, or even to trade for them, to catch fish—it seemed we did nothing but build houses, nurse the sick, and scratch for food!"

"So we felt. But Weston was in disagreement. He accused us of greater weakness of judgment than of hands."

"I wish he had been here," I said indignantly. "I wish he had seen how it was!"

"Ah, but he wasn't here, and he could not see. And though we told him, he did not believe us. And then the "Fortune" came. You know, Con, that London group seems never to mind sending us more mouths to feed, but they never supply the wherewithal to feed them! In any case, when the "Fortune" sailed back to England she carried £500 worth of beaver."

"I remember," I said. "And it was pirated. It never reached them."

"True. And although London could hardly blame us for this, still and all it did not sit well with them."

"How much do we owe them, Father?"

"Close to £1,400, Con."

I sighed. It seemed a staggering sum, and I could not imagine how we might ever amass that much. I asked Father.

"It can be done, if London will be patient. Ed Winslow plans to negotiate with them when he arrives, hoping to work out some plan which will be acceptable to both parties." Father thumped his fist on the arm on his chair. "What they in London cannot realize, Con, is how we must work to keep ourselves housed and fed, and to create a strong settlement here. There is never a moment when any man in Plymouth can sit quietly, knowing there is nothing he should be doing." Again he rose, smiling at me. "And that is true for me. Enough talk for tonight. Do you feel more knowledgeable now, poppet?"

"Yes, Father, and thank you."

Roughly he patted my cheek. "You're a good girl, Con. I'm proud of ye!" And with that he went out.

It seems odd that I did not understand all of this before, for certainly the "London debt" is talked of a-plenty. Already, having learned these facts from Father, I could wish to work twice as hard would it help to speed our freedom from this burden.

October 1623 continued

Since my talk with Father I have taken a satisfaction in being of as much assistance as I can about the house, preparing food to be kept against the winter—smoking some fish for our own use, pounding corn and storing it in our wooden casks, drying those of the fruits that may help make a meal more tasty. Though these small acts may make no change in the Plymouth debt, they give me a pleasant feeling of being a part of our town's unrelenting effort. The nearest I come to any sort of leisure is when I am sewing (and now there is little to sew, save to lay another patch on some worn garment) or searching for berries, nuts, or shellfish.

I was thus engaged but a day or two ago, hunting for mussels along the shore, when our shallop came in from fishing. I saw Stephen Deane's flaming head in the bow, and he was the first ashore, helping to pull the little boat safely onto the sand. I watched with pleasure the way his long legs braced and his brown arms bulged. I consider him a most well-bodied man!

Seeing me, he left the gathering up of their catch to the other men, and joined me halfway up the beach.

"Sit down a moment, Con," he said. " 'Tis weeks since we have had the chance for talk."

"I cannot take the time, Stephen," I told him. "See, here in my basket, how few mussels I have found. I need many more."

"Then I will help, and we will find the right amount in

half the time, and then you will have no excuse!" His sea-colored eyes laughed at me, and before I could stop him he was scrabbling about at the water's edge, digging up the small shellfish with his fingers at amazing speed.

"How can you find them so quickly?" I asked.

"They call to me, to tell me where they are."

"You're jesting!"

He looked up at me in disbelief. "You mean you have never heard a mussel call you? Why, my poor Con! No wonder you have trouble searching them out!"

"Stephen! They make no sound at all!"

He let a double handful fall into my basket, almost filling it. "You think not?" he said. "Come here. Put down the basket—now bring your ear close to the sand."

Not knowing whether to believe him or not, and feeling a fool, I put my basket down carefully, and kneeling on the sand, leaned my head down.

"No, you are not close enough. Like this." He stretched his length on the cool beach, pulling me down beside him. "Now, be very quiet. Don't make a sound!" I strained my ears to listen—he seemed so serious. "You hear nothing?" Stephen asked. I shook my head. "Then close your eyes, you will concentrate the better."

Laughing a little, I did as I was bid, waiting for him to make some silly sound, perhaps—pretending it was that of the fish. Instead, I felt his lips on mine, warm and firm. My eyes flashed open, and I struggled to move away. Stephen's arm lay across me and its pressure held me down, as his other hand gently covered my mouth.

"Did no one ever tell you to close your eyes when you are

being kissed?" he asked softly.

Wide-eyed, I tried to answer, but was stopped by his hand, so that I just shook my head a little.

"Then I tell you now, Constance," he murmured. "Close your eyes. You have enough mussels for the King's army! Stop fretting, and close your eyes!"

Again he kissed me, slipping his hand from my mouth to let his lips rest there. I closed my eyes, and felt the warmth of the autumn sun, and heard the gentle swishing of the waves near my head, and tasted the salt on his lips. For a moment all the world seemed so far away that it was of no importance, and I could think of nothing—nor wanted to. Then suddenly I recalled the great feasting time when I had lain back, eyes closed, to feel the beat of Indian chanting throbbing through the ground and into my body. Ted Leister had kissed me then, as Stephen was doing now, and heaven knew what havoc *that* had caused! Before he could stop me, I rolled quickly away from Stephen and scrambled to my feet. Surprised, he rose to his knees, reaching for both my hands.

"Don't go away, Con—sweet Constance! Please don't go!"

"I must, Stephen!" My voice was breathless, and my hands shook as I settled my cap straight on my head. He stood up, tall beside me, grinning down.

"I vow you're scared of me!"

"Pish! I am not!" I said stoutly. "It is just that . . . that I must get home!"

With a rueful great sigh he picked up my basket and handed it to me, and we started walking together across the sand. I felt quite distraught, and knew my cheeks were red, and I feared what Stephen must think of me for permitting such liberty. Stealing a glance sidewise at him, I found him looking at me, his eyes filled with laughter.

Surprised into something close to anger, I said hotly, "And what do you find so amusing?"

"My sweet innocent Con! Just tell me one thing. Did you find the wild cry of the mussel . . . pleasurable?"

I could not help it. My lip twitched as I tried to hide a smile. Stephen is indeed a scoundrel!

" 'Tis a strange sound," I said carefully, "and wild in truth. I think it would be most unwise to hear it often!"

Putting his head back, Stephen laughed with delight, and without meaning to I joined him.

"Here, give me your basket," he said, "and gather up your skirts. I'll race you to the Street!"

By God's grace no one saw us as we ran across the beach, the wind full in our faces. He was so far in the lead when we reached the Lower Gate that I stopped, smoothed my gown, tucked back my hair, and arrived home in maidenly calm, the basket—filled with mussels—on my arm. But within I am still in a turmoil of excitement!

November 1623

Elizabeth sees so much! This morning, as we were sorting herbs and tying them into bunches with long grasses so that they might hang to dry, she said quietly, "Art thou well, Constance?"

I looked at her in surprise. "Perfectly well. Why do you ask?"

"Thou art moon-eyed, child."

I blushed. I could feel it. I do wish I would not blush! "Naught ails me," I mumbled, my head lowered over the fragrance of rosemary. Rosemary for remembrance!

"Thy heart. Is it well, too?"

"I know not what you mean," I managed.

"If thou art in love, Constance, I am happy for thee. If he loves thee back, that is."

"I know little about love, ma'am," I said. "I might not know . . . were I in love or not."

"That is a situation common to many women. Sometimes 'tis truly love, and other times just the pleasure of knowing a man finds thee desirable."

"But there must be a way to tell."

"There are many ways. Love is a strange thing, Constance. Rarely is it the thunder and lightning, or even the moonlight and tender words that the poets might have us think. More often it is knowing that your happiness lies in being always near a certain person—the realization that without him you are incomplete."

I thought about Stephen for a moment. I longed to be with him again, and—shamelessly—longed to be kissed again. I could think of no nicer lifetime than one of having Stephen hold me and kiss me as he had on the beach. And so, therefore, I must be in love! But did Stephen feel the same way? Surely he must! He was not the sort of man to give kisses lightly—or was he? Did it mean that we were now betrothed? Would he talk to Father and ask to marry me? And what would Father say? And what would marriage to Stephen be like? I felt in such a twitch with questions I could not ask that I broke the grass I was trying to tie.

"Oh, pox!" I said crossly, and felt strangely like weeping. Elizabeth was sitting near the open door. She looked at me with her very soft dark eyes, and then turned her head slowly and sat gazing into the Street, her hands still busy with the herbs.

"Ah, there goes Stephen Deane," she said, and my head jerked up to see him. "He is walking with Fear Brewster. In truth he has an eye for a pretty girl." I wondered if she had noticed my quick movement and decided she had not. "Like many men," she went on calmly, "Stephen has much charm, but I doubt he will make a good husband. He is like a great bee, going from flower to flower, but settling on none."

"But in time he will settle," I ventured. "He will want a wife—and a home."

"I suppose you are right. In time he will most probably take a wife. But he seems in no hurry to give up his present enjoyable habits. Come to that, he may never give them up!"

"What do you mean, ma'am? Surely, if Stephen were married—"

"If Stephen were married he would still have eyes, nor does marriage change a man's nature. In truth, I think whoever Stephen marries—*if* he marries—had best be either blind, or tolerant, or very, very clever." She paused, and then looked at me, smiling. "Best mend the fire, Constance. 'Tis getting low, and you look as though you might have taken a slight chill."

January 1624

The many newcomers to Plymouth have wrought many changes, and in several different ways. There has been such a spate of courting and marrying as makes Father say the Plymouth air is turning pink with romance. The Governor wed his Alice Carpenter Southworth, and they are as content and pleasant a couple as would be hard to duplicate.

Myles has married his Barbara, and from the moment she set foot on Plymouth beach 'twas certain he had no choice. But she is a good wife for our little Captain, energetic, jolly, and hard-working, and quite equal to his occasional tempers which she matches with lusty scoldings of her own. 'Tis not uncommon to hear the two shouting fiercely at each other over some trifle, only to have one or t'other make a statement so wild as to cause the mate to burst into laughter, where- upon they kiss good-humoredly and the quarrel is forgotten. Mayhap it does them both good to clear the air this way, though I think I could not like such a marriage.

Although not yet married, young John Howland has his eye on Bess Tilley for sure. John was indentured to Master Carver, and when both the Carvers died that first summer, John in- herited all their goods, they having no children and being most fond of John. He thereupon bought his freedom, and is now well fixed for a young man, so that Bess, who is an or- phan since the Sickness, would do well to take him.

Now that I am eighteen I, too, should be marrying, I expect, and yet my mind is such a turmoil I know not how I feel. I see Stephen often, but though he has sometimes suggested a walk along the shore, I have refused. I do not think I trust the "wild cry of the mussel," or is it myself I do not trust? Perhaps I am a fool not to go with him. Others do. I have seen them. He has strolled past the house with the Brewster girls, and with Mary Chilton, and I see him laughing and bending his bright head close to hear what they say, and often he casts a quick glance at our house to see am I watching. I think that were I to put my mind to it I could take his interest away from all others but me, and sometimes I plan to try, but then comes the fear that mayhap I could not. It may be that I am no more to him than another female to laugh with, and cosset, and tease, and that he may be well contented so, and feel no great need to settle down with one as wife.

All of this puts me in a ferment, and although I mean it not, my temper sometimes runs short. Elizabeth knows this, I think, and the cause as well, and sometimes she sends me off on errands I feel sure she designs to help me achieve a sweeter mood.

Just last evening she asked me to take some of our finest hollyhock seeds to Priscilla, of whom she knows I am greatly fond.

"I promised them to her and it keeps slipping my mind to take them. Tell her they are a mixture of the white and the pink that did so well for us."

"But she cannot plant them until spring, ma'am—certainly there is no need to take them tonight."

" 'Tis a clear evening, Constance, and not too cold. 'Twill do you good to visit for a while."

"You think that because I was cross with Giles at supper—"

"My dear child! I think nothing save that you might find it pleasant to sit with Prissy for a bit. If you do not choose to go it is of no great matter."

Perversely, of course, I took my cloak—or what is left of it

—from the wall-peg, and went. It was a fine evening, dark and crisp, but lighted by a million stars and a thin slice of moon. There was the smell of woodsmoke from the chimneys along the Street, and a soft glow from every window. By the time I arrived at the Aldens' door I felt more like smiling than I had all day, a feeling that was immediately undone when Prissy answered my knock and I looked past her to see John and Nicholas Snow sitting by the fire. John was comfortable in one of the two great chairs he made for himself and Priscilla, and Master Snow was enthroned in a corner of the new settle that John had only just finished, one long leg bent so that his foot rested on the seat beside him. They were both wreathed in clouds of smoke from the pipes on which they contentedly puffed.

"Here's Constance, John," Prissy said, openly pleased as she always is to see me. John greeted me in friendly fashion, and turned to Master Snow.

"Do you know Mistress Constance Hopkins, Nick?"

The dreadful man rose and came toward me. "I have met Mistress Hopkins," he said, "but under rather less formal circumstances." He took my hand and bowed over it as though I were some great duchess, making me feel an utter fool.

"When was this, Nick?" John asked, and I could see Priscilla throw him a look of caution, which he blandly ignored.

"Oh, 'twas nothing," Master Snow replied. "Mistress Constance and I but spoke for a few moments of . . . ah . . . food, and public rights, and other such topics." In surprise I glanced up, thinking it most tactful of him to say no more, and then he added, "She has a most forthright way of speaking that impressed me greatly."

Priscilla giggled, and John was just ready to ask some further question which I am sure would have embarrassed me, when Nicholas Snow led me toward the settle.

"Do sit down, Mistress Hopkins, and admire the comfort of John's latest achievement."

"I really cannot stay," I said. "I came only to bring Priscilla some of the hollyhock seeds my mother promised her."

"Oh, Con! Those lovely pink and white ones? How pretty they will look planted about the house, John! Isn't it kind of Mistress Hopkins?"

"Very kind," John said. "Now do sit down, Constance. We were just discussing the rulings Will Bradford has made regarding those who came with Master Oldham on the "Little James." Surely your father, working so closely with the Governor, has spoken of this."

"Yes, I have heard Father talking about them—but I do not think I had better stay."

"Please, Con," Prissy pleaded.

"Yes, please do," Nicholas Snow said, and before I quite knew what had happened I was sitting on the settle next to that great butter-headed man, and Prissy was taking my cloak from me.

"But why must they have different rulings from everyone else?" Pris asked. "I don't understand."

"They do not belong to the general body," John explained to her. "They have come quite on their own behalf—in a particular way—and owe nothing to the group of merchant adventurers to whom the rest of us are beholden until our debt is paid. Yet, since they are to live in the colony, they must be in certain ways responsible."

"I believe the Governor thought well," Nicholas Snow said. "He seems a fair man in his judgments, and most determined that all things be of benefit to the settlement."

I was pleased at the way Master Snow spoke of Governor Bradford, and added a few words of my own to the discussion.

"He will see that they are," I said. "He has insisted that Master Oldham and his people be subject to all the laws and orders that are made now, or that may be made—all that pertain to the public good, I mean."

"But they do not have to work for our company," John put in.

"They do if it is for the perpetual good of the colony," I said, pleased that I had listened when Father spoke of this. "They must participate in Captain Standish's defense training, for example."

"And to assist in maintaining the government and the public officers, every male over sixteen must pay a bushel of Indian wheat, or its value, into the common store," John went on, "so they cannot sit in the chimney corner hoping we will support them."

"Nor can they trade with the Indians," I said, "not as long as this contract endures."

"It seems to me strange that such people would come," Priscilla said. "They are not as we are—here by reason of religious belief, or family tie, or even willing to throw in their lot with our company for the sake of eventual gain. Why think you they would come here?"

Nicholas Snow blew a long thin stream of pipe smoke toward the fire, and watched it drawn up the chimney. "It may be they dreamed of a golden world," he said quietly, "where riches would hang like plums for the taking. They would not be the first so to dream."

It was on the tip of my tongue to ask whether *he* had dreamed so, his remark seemed so sincere in its feeling, but something held me back. I could not be sure with this man when his barbed tongue might exercise itself at my expense. Instead I looked for some safe topic to enter into the conversation.

"Such dreams are much like your pipe smoke," I said. "They disappear so quickly. But 'tis pleasant to see men smoking. I did not think there was any tobacco left in Plymouth."

"Nick brought some," John said. "He came well equipped, it seems, which very few do."

"And do you know what else he brought?" Prissy asked, leaning a little forward in excitement. "Ells and ells of fabrics! All sorts!"

In spite of myself I turned to him quickly, and I know my eyes were shining. If there is one thing I do admire, it is great lengths of uncut cloth! "You truly did? Of what kind are they?"

"I know not all the names," he said. "There is something called linsey-woolsey, I believe, in a color much like claret wine, and some blue stuff, and some white linen—"

"Linen!" I breathed, and could almost feel its fresh coolness under my fingers. "But for whom are they? Why did you bring them?"

"Look at Con," Prissy teased. "She is nigh licking her chops at the thought of such pretties."

"Perhaps they will be of more value than I thought," Nicholas Snow said, and I could see a sparkle in his dark eyes.

"But you haven't told me why you brought them," I insisted.

"Oh," he drawled, "I thought they might be useful for negotiating with the . . . natives."

"But you are wrong," I said quickly. "The Indians much prefer cheap baubles and beads, and knives and coats and suchlike! They rarely sew—"

John threw back his head in laughter which I did not understand, and Priscilla hushed him.

"Nick didn't mean Indians, Con dear," she said. "He meant . . . well . . . females!"

"Oh!" I murmured, and could feel that fearful blush to which I am prone mounting to the edge of my cap.

"Nick, the wise old fox, thought he might catch himself a wife—or something," John explained, "and I vow, from what Pris tells me, he couldn't have found a better lure."

"I see," was all I could manage, and to cover my discomfiture I rose and picked up my cloak. "I must go now, Prissy. I thank you for a pleasant evening."

"And do you thank your mother for the seeds," Priscilla said as she rose to walk to the door with me.

Nicholas Snow got to his feet also, his great height making the room look smaller. "I will walk Mistress Hopkins home."

"There is no need," I murmured hastily. " 'Tis only down the Street—"

"Ah, but think of the perils that might lie in that short distance! Wolves, and savages—" He knocked his clay pipe out carefully against the chimney, the small remaining dottle falling onto the hearth. "Thank you, John, Priscilla, for your hospitality."

"Come often, Nick," Priscilla said. "You are pleasant company."

The door closed behind us, and I was surprised to find how cold it was. Coming from the warmth of the Aldens' fire I shivered a little, pulling my cloak closer about me, and watching my breath make white puffs in the air.

"New England nights are colder than those in London," Master Snow said.

"You know London? You come from there?"

"From Hoxton, which is not a great distance. I know London well."

"We lived there."

"Yes, I know."

"How did you know?"

"I asked Priscilla," he said calmly.

I looked up at him in surprise. "You asked Priscilla where we came from?"

"Should I have asked you instead? You did not seem inclined to chat about yourself the one time we met. I feared you might tell me 'twas none of my affair."

"If I was hasty in my speech and judgment on that occasion, I pray you will forgive me," I said. "I sometimes speak ill-advisedly, I fear."

"Ill-advised or not, I found it stimulating. I was quite convinced that sparks shot from your eyes—but then, when I saw them again tonight, they were as deep and quiet as a midnight sea."

I did not know how to talk to this man! The things I said

he seemed to twist to his own ends. "We were speaking of my undue haste in criticizing you," I said in my coolest voice, "not of my eyes."

"*You* were speaking of your undue haste," he corrected. "I would far rather discuss your eyes. They are, for example, the only blue eyes I ever saw that can look quite black."

"I should appreciate it if you would be less personal in your remarks, Master Snow. I find it unbecoming in one who is virtually a stranger."

"Oh, no, you don't. I wager you would far rather hear my views on the strangeness of your eyes than have me sing about pumpkins."

"It is not of the slightest interest to me *what* you do," I said angrily. Truly, the man was very forward!

"Then, if it matters not, I shall continue to discuss your eyes. I also noted that they are remarkably fringed in black, the which is most surprising since your hair is as pale as silver, and—"

"I bid you good night, Master Snow," I interrupted, my hand on the fence post by our house.

"So quickly? How unfortunate it is that Plymouth is not a much larger town, that we might have had farther to walk."

"Unfortunate, indeed!" I snapped at him. "I could wish it were as big as London, and that we lived at opposite ends! Good night, Master Snow!"

"Good night, Mistress Hopkins," he said softly, and bowing like the gentleman he most obviously is *not,* he kissed my hand.

As I opened our door he turned and went walking down the Street to the Common House, singing at the top of his powerful lungs, *"Pumpkin at morning, and pumpkin at noon, if it was not for pumpkin we should be undoon."*

My lips set, I closed the door behind me, and taking off my cloak, hung it on the peg.

"Who was that singing so lustily?" Father asked. "I did not recognize the voice, though I know the song well."

"It was a most impossible young man named Nicholas Snow," I said. "I cannot think why John Alden chooses such people as friends."

I thought Elizabeth looked at me very oddly as I went into my room to prepare for bed, letting the door latch fall with a sharp click. And oh, what would I not give for my mother's little silver mirror! Are my eyes truly as remarkable as he said?

February 1624

Winter lies deep and still around us, and never a day goes by without my giving a silent prayer of thankfulness for the fact that this year there is no hunger in Plymouth. Our storehouses are full, and while our daily diet may lack much in the way of variety, at least our bellies no longer growl. And this is true of everyone in Plymouth, even though our number is now close to two hundred people.

Governor Bradford and his Mistress Alice visited us last evening, and the Governor and Father talked of Plymouth as compared with the Virginia colony. Seems the "Virginians" have been there for sixteen years, whilst we have been in New

England but three. Master Bradford brought out the shocking information that out of every ten who have shipped to Virginia, close to nine have died—almost nine thousand lives! God has blessed us by taking no more than one a year from our little company since that first fearful spring. Much money has been poured into the Virginia colony—the Governor says it might be as much as £200,000—and we have had no more than a bare minimum of aid. And yet, as of this moment, Plymouth flourishes, and poor Virginia is not yet secure nor self-sustaining. It makes me consider soberly Minnetuxet's explanation—"WillofGod."

My friendship with Minnetuxet continues and waxes stronger, for though I see her but rarely, each time she comes we resume our relations from where they left off the last time. Earlier in the month, during a heavy snowfall, she came, bringing a rug for baby Caleb made of the softest beaver skins. Giles had been making a small sledge for him, and Minnetuxet showed Giles how to twist some long dried grasses that she found into a rope with which to pull it. We sat the baby on it, bundled in his new rug, so that only his little face emerged, and pulled him across the snow, the while he laughed and crowed with delight at this new white drifting world.

"Baby happy," Minnetuxet said.

"Yes."

"Minnetuxet happy, too." She glanced at me shyly. "Samoset has found husband for Minnetuxet."

I stared at her in amazement. "Minnetuxet! You're going to be *married?*"

"Yes."

"But . . . but . . . you look so young!"

"Minnetuxet has seen nineteen winters. That is not young for an Indian girl to marry."

I smiled ruefully. "Not so young for an English girl, either." I touched her arm. "Do you like him, Minnetuxet? The man you will marry?"

"He is very brave and strong."

"But do you *like* him?"

"Minnetuxet think he will bring great happiness."

"Oh, I am glad for you! I *want* you to be happy!"

"Constance will find a man soon. Then Constance be happy, too."

After Minnetuxet had gone I thought about what she had said. Does a woman's happiness depend on her finding a man and marrying him? I am eighteen, and quite old enough, heaven knows, but my heart is so unsure! In truth there are as yet in Plymouth few young men well enough provisioned as to be able to take a wife. Save for the Aldens, all the other marriages have been between more mature folk, and in each case the man had been widowed early in our stay here. It does speak well for marriage that those who have tried it are anxious to try again!

But then others, like Stephen Deane, seem not truly anxious to try it at all! A few days ago, when the afternoon sun cast long blue shadows on the snow, I met him down near Town Brook. He was coming back from hunting and carried his gun across one shoulder and three rabbits across the other, and he was whistling gaily as he strode along the path. He stopped when he saw me.

"Constance!" he said, and his voice sounded pleased.

"Hello, Stephen."

"What do you here?"

"We needed more water, and since the day was inviting—"

"Carrying water is no chore for you. Why cannot Giles do it? Or the Two Teds?"

"Giles is off somewhere on his own ventures and the Teds were busy with Father. And I truly wanted to be outdoors."

"Let me carry your pail."

"You have enough to carry as it is. It looks as though your hunting had been successful today, Stephen."

"Most especially since I have returned."

"I don't follow you."

" 'Tis certain that you don't, Constance. It seems weeks since I have seen you alone."

"I am sure you have not lacked for company," I said, my voice as cool as the snow.

"Oh, there is always company in Plymouth, but not always of my choosing." He took the pail from my hand. "You know I would rather be with you, Con. Do you avoid me?"

"Certainly not," I said, my chin high. "Why should I?"

"I thought perhaps—but surely a kiss would not have frightened you!"

"Frightened me? Come, come, Stephen! What is there in a kiss to fright a girl?"

"Exactly!" he said.

He set the pail down on the path, and carefully laid his gun beside it, with the three small rabbits making a furry heap in the snow. Then he laid his hands on my shoulders, turned me toward him, and added softly, "Remember, Constance, close your eyes!"

And then I felt his lips on mine, cool, and not salty as they were that first time. His arms were strong and tight, and I stood so close I could hear his heart beat in rhythm with my own. He smelled pleasantly of leather from his jacket, and of cold fresh air, and suddenly I knew a deep response, so that I raised my arms and clasped them around his neck, feeling the soft wool of his black knitted Monmouth cap. At last he took his lips away, and I opened my eyes, still standing close a-gainst him. His face was very near, and looked more serious than I had ever seen it.

"Constance," he said very softly, but his voice was unsteady, and he cleared his throat and said my name again. "Constance!"

"Yes, Stephen?"

As though against his will he put me gently away from him. "You are a dangerously beguiling wench," he murmured, and ran his fingers around the inside of his collar, as though his jacket constricted him, though in all faith it looked loose enough.

"Am I, Stephen?" Without his body close to me I felt cold, and longed to move in to him again.

"I am . . . I am most fond of thee, Con."

"Are you, Stephen?"

"And you. Do you . . . do you . . . *like* me, Con?"

"Yes, Stephen."

In a sudden loud burst he said, "Lass! Stop saying 'Yes, Stephen,' 'No, Stephen,' 'Of course, Stephen!' Here I stand in a tremor and you babble like a silly schoolgirl!"

"What would you have me say, Stephen?"

With an odd little groan he pulled me close once more and

spoke softly into my ear. "It may be better not to talk at all," and then I was being kissed again, the which I found to be a truly interesting and pleasurable experience, until I felt my feet becoming fearful cold from standing so long in the snow.

"Stephen," I whispered against his lips.

"Yes, love?" His voice held a note of eager expectancy.

"My feet are cold."

For a second it was as though he froze. His lips, just above mine, did not move, not a muscle in his arms shifted, even his breathing stopped. Then he dropped his arms and stepped back, taking a great deep breath and letting it out slowly.

"Your feet are cold," he repeated flatly.

"Yes, Stephen."

He stood looking at me, his lips tight. Then he bent down and picked up the rabbits, the gun, and the pail.

"I can carry something," I said helpfully. "No reason for you to have both your hands so filled."

"It is best they are," he said grimly. "Otherwise one of them might very likely spank you as you have not been spanked in years!"

I looked at him in surprise. "But why, Stephen? What have I done? I thought you liked kissing!"

"Girl, just walk, will you? Please! Walk!"

I started along the path toward the Lower Gate, Stephen behind me. I did not know what I had done to anger him, and yet he did in truth seem angry—it was most bewildering. Of a sudden he started to laugh, and to my embarrassment he continued to roar out his mirth as we approached the gate.

"Stephen!" I said, turning to face him. "Such noise is unseemly! People will wonder! Please hush!"

"Constance," he gasped, "there can be no other woman like you in all the world! For which I do truly thank God!" And with that strange remark we walked up the Street, Stephen letting out occasional chuckles all the way.

I wish I could talk to Prissy about this, for I do not understand such things, but I find it difficult to discuss. There was that moment when I felt sure Stephen found me not displeasing—in fact, quite the opposite. And then, to have him laughing at me for no reason that I can see makes me confused. As for the kissing, it was most enjoyable, which I believe Stephen found it also, for he seemed quite affected by it. But it took nigh an hour for my feet to be warm again.

March 1624

Father has been elected one of five Assistants to the Governor, and though he does try to hide his pleasure, Elizabeth and I smile to see that he stands a little taller, and spends much time being friendly with the Plymouth folk.

Master Bradford had asked that someone else be elected Governor, and said that if it was an honor, then it was fit that others should partake of it, and if it was a burden (as I am sure he often finds it), then others should help to bear it. The townspeople would not hear of his retiring, but they did agree to give him five Assistants, instead of just one as it has been heretofore. Isaac Allerton is still the first of these, with Father, Edward Winslow, Captain Standish, and Richard Warren as the remaining four. All being of the "Mayflower" group, they are compatible and work well together, and it is to be hoped they will spare the Governor some part of the work and problems that arise.

One of these problems is the sad fate of the "Little James," which was to do so much for us. She was a fine vessel, bravely decked with flags and streamers, making an excellent showing as she entered or left our harbor. But save for the master, all her men were upon shares and received no wages, and this made for great inefficiency in the handling of her. Her crew declared that they had been told they could expect great profits by taking some French or Spanish man-of-war, and to this they were agreeable. But that they should spend their time in fishing or in trading did not please them. They were a surly and unruly lot, and it was only when the Governor told them he would pay their wages that they were persuaded to work for us.

At first she was sent around Cape Cod to trade with the Narragansetts, but the whole trip was unsuccessful. On her return home, at the very entrance of our harbor, she ran into a storm so severe they had to cut off her mainmast and her tackling to save her from driving onto some flats called Brown's Islands. This required the putting up of a new mast and the general repair of the pinnace, and then she was sent off eastward on a fishing trip early this month.

Poor "Little James." Another storm took her and drove her against some rocks with such force that a great hole gaped in her side, letting the sea rush in, and driving her into deeper water where there was no hope for her. The "Little James" lies on the bottom, and all the goods aboard her are lost. The master and one of the crew drowned—the rest of the men managed to save themselves. So now we no longer have the "Little James."

But a great and good thing did occur, bringing much pleasure to Plymouth. A sweet small ship, the "Charity," came into port, bringing all our people down to the shore to greet her. Although ships come more often than they did, it is still a great event in our lives, and of sufficient importance to stop daily chores for the time. So there we gathered, on a blue, windy morning, watching to see whom the shallop would bring to shore. There seemed to be a great to-do on the "Charity," but we could not see what the cause was. At last the shallop pulled away from the far side of the little ship, and as it bent its oars toward the shore, a great, lusty cheer went up from every man in Plymouth. For there, standing proudly in the bow, was Master Edward Winslow, and behind him, securely held and bawling frantically, rode three heifers! No pretty woman was ever helped so gallantly from a rocking boat as were those three cows! They were led tenderly up the beach, stroked and soothed, admired and cosseted, fed and watered, and I do believe they could have had their choice of any bed in Plymouth! When the shallop, on its next ferrying trip, brought a pawing, bellowing, fire-breathing bull, our joy knew no bounds!

John Cooke and Giles stood near me, their eyes awe-struck at the magnificence of the bull. Giles, being London-bred, had never been so close to such an animal before.

"Faith, he's a big one, isn't he?" he murmured. "I vow he should be treated with respect!"

"He is naught to fear," John said. "I saw them often in Leyden. See, I am not afraid of him." Approaching the bull, he put out one hand to touch its glossy hide. The bull lowered his head, gazed at John out of bloodshot eyes, dug its hoof repeatedly into the sand, and let out such a roar as sent brave Master Cooke scuttling for safety.

At last our "herd" was led away amid great jubilation, for while the four beasts we have now will be communally owned by all of Plymouth, the understanding is that in a few years when (we trust) their number will have increased, there will be a dividing up of cattle amongst the households. And thus we have gained one more essential of a comfortable existence.

There were three Plymouth-bound passengers on the "Charity" who are sure to make a difference in our lives. One is a ship carpenter, who is to build us various small boats to use for fishing, trading, and sailing up and down the coast; and one is a saltmaker. The third is a minister, a Master Lyford, who was so filled with emotion at a safe arrival—which he seemed not to have expected—that he made a great display on the beach, falling upon the shoulders of the Governor and some of the men to whom he was introduced, and weeping openly while giving thanks to God for his deliverance. It seemed to me lacking in dignity for a man of his position, but should these three prove themselves in their respective ways, both our souls and our bellies should fare the better.

To add yet another cause for thankfulness, each of us has been granted additional land for farming. Father, as one of Will Bradford's Assistants, had a voice in this decision, and told us of it.

"It is clear now that men will work harder for themselves than for their neighbors," he said. "The crop which has taken us well through the winter is proof of that."

"I told you that was true, Father," Giles put in.

"You and many others," Father said drily. "And you were right, all of you. So now we have agreed that there shall be an acre allotted to each person, as near the town as possible."

"And will these new acres belong to us year after year?" I asked.

"That is what we agreed," Father said, and I could hear the satisfaction in his voice when he said "we." "And I do believe that now we have seen the end of hunger in Plymouth!"

"Providing that now we have the land, we farm it well," Elizabeth remarked from the corner where she was feeding young Caleb his supper. "It will take many hands and much work to use properly the several acres we will have."

"Giles and Constance are strong and willing," Father said, "and with the Two Teds—"

"And what about you, Stephen? Will you not be working also?"

"Of course I will, whenever I can take time from the duties of Assistant to the Governor. But you must realize, Elizabeth, that I have responsibilities now which are of great importance to the town. I must devote many hours to them."

Elizabeth spoke solemnly to the baby. "Dost thee hear thy father, poppet? Thee must learn to bow to him quite soon, for surely he is a man of great position!"

Father rose from his chair and going to Elizabeth, lifted the babe from her lap.

"Son," he said, "thy mother is a sharp-tongued creature who has no respect for her master. See that when thee marry, thee choose a docile wench!" To young Caleb's great delight Father tossed him high in the air again and again, catching him safely each time.

"Stephen," Elizabeth warned, "the baby has just eaten—"

"One would think I had never had a child before," Father told his son, throwing him high once more, and then roared, "Thunder! Here, Bess, take the boy!"

As Father wiped porridge from his coat, Elizabeth cuddled the baby close to her, smiling over his dark head.

"Dost thee not realize thy behavior is not respectful to thy exalted father?" she murmured to him. "In future, best keep thy little mouth tight closed in his presence, lest the Governor's Assistant chastise thee."

"Better the Governor's Assistant should chastise his wife for insubordination," Father growled, and jamming his hat on his head, he strode off to seek more understanding company.

June 1624

And now it seems there is trouble a-brewing in Plymouth. The first that was known of it was from letters which the Governor received when the "Charity" arrived, written by a Master James Sherley who has succeeded Thomas Weston as the chief officer of the merchants' group which sponsored the "Mayflower" voyage, and to whom we still owe much.

There is one John Oldham who came on the "Little James" with his wife and some several others, the same man of whom we talked the night Nicholas Snow and I met at the Aldens' (and though I see Master Snow from time to time in passing, we have not again exchanged words, a situation I find to my liking and would have it continue!). This Master Oldham will not join with us in anything, and yet he seems to find much to discontent him, and writes of it to Master Sherley and others, hoping, for reasons I cannot understand, to discredit us and put us in the poorest light possible.

Father has told us some of the things of which John Oldham complained (and which Master Sherley apprised us of, seeking to know if they were true), for now that he works with Governor Bradford he is more aware of all that goes on. This faithless Mr. Oldham wrote that the children of Plymouth are not taught to read nor write, nor are they taught their catechism, a thing I know to be untrue, for often have I seen Mistress Brewster and Master Warren and Francis Cooke and many other parents spending long hours at teaching their children. Master Oldham wrote too that the water here is unwholesome, to which Father says that the Governor replied, "If he means not so wholesome as the good beer and wine in London, I will not dispute him. But for water, it is as good as any in the world."

"What else did the wretched man say of us?" I asked Father. I was sitting at the board, shelling the first batch of early peas, enjoying the cool, smooth, firmness of the pods in my fingers.

Father reached his hand into the wooden bowl, pulling out a few peas and flipping them into his mouth. "He said that many of us are thievish, and steal from one another." He helped himself to a few more of the crisp little green pellets.

"There are times when I do believe that to be true," I admitted, slapping his hand lightly, "although I do not like to allow John Oldham to be right. Was there more?"

"Indeed yes. He wrote that the Dutch are planted near Hudson's River and are likely to overthrow our trade. Will simply said that the Dutch will come and plant in these parts also, if we and others do not, but go home and leave it to them. In fact, the Governor feels the Dutch should be commended, rather than condemned."

"This Master Oldham must be *mad!* What else did he froth about?"

Father's face became more sober. "There were other things, some of a far more serious nature, having to do with religion and the like, but none were true in our eyes. But now, Con, Oldham and the new minister, Lyford, have become most intimate, and there is a deal of whispering and gossiping between the two, so that I mistrust them both."

This amazed me. "But Master Lyford seems so . . . so filled with kindness and reverence and humility! I cannot think he would have any dealings with such a man as Oldham seems to be."

Father shook his head. "I do not trust Lyford. I watched him, that first day he came ashore from the "Charity" with Ed Winslow. He bowed and nigh cringed as he was brought to meet the Governor and some of the others of us. I think he would have kissed our hands if we had let him."

"But you cannot hold these things against him."

"Except that they do not indicate a man of strength, suitable to lead us spiritually. No, Con, I think Lyford's coming was a mistake, and I think it will not be long before others agree. If he and Oldham are of the same stamp, they can do much damage to Plymouth—unless we are aware and can prevent it." Father rose and stretched. He can never sit still for very long without becoming restless. "Mind you say nothing of all this, lass. We can better catch them at their own game if they do not see us coming."

"I am not a gossip," I said indignantly. "To whom would I talk of such things?"

"Oh, that red-headed giant, perchance, with whom I sometimes see you walking. Should I expect him to approach me soon?"

I set the basket of shucked pods on the table, avoiding Father's eyes. "Approach you? Why should Stephen approach you?"

"I thought the man might have marriage on his mind, daughter, that is all."

"If he does, he has said naught of it to me," I replied. "I doubt he will be bothering you."

Father patted my head in the vigorous way he has that nigh rattles my brains. "Take your time, Con," he said. "We're in no hurry to lose you." Taking a last handful of peas, he went out.

But I do have the feeling that he expects I will marry Stephen Deane.

July 1624

It seems Father was not the only one who assumes that I will wed with Stephen. I walked along the shore one afternoon with the baby, for now that he is nigh a year and a half old he must needs run all day long, keeping both Elizabeth and me in a fret trying to stay him from trouble. He trotted along, his fat bare feet marking the sand, so that he stopped every few steps to investigate the prints with great wonder. After some distance I looked up from watching his amusing antics, to see John Alden and Nicholas Snow. They were standing with the boatbuilder (who has already made us two good shallops and is now building a lighter), trying, I suppose, to learn something of his craft. It was in my mind to turn quickly and head Caleb the other way, since I felt no need of Master Snow's exasperating conversation, but it was too late, for they had already seen us. John waved, and Nicholas came slowly along the shore to meet us. We exchanged greetings, and he crouched down on the sand to chat with the babe.

"Good day, young Master Hopkins," he said solemnly. Caleb stared at him as he does at strangers, and then grinned engagingly. "What is your name?" Nicholas Snow asked.

"Taleb," the child offered politely. Then, with no warning, he reached out and grasping Master Snow's nose firmly, pulled it. The gesture was unexpected, the child is amazingly strong, and Master Snow, taken by surprise, let out a snort of extreme displeasure. I could not help it—I laughed. The man stood up, rubbing his nose tenderly, his eyes watering a bit from the smart.

"He is devilish strong," he said. "Do all children act thus?"

"Perhaps he does not like you," I said demurely, although I knew it to be untrue, for Caleb will have nothing to do with those he does not care for.

"There are people *I* don't like, but I don't delight myself by tweaking their noses," Nicholas said. He sounded very aggrieved, which amused me vastly.

We stopped for a few words with John and then continued walking slowly along the sand where the small waves rolled up and wet the baby's feet.

"Although, on further thought, tweaking a few noses might relieve me greatly," Nicholas remarked.

"Have you any special noses in mind?" I asked idly.

"Indeed I have. One, in particular, which juts out from beneath a thatch of carrot hair. And I do *not* mean Captain Standish!"

"I did not really assume you did. But what have you against that particular nose?"

"It is far too often far too close to yours! And if I may say so, Mistress Constance, your nose is a distinctly pretty one, even when elevated, which it is at this moment, and I should not like to see it contaminated by contact with a much inferior nose."

"You speak nonsense," I said.

"Do you prefer I speak more openly?"

"I would just as soon you did not speak at all. In any case, I cannot see that it is in the slightest your affair."

"And that is the whole unfortunate crux of the situation! I should like to make it my affair."

"Would you, indeed! And how would you propose to go about it?"

"By so endearing myself to Mistress Constance that she would find it quite unthinkable to consider anyone else."

Again I laughed at him. "You have a long way to go, Master Snow."

"If you would call me Nicholas we would already have taken one step of the way."

I gave him one of the sideways glances from under my lashes which is sometimes, it seems, quite effective. "But with such a long distance to travel, that small step seems insignificant—*Master Snow.*"

Little Caleb chose that moment to wade into the water up to his knees, whereupon he lost his precarious balance, fell headlong, and roared with surprise at the mouthful of salty water he received. Nicholas Snow reached down easily and plucked him out. Taking a kerchief from his pocket he dried the child's face, and then hoisted him atop his shoulders as Father sometimes does, which pleased the babe mightily. In this way we continued our walk, turning our steps back toward home, and luckily the mood had been somewhat changed. We talked a bit of the boatbuilder whom Nicholas and John had been watching earlier.

"He is an excellent workman," Nicholas Snow said. "If he will remain here, we should have a good number of boats to aid us in fishing and trading, and even exploring the coast a bit further. Did you know he is going to assist in raising and rebuilding the 'Little James'?"

"Raising her! But I thought she was lost! Completely sunk!"

"So she is. But the water at Damarins Cove is not so deep but what she can be raised. At least that is what I have heard."

"But how will they do it?"

"John explained it to me. They will gather all the casks they can lay their hands on and fasten them to her at low tide, so she will float as the tide rises. Then they feel that, be there enough men, they can pull her onto shore where she can be worked on. Of course they may find her past repair, but they do not feel they will."

"She would be of great help to us, would she not?"

"Indeed. People who choose to live at the edge of the sea must have ways to travel on the sea."

My eyes wandered out over the endless expanse of ocean, brilliant now under the summer sun. "I never knew the sea before," I said.

"It has much to give us. Fish, which are both food and money; a means of travel up and down the coast; salt—"

"What of the saltmaker who came on the 'Charity'? Is he going to be an asset to us also? As the boatbuilder is?"

"The saltmaker is an ignorant fool!" Nicholas Snow said forcibly. "I have listened to him talk, and heard his great plans, but I have as yet seen no results."

"But he found a piece of land which he told the Governor would be an excellent spot for a saltworks—"

"Yes, and then demanded eight or ten men to work constantly for him—far too many to assign to just one aspect of improvements."

"Did the Governor not give him the men?"

"He gave them, grudgingly, feeling that he must give this fellow a chance to prove himself. They built a great frame for a house to receive the salt, and then this do-nothing announced that the ground was not, after all, precisely right; either the bottom was too wet, or not wet enough—he seemed unsure. So all that work has come to naught."

"And now what?"

"Now he waits until the lighter is finished, the one on which our boatbuilder now works, and says that he must use this to carry clay to aid him—ah, 'tis all empty talk! The man knows nothing!"

We had reached the foot of the Street, and Nicholas swung Caleb down from his shoulders and set him on the ground.

"Thank you for your kindness in walking with me, Mistress Constance," he said politely, but I could see the glint in his dark eyes like silent laughter.

"You are most welcome, Master Snow," I said with equal formality, and then added, "I am sure Caleb enjoyed it." I took the child's hand and had moved a few steps away when he said, "John Howland married Bess Tilley a few weeks back."

I turned, surprised. "I know," I answered.

"And Mary Chilton and young John Winslow are wed."

"I know that, too."

"And Jonathan Brewster has married John Oldham's daughter Lucretia."

"What is all this to me?"

"And I understand that Patience Brewster and Tom Prence are to be next."

"This is not news, Master Snow!"

"Agreed. I only bring it to your attention. Marriage seems to be in the air. You might dwell upon the thought."

He bowed, and I looked at him a moment, perplexed, and then started up the Street with Caleb. I could feel Master Snow watching me as I walked away.

He is a most bewildering man! At moments I feel quite drawn to him, and then of a sudden he becomes so mocking, teasing, or exasperating in his manner that I could wish him a thousand miles away! Surely this is no man to take seriously!

August 1624

The boatbuilder caught some sort of fever and died; the saltmaker has proven himself useless; and the trouble caused by Master Oldham and John Lyford finally reached a great proportion.

The boatbuilder we will miss sorely, both for the work he did and for the goodly man he was. The saltmaker we are pleased to be rid of. The last item takes a bit more telling, for few of us knew all that went on until a short time ago when Governor Bradford—a most worthy man!—brought it into the open.

The "Charity" stayed here for some several weeks, making fishing and trading trips for us. When the time came to leave for England, it was noted by some that the Reverend Mr. Lyford was busily writing scores of letters and delivering them to the ship. The Governor and his Assistants have been deeply suspicious of John Lyford almost since his arrival, and they did not trust him to picture things in Plymouth in their proper light, so that when this great correspondence was known to them, the Governor and a few others waited until the time of the "Charity's" sailing, and then went out to sea with her for a few leagues. There, in the knowledge that fire best fights fire, the Governor called for all of Oldham's and Lyford's letters to be brought to him, the which they were.

As Governor Bradford had thought, the letters were filled with slander and false accusation of Plymouth, its people and its ways, which might well have meant our ruin had they been read and believed by those in England. So our men busied themselves in copying many of the letters (although 'twas said later that Oldham wrote such an illegible hand, little could be done to decipher his), and in a very few cases keeping the original lest the writer try to deny its existence, and sending in its place a copy. With those which he sent on, the Governor added a letter of his own, and after such activity he and his Assistants returned to Plymouth after nightfall.

The Governor chose to say nothing of his night's work, and although there was some unease at first among those who knew he had visited the "Charity," when nothing more came of it they put it from their minds. Oldham and Lyford, believing their treachery to have been undiscovered, continued their whispering and gossiping, indicating that they would soon be the leaders of the settlement, and trying to induce others to join with them. They managed to attract a few followers, which so encouraged them that they dared to become quite insubordinate.

When Captain Standish called Master Oldham to take his turn at the watch (as all Plymouth men do in order) the man refused to obey. Instead he called the Captain a rascal and other far worse terms which Father will not tell me, and set upon him with a knife. Our Captain being not the sort of man to take such treatment meekly, a lively scuffle followed, the noise of which brought the Governor a-running. There was a great roaring and raging and much vile language which was heard over most of the Street, and at last Master Oldham, behaving more like a wild beast than a man, was clapped into the Fort. There he stayed until he cooled down, at which time he was punished and then set free.

But the cooling off did not last, and Oldham and Lyford were soon at it again. Without the permission of our Governor, our church, or Elder Brewster, they set up a public meeting on a Lord's Day, which was against all the teachings of Plymouth church. 'Twas about this time that the Governor determined to put an end to such undermining behavior before excessive damage was done, and he therefore called a court to meet in the Fort, and summoned all of Plymouth to appear.

So little had this matter been discussed abroad that there were many who had no knowledge of why the meeting was called. While I knew of the subject, I could not have imagined the dramatic happenings that would take place before the day was done. As we gathered in the big room of the Fort, seating ourselves on the long, backless benches, there was much whispering back and forth among the curious as to why we were there. The room was hushed, for no one spoke out in his normal voice. It was clear that this was a matter of import, and a solemn occasion.

The Governor, dressed in his best blue suit—which becomes him well—sat at a table facing us. On either side of him were ranged his Assistants, each of them carefully groomed, looking impressive and forbidding with their serious faces. I noticed that John Oldham and John Lyford did not sit near each other, but both kept casting furtive glances about the room as it filled with the townspeople. They looked uncomfortable and ill at ease, but tried to appear totally innocent and unsuspecting. I am sure they did not *know* whether or not they were the cause of the gathering, but their consciences must have told them that it was highly likely.

At last the room was filled nigh to bursting. The Governor quietly asked Captain Standish to close the great door, the which he did, dropping the bar into place with an ominous thud. Then he stood against it, feet apart, arms behind his back, a very formidable guard indeed. After a few seconds of utter silence that seemed as long as eternity, the Governor rose slowly to his feet.

"Townspeople of Plymouth," he began, "I have called you here today so that we may sit in fair judgment on two who, it seems, would do our Colony harm."

There was the faint flutter of a sigh, and a gentle rustling, as everyone, now aware of the purpose of the meeting, settled into his seat. Speaking slowly but clearly, choosing his words carefully, Governor Bradford continued.

"As Governor of Plymouth Colony, I do hereby charge John Oldham and John Lyford, both late of London, with intent to plot against the Colony, and to disturb its peace, both in civil and churchly matters. This I proclaim to be most injurious, since these two men, and all the others in this room, as well as many more in England, know that both John Oldham and John Lyford came here to enjoy the liberty of their consciences, and the free use of God's ordinances. I ask these two men to rise."

I saw each man glance at the other, then they both got to their feet, standing stiffly, their mouths tight.

"Mr. Lyford," said the Governor, "do you admit the truth of these charges?"

"I do not," Lyford murmured. "There is no truth in them."

"And you, Mr. Oldham?"

" 'Tis all trumpery and nonsense! I have no knowledge of any of this!"

"Mr. Lyford, is it not true that you have often written to friends in England?"

The minister's voice was impatient. "Surely you will not say that to write letters to friends is a sin?"

"I consider it a sin if the letters are designed with malice to twist and distort the facts in such a way as to do harm to innocent people, and I consider it a sin if these letters are directed to the company of merchants who are our sponsors in London. I say that the letters you wrote, Mr. Lyford, were such letters!"

"The letters that I wrote were what any man might send a friend, telling of a new country, a new life—"

"But not telling it truthfully," the Governor interrupted.

"And I know nothing of any London company of merchants," Lyford went on, "nor of any business you may have with them! I consider your imputations slanderous, sir, and I could only wish that the letters were available so that I might prove my innocence. But never thinking that I, your minister, would be so maligned, it did not occur to me to keep—"

Governor Bradford raised his hand slightly to stop the defensive words, and when he spoke his voice was silken smooth.

"I am pleased to put your mind at rest, Mr. Lyford. The letters *are* here." He smiled. "So it will be an easy matter to read them aloud, and let the people of Plymouth decide for themselves concerning your innocence."

Lyford stood for a moment, dumbstruck. Then, his voice climbing like a weeping woman's, he said, "This is some trick! The letters were sent to England weeks ago! You can prove nothing!"

The Governor turned to Isaac Allerton, who sat next to him. With the greatest deliberation Master Allerton reached into the pocket of his jacket, and bringing forth a neat sheaf of letters, handed them to Bradford. The minister stood, his eyes fastened on the sheaf, the sweat pearling on his forehead. Nervously he wiped it away with his hand, while the Governor slowly withdrew one letter, glanced through it, then cleared his throat and started to read.

"This letter, signed by John Lyford, is directed to Master James Sherley." Again there was that small sound of exhaled breath among the listeners as they sat craning forward to see and hear the better. "In this letter Mr. Lyford writes, 'These self-called saintly people of Plymouth will allow no one to live amongst them except he be of their particular church and belief.' "

There was a gasp as the Governor lowered the letter, looking over it at the crowded room. Then he turned toward Father, sitting at the table.

"Master Stephen Hopkins," he said. "Would you please to stand?"

Father rose, and from the look he threw at the Governor I knew that much of this had been well planned, and I was glad! I could not have borne to see these two, Oldham and Lyford, get the best of us!

"Master Hopkins," said the Governor formally, "are you a member of the Plymouth church?"

202 · 201 ·

"No, sir," said Father, his voice strong.

"Do you subscribe to the beliefs of those of us, sometimes called Separatists, who first arranged the voyage to New England?"

"No, sir," said Father.

"Have you, because of this difference between us, ever been treated with anything less than affection and courtesy?"

"No, sir," said Father.

"Thank you, Master Hopkins. You may sit down." With a suggestion of his grin, Father sat. "Captain Standish," the Governor called. From his post beside the door, the Captain answered.

"Yes, sir?"

"I ask you the same questions that I asked of Master Stephen Hopkins. Are you a member of the Plymouth church?"

"I am not," thundered the little Captain, his face as red as his beard. From near me I saw Barbara, her eyes on him in admiration.

"Do you subscribe to our beliefs?"

"I do not!"

"Have you, since arriving in Plymouth, ever been treated with aught but affection and courtesy?"

"Only by these two rascals," blurted the Captain. "And what I say is that they don't deserve a hairsbreadth of—"

"That will do, Captain Standish," the Governor barked, and our little warrior subsided, muttering to himself. The Governor continued, "Master John Alden! Rise, please."

From beside Prissy, John stood up, his tall body straight, his blond head high.

"I am not a member of the Plymouth church," he said, "although it comes to me now that I want to be. What is more, I was under no contract to remain in Plymouth longer than a year, and yet I would not go elsewhere! I am a free man, and as a free man I choose to remain and work for a Colony which has given me more happiness than I have ever known!" He put his hand on Priscilla's shoulder, and when she looked up at him I saw tears shining in her eyes.

"Thank you, Master Alden."

Just as the Governor was about to call another name John Lyford's whining voice interrupted. "But these men all came with you on the 'Mayflower'! Of course you will stand together, for if you do not you will be overthrown by others who are stronger! You do not dare to call on any who are not of the sainted company!"

Governor Bradford merely looked at Lyford. Then in his strong voice he called several names. "Edward Bangs, Thomas Prence, John Jenney, Nicholas Snow, Stephen Deane—"

My heart gave a strange lurch as I saw Nicholas and Stephen rise in different parts of the room. Both stood so tall and straight—the one with his thick yellow thatch, the other with his banner of bright hair—both faces stern, unsmiling.

"Gentlemen," said the Governor. "Were you passengers on the 'Mayflower'?"

Almost as one voice the answer came from all of them. "No, sir!"

"You have heard a statement written by Master John Lyford to James Sherley. Do you agree with the truth of this statement?"

"No, sir!"

"Are you in a position to deny its veracity?"

"Yes, sir!"

"Thank you, gentlemen." Quietly they resumed their seats. "Now, if you will bear with me, I should like to read you more of the scurrilous charges that Masters Oldham and Lyford have brought against us." Whereupon, from one letter and another, Governor Bradford proceeded to read such statements as it seemed could hardly have been written by other than madmen. That we sought the ruin of anyone who had come on his own behalf, with no need to work for the repayment of the Colony's debts; that we took no care of our vessels (poor "Little James"); that Captain Standish was no more than a silly boy and not fit for his position (which remark I feared would bring our Captain to apoplexy, so crimson did he become); and that the distribution of food was unjust, giving some favorites more than was allowed to others.

After reading the last item, the Governor raised his head to say: "It is true that some men have received a larger allowance of provisions than others. Those whose work permitted them no time for farming or hunting or fishing have been given a greater amount of food than those who could raise their own. Among these 'favorites,' as Master Lyford calls them, were the boatbuilder, the saltmaker, and the Reverend Mr. John Lyford himself." Gazing levelly at Lyford for a moment, he added, "I can see now that that was a mistake."

Reaching for still another letter, the Governor was interrupted by Master Oldham, who turned to the room at large, throwing his arms wide. "Masters," he pleaded, "where are your hearts? Show your courage! You have often complained to me of these things—you have told me they were true! Now is your time if you will but do something! I will stand by you—I will not desert you." Wildly his eyes searched the room, finally lighting on John Billington. Had he tried, he could not have found a worse man to speak for him! "John Billington," Oldham screeched. "Confess that you have told me these things!"

There was complete and absolute silence. Billington, unmoving, stared back at Oldham as at a man he did not know.

"Will none of your speak?" the enraged Oldham yelled, and now the veins stood out sharply on his skull and neck. "Do you not at least condemn your Governor for the breaking open and stealing of other people's mail? Have you nothing to say openly against him—you, who had much to say to me in private?"

And still there was not a sound. Then the Governor spoke again.

"Perhaps I should be condemned for the opening of mail," he said. "And yet you have appointed me your Governor and magistrate. As a magistrate I had no choice if I was to endeavor to prevent the mischief and ruin that these conspiracies and plots would bring on this poor Colony. And be it noted that our revered minister and Master Oldham have both not only opened letters which many among *you* have written, they have also taken copies of them, sending them—with disgraceful annotations—where it was felt they would do the most harm."

At hearing of this invasion into their privacy, there was a hushed commotion among the people in the room, and I could not but think how odd it was that what was permissible for the Governor to do was regarded as deepest treason when performed by men they frowned upon.

Then the Governor called on each of the two men in turn, asking them what they had to say in their own defense. Oldham, head hanging, could only continue to mutter that there were many there gathered who had told him the things of which he had written, but that now they were too cowardly to speak for themselves or for him.

But Lyford, when he was addressed, suddenly burst into amazing tears. "Have pity on me," he cried. "I am a reprobate! My sins are so great that I doubt God will ever pardon them! I have so wronged you—you who were my friends and my spiritual charges—I can never make amends! All I have written was false, all I have charged you with was nothing! Pity me—pity me! Let me but stay among you and I will show my gratitude by working for you so long as God will let me stand!"

I could not help but be touched by the man's tears and obvious repentance, but looking about the room I saw Father's eyes resting on the weeping minister with a most doubtful look, one of his eyebrows raised slightly. There were others, however, who appeared to feel as I did—that surely the man should be given another chance. But as for Master Oldham, I could see no gleam of pity anywhere for him.

At last it was agreed that John Oldham would be expelled from Plymouth at once, although his wife and children would be allowed to stay throughout the winter, or until he could make comfortable provision for them. John Lyford was also punished by expulsion, but in view of his sorrow and shame over his misdeeds, he was to be permitted to remain for six months in the Colony, and given a chance to redeem himself in the eyes of Plymouth. At hearing this, the wretched man fell to his knees, blessing the Governor for his charity and kindness, and saying it was far more than he deserved. From the expression on Father's face I felt sure he agreed. And thus did the trial come to a close, and whether we are to be glad or sorry that we have allowed Master Lyford to remain, we do not yet know, nor whether there may be further troublesome results from those in London who have authority over us. But this I do know and am sure of—that our Governor is a strong and unshakable man, and without him Plymouth would be in sorry state!

November 1624

   And now, albeit Father says it took longer than he had supposed it would for "Plymouth to come to her senses," the disturbing chapter of John Oldham and John Lyford has, we think, truly come to an end. What is more, it has brought about an unexpected consequence.

After the trial Oldham departed promptly, fuming and muttering that we had not seen the last of him. We heard later that he went north some thirty miles and is endeavoring to start a settlement at Nantasket with some of his few followers from here—people, I might add, we are pleased to do without. His daughter Lucretia, now Mistress Jonathan Brewster, remains here, and seems quite agreeably unlike her father.

John Lyford bided amongst us, as he was privileged to do,

and never was there such a paragon of kindness and sanctimony. He continued to preach and confessed his sins openly in church meeting, weeping even more copiously than he had that day at the hearing. Although Father continued to view him with suspicion, it seemed that his reform was complete, until a small ship put into port with some mail and assorted goods for us, before continuing to Virginia. While it lay in the harbor Master Lyford took to his old habit of letter-writing, but this time in such secrecy that the epistle nigh departed with the ship. However, John Lyford misjudged his messenger, and the letter was delivered instead to Governor Bradford.

Our Governor, having reached the limit of his long patience, spent no time on public meetings, but called his Assistants together forthwith and had Lyford brought in. In a very short while our so-called minister and his wife were headed for Nantasket, taking with them Mistress Oldham, who most prudently felt it was a strain on relationships for her to remain longer in Plymouth.

That evening Myles and his spirited Barbara sat before our chimney, talking with Father of the afternoon's affairs.

" 'Tis good riddance to those rotten apples," Father said. "They brought us naught but trouble! I always said they would!"

"The wonder is that, rotten apples as you say they were, the Plymouth barrel was not more tainted by them!" Barbara leaned forward, speaking forcefully. "Why do you suppose the blight did not spread further?"

Elizabeth spoke softly from where she sat sharpening the ends of quills into fine writing points. "I have wondered that myself," she said, "and it came to me that the strength of many of our people comes from . . ." She paused, almost as if embarrassed, and then finished firmly, ". . . from their godliness! I intend to join the Plymouth church, Stephen, and I think it would not be amiss if you were to do the same."

Father stared at her. "Oh, now, Elizabeth—" he began, but he was interrupted by Barbara.

"Elizabeth is right, Stephen," she said. "I have had the same thought myself! Heaven knows it can do no harm!"

Myles laughed aloud. "Fancy Barbara in church-meeting," he said. " 'Tis a good thing those guns rest strongly atop the Fort, else when my girl lifts her gentle voice in the hymns, the roof might well fly off!"

"Loud I may be," Barbara flared at him, "but at the very least I stay with the tune!" She turned to Father. "When *Myles* sings one might take it for the agony of a bull with a griping in his belly! I pity those who must hear him!"

" 'Tis a needless waste of pity, lass," Myles replied, "there is no danger of my appearing in yon church!"

Barbara looked at him, and her wide mouth turned up in a sly smile. "Oh, you will be there," she said silkily. "You, and—I daresay—Stephen too. Just think, Myles, how much like an insult to our good Governor it would look if the *wives* of his respected Assistants became dutiful members of the church, and the Assistants themselves refused. It might truly make him reconsider his choice."

Myles stared at her, his mouth opening and closing in silence. After a moment Father rose abruptly, tramped noisily twice around the room and came to stand by Elizabeth's stool.

"I . . . er . . . I had been meaning to speak of this to you,

Bess," he said gruffly. "I deem it time for our family to appear regularly at all churchly meetings. 'Tis right that we set an example."

Elizabeth smiled demurely up at him. "As you wish, Stephen," she said.

"You will see that the children are prepared to join us next Sabbath Day," Father went on. Then he turned to the Captain. "We will stop by your house on our way up the hill, Myles. 'Twould look well, I think, were we all to walk together."

Myles glared up at Father from his hot blue eyes. "Traitor!" he muttered.

But the fact of the matter is that the following Sabbath we did indeed all file up the hill to the square little Fort where Elder Brewster had resumed his preaching, and were amazed to find how many others were becoming members, just as we were.

When the hard benches were filled Elder Brewster took his place behind the long table at the front of the room, looking out over the lifted faces. There was quiet for a moment until at last he said firmly, "Mayhap there was some purpose to the turmoil caused by John Lyford if it brought here today these newcomers to our church. It seems God chose to hold a charlatan up before you, that you might see and know His need for strong and loyal followers. If this be true—blessed be the name of the Lord!"

"Amen!" rang out the many voices, and those of Father and Myles seemed loud indeed.

January 1625

It is a cold, snowing, blowing, freezing winter, but Plymouth does not suffer. Our storehouses are full, our fires blaze cheerily, and life is busy, peaceful, and good. Father has been trying his hand at making a chair, with Giles weaving a seat of rushes, and though Father does not excel at wood-working, John Alden aided him, and the result promises to be sittable, at least. Elizabeth, who has been saving wild goose feathers almost since we arrived, now has enough to make a featherbed, and with cloth brought by Edward Winslow on the "Charity," she is busily sorting feathers and fashioning the covering. We obtained more cloth from the replenished sup-plies, and I have made myself *two* dresses and a warm little coat for young Caleb. Elizabeth is wearing the expanded dress of Rose Standish's again, for there will be another baby in the summer. My two gowns are plain, but it is exceeding good to have something to wear that is not a mass of rags and patches! One of them is of the deepest blue woolen, which is soft and warm (and Elizabeth tells me it makes my eyes seem enor-mous, but since we have no mirror I cannot tell). The other is the shade of the ripest raspberries—not red, nor yet purple, but something in between. I have made fresh white linen caps for Elizabeth and me also, and new broad, square collars, those we call falling bands, for Father and Giles, and all in all we look most respectable once again.

Not many evenings ago Elizabeth invited Stephen Deane to sup with us. I think she did this because she feels that any man without a woman to cook for him is improperly fed, for she does not consider him highly as a husband for me. I was of two minds about his coming. I am most fond of Stephen—I may as well admit it here, where it cannot be seen—and yet so often he walks with other girls, looking as if he well enjoyed their company, that I do not know what his feelings are to me. He has kissed me, but perhaps he has kissed the others too. He seems always glad to see me, but mayhap he is glad of any female society. It is most puzzling! In any case, Stephen arrived, stamping snow from his feet and brushing it from his shoulders and his Monmouth cap, and bringing into the house with him a loud jollity which was most pleasant. Having lived with us for a while when he first came to Plymouth, he feels at his ease with all the family, and makes himself popular with each of us. He greeted Elizabeth cordially, commented on the savory smells that filled the room, shook Father's hand and called him 'sir,' discussed the respective merits of matchlock rifles and flintlock rifles with Giles (who, now that he is seventeen, trains with Captain Standish), endeared himself to Caleb by giving him a small wooden soldier he had carved, and finally turned to me.

"And Mistress Constance," he said. "The maid with the warmest eyes and the coldest . . . *heart* in Plymouth." Silently I damned him! He had paused so long before he said "heart" that I was certain he was about to say "feet," and I blushed to the edge of my cap. Ever since that day last winter when we met by Town Brook and my feet became so fearsome cold whilst we were kissing, I have tried without success to put it from my mind, for I know now that it must have been a great blow to any man's pride to have a girl thinking

only of her feet while he was a-kissing of her most profi-
ciently. But Stephen will not let me forget it! On one or two
occasions he has asked, with mock concern, about the state of
my feet, which generally leaves me with naught of sense to
say. Why must men have such devilish ways? At all events,
his remark now caused Father to ask, "Has Constance a cold
heart? I should have thought just the opposite!"

"Perhaps the fault is mine," Stephen said, "for not yet being
able to kindle it into a warming glow. Mayhap with time—"

I wished greatly that I could say some of the things I was
thinking, such as "You had the time, my lad, but you
choose to evade the issue!" but it seemed better to let him go
unchallenged, lest the conversation become even more embar-
rassing to me. I was relieved when we gathered around the
board, though Father's blessing seemed longer than necessary,
for now that he is a member of the church he has become
most enthusiastic about religion. While Father prayed, loudly
and fervently, I made the mistake of looking up a little and
found Stephen gazing at me, his sparkling green-blue eyes
surprisingly thoughtful. All through the meal I kept wondering what he was thinking of, but everyone chatted together
and there was no further personal turn to the conversation.

Soon after we had finished, when Elizabeth and I had
started to clean the trenchers, there came a knocking at the
door. Father opened it, letting in a scattering of white flakes
and Master Nicholas Snow! My mouth fell open in amazement, for he has never been in this house since he first arrived,
and now here he stood, holding out a small auger to Father.

"John Alden sends it to you," he said. "He bade me tell you
it would be of great service in completing the chair you are
building."

As Father thanked him I felt both Stephen and Nicholas looking at me. Hastily I filled my hands with trenchers from the table and turning my back, occupied myself in scraping them clean. Behind me Father was saying, "Sit down, man, sit down! You know all my family, of course."

"Of course. Good evening, Mistress Hopkins, Giles, Mistress Constance—"

"And this is my youngest, Caleb," said Father, swinging the child up into his arms.

"Yes, I have met Master Caleb before," said Nicholas, and he touched his nose reminiscently.

"And this is Stephen Deane. But I am sure you have met."

"Indeed we have," Stephen said. Nicholas merely nodded.

I hoped sincerely that the man would leave, but Father was so insistent in his invitation to stay, and Elizabeth so hospitable in supporting him, that presently we all sat about the fire, greatly to my discomfort! Presently Father embarked on his theories of why he felt the people of Plymouth were poor fishermen.

"'Tis the hooks, I feel sure. Even those that Winslow brought last spring are not of the right size. The waters teem with fish—we can *see* them—yet in proportion to what is there, our catch is small."

"How do they fare at Cape Ann?" Stephen asked. "I know the station there is new; has there been time for it to prove its worth?"

"That station, or fishing stage, as Will Bradford calls it, is meant to clear the boats of their catch so they need not make the long trip home to unload before going out again. With the drying done at the stage, and the vessels sailing out again immediately, much time is saved. But none of that is of great

help if the catch is not sizable. And *that* is where our trouble
lies!" Father smacked his hand against his knee in exaspera-
tion. "Thunder, 'tis enough to drive one mad! The fish are
there, waiting to be caught, waiting to be dried and smoked
and shipped back to England as payment on that strangling
debt—and we seem as incapable as boatloads of donkeys!"

"I understand it takes great patience to fish," Nicholas remarked, his eyes lowered over his pipe as he filled it. "Perhaps
our men are not patient enough."

"Of what use is patience when the equipment is poor?" Stephen said. "Sitting and waiting never caught fish."

"Not in itself, perhaps. But if you are waiting for the fish to
draw near so that they become catchable . . ." He let the sen-
tence drift off, raised his eyes and looked at me through the
little cloud of pipe smoke.

Stephen noted the look. His eyes sparked with quick surprise as he glanced first at me and then at Nicholas. Then he
seemed to stretch his long legs out a little farther and settle
himself more comfortably.

"I can't agree," he said smoothly. " 'Twould seem to me
that with the number of fish in the sea, and truly there are a
great many, a man need only make up his mind that he wants
one, and then take it. If the hook is not right—well, there are
always nets. Or perhaps he could grasp the fish in his hands."

"I've known those who caught eels in their hands," Father
put in, "though I for one have never been able to manage it."

"Those methods may do very well for someone who cares
not what he catches," Nicholas said, "but to a discriminating
fisherman, it is often worth his while to wait."

Stephen balanced the heel of one foot on the toe of the

other, waggling the top foot to and fro. He seemed to be enjoying himself enormously. "I think it quite possible that while one fisherman is patiently waiting, another might catch the fish," he said, gazing at his foot.

"That is, of course, something to consider." Nicholas appeared to ponder the question. "However, it would make little difference unless both were after the same fish."

"Quite true," Stephen agreed. He looked straight at Nicholas, whose eyes met his squarely, and they smiled slightly at each other.

Poor Father! He seemed to have no notion that the conversation concerned anything but fish! Impatiently he looked from one young man to the other.

"Blow me," he said, "what matters it *which* fish? The important thing is to get fish—any fish! As many as possible! They are there for the taking—if we weren't such fools in the practice we would have sent shipfuls back to England by now! Aside from beaver skins, which we can best get by trading with the Indians, fishing is our best means of paying off the debt. And yet even Will Bradford says that fishing seems to be fatal for us. We have no success with it at all!"

Nicholas puffed a lazy stream of smoke toward the roof. "Some people are better fishermen than others," he said equably. "I still believe in patience."

Stephen Deane disentangled his feet and sat up. "You try your methods and I shall try mine. Enough of fishing! Has anyone heard news of Oldham or Lyford recently?"

And thus they talked of other things, and I sat quiet, trying to assort my emotions which seemed in a monstrous tangle. Elizabeth gazed at me speculatively from time to time, until at

last I rose and took the babe into a corner where I undressed
him for bed. It seemed almost to be a signal to Stephen and
Nicholas, for they rose, too, almost simultaneously, and took
polite leave of Elizabeth and Father.

"Come again," Father told them. "We enjoy visitors."

"Thank you, sir," Stephen said. "I will, indeed."

"I appreciate your kindness," Nicholas said, "and I shall
avail myself of it—often!"

And together they left, disappearing into the snow which
still fell heavily, so that, peeping on impulse through the
slightly opened door, I could not see whether they walked together or apart.

March 1625

And now has begun such a procedure as makes me
feel a very fool! It seems I no sooner set foot out of the house
than either Stephen or Nicholas appears at my side. If I manage to slip next door to visit with Bess Howland for a few
moments, I come back to find one or t'other sitting by the fire,
waiting for me! I hardly dare stop at Prissy's, for Nicholas
lodges with them, and if I go in the other direction, down the
Street, I must pass the two Common Houses, in one of which
Stephen lives with several of the unmarried men. If I am with
Stephen, we are *bound* to pass Nicholas somewhere. He will
bow formally, and then stand, with all the dreadful patience
of Job, watching us pass. If I am with Nicholas, Stephen's
blazing head will pop out from some corner, and he will greet

us with much to-do of waving and hallo-ing. I cannot see when either one accomplishes the chores that each man must do, but Elizabeth tells me that Father has remarked on how much harder they both are working than ever they did before. He is both pleased and puzzled, Elizabeth says, and has no notion of what has spurred them so noticeably.

"Did you tell him?" I asked her, for there is little sense in pretending Elizabeth is blind to these goings-on.

"No, I did not think it was necessary. When the time comes he will find out."

"*If* the time comes."

"They are two excellent young men," Elizabeth observed mildly. "They work hard for the Colony and for themselves. It should not be long before one or both will be in a position to marry."

"They are *horrible* young men! I think each is far more interested in outdoing the other than in me. I am—I am just the *fish!*"

Elizabeth laughed. "Still," she said, "it should make you proud, Constance, to have the interest of two such worthy men."

"Ma'am, each cares far more about being victor over the other, than about me. They only make me conspicuous and laughed at by all Plymouth!"

"Then perhaps 'tis up to you to show your preference, child."

"There's naught to choose between them," I said sharply. "Who would want a man whose great delight is in making a girl look a proper fool? They are impossible!"

Elizabeth stopped grinding corn in the mortar, and straight-

ened up. Half-amused and half-serious, she brandished the
pestle at me. "Do not be too vaporish, Constance. Nicholas
and Stephen are two of the most promising young men in
Plymouth. You would do well with either."

" 'Twas not so long ago you did not approve of Stephen as a
husband," I reminded her.

"It is true that I felt he did not want to give his attentions
undivided to anyone. He seemed to thrive on variety. But of
late I think perhaps he has changed his mind." Putting the
pestle down, Elizabeth came to me, laying her hand against
my cheek. "I want you to be happy, child. I want you to wed
a man of whom you can be proud. There is much to be done
in this new world, and a man and wife working together are
the best people to do it. Were we still in London you might
play the coquette with better grace, but here in Plymouth—
there are more important things to do."

I held her hand where it was, finding comfort in her touch.
"Certainly coquetting was not in my mind," I said. "I like
them both when they do not make me look ridiculous. But
somehow . . . I had hoped for more. More than just *liking,* I
mean."

"It may come, child, it may come. Perhaps if you—" But
here she was interrupted by a great shouting from the Street.
We opened the door onto the gray March day, and felt the
damp, chilling wind in our faces as we looked out. To our
right, outside our small fence, a new road cuts across the
Street, leading from the South to the North Gates in the palisade. Just on the other side of this, with its door facing away
from us, to the west, stands Governor Bradford's house. A
great many people were gathered close to the Bradfords' gate,

their attention seeming to be on the doorway, which we could not see.

"Whatever is happening?" I wondered aloud.

"Fetch our cloaks," Elizabeth said briskly. "Let us find out." Taking Caleb by the hand from where he had been playing with wooden blocks in the corner, she stepped outside. I lifted our cloaks from their pegs, and put Elizabeth's around her shoulders, adding a shawl for Caleb, and together we walked through our gate and up the Street. Elizabeth was a few steps ahead, and saw him first.

"It's John Oldham!"

"But he was forbidden to come back to Plymouth!"

"See for yourself!"

She was right. Craning through the crowd, I saw him standing at the Bradfords' door, with the Governor in the doorway. With Master Oldham were several men I had never seen before, all facing the Governor with most threatening expressions. From the direction of the Fort, Myles Standish came hurrying down the hill, with Father at his heels. Behind them came the men who had been doing their military drill when the interruption arose, and I noticed Giles and Stephen and John Cooke and John Howland and Richard Warren among them. Each carried his firing piece, and they looked as though they expected an attack by the entire Massachusetts tribe at the very least. I wondered where Nicholas was, and why he was not among the others, when I felt a touch on my shoulder and turned to see him standing beside me. I should have known!

"What's Master Oldham doing?" I asked. "I cannot see."

"He is being thoroughly unpleasant," Nicholas said. Then I heard Governor Bradford's voice, quiet, but strong.

"John Oldham, what do you here in Plymouth?"

"Why should I not be here?" Oldham's tone was defensive and rough. "My daughter lives here, more's the pity for her. If I choose to visit her, what right have you to say me nay? Is this not a free land? You have often said so!"

"It is free for those who live in consideration of others. This you did not do. It will be better for all of us if you leave now —with your friends."

Turning to the men with him, Oldham shouted, "You hear him? He thinks himself the King of New England! He has much to learn!" Then he caught sight of Myles. "Ah, here comes the doughty Captain Shrimp! See how he backs himself with his army for protection!"

There was the braying sound of laughter from these unwelcome visitors, and Nicholas said, "Constance, you and Mistress Elizabeth had best return home. I think this is not going to be pleasant."

"I would not leave for worlds!"

"Please?"

"Will you kindly stop telling me what to do? I am quite able to take care of myself, thank you!" I pulled a little away from him.

He looked at me and for a moment I feared he might pick me up bodily and move me from there, but instead he cocked an eyebrow at me and merely said, "Then see that you do!" With that he moved closer to Oldham.

There must have been further words between Master John and the Governor which I had not heard, for by now Oldham was seething with anger. He shouted madly, calling us rebels and traitors, though for what reason I could not be sure, and announcing that Plymouth was a useless, bigoted, unfriendly settlement that would come to naught. His raving became most violent, and still our Governor stood quietly, allowing Oldham to make a sorry spectacle of himself indeed. I noticed that even his own men, one by one, seemed shamed and disgusted by such a display, and gradually they sifted quietly through the Plymouth gathering and moved down the Street toward the Lower Gate. This only caused Oldham's fury to double, and he turned on his own people with such obscenities as I had never heard before. In shock, I clapped my hands over my ears, and suddenly saw Nicholas laughing at me, which made me so angered that I took my hands away again, only to hear the vilest sort of language. But then, at some signal from the Governor, Nicholas grasped Master Oldham on one side and Father took him on the other, and with the Captain leading the way, and followed by most of the men who had been training, they marched up the long hill to the Fort. With the source of the excitement gone, all of us who had stood together started drifting back toward our homes, Elizabeth and I walking side by side.

"What will they do with him?" I asked her.

"Let him cool off for a bit, I trust," she said. "Never have I known such a mad jack!"

As we walked the short distance to our house I saw that the men who had come with Oldham were now through the Lower Gate and on their way, and pointed it out to Elizabeth.

"Aye," she said. "Not even his own people have respect for him!"

The afternoon was drawing to a close and Elizabeth and I

were preparing supper when we heard the even beat of marching feet passing the house. We snatched our cloaks from the pegs again and ran outside. From where we stood in front of our house we could see a good score of our well-trained men stepping in neat formation down the hill toward the Lower Gate. Before them, firmly escorted by the Captain and John Alden, walked Oldham. As we stepped out into the Street we saw them stop just inside the Gate, where the men formed two lines, facing each other. Lifting their muskets from their shoulders they held them by the barrels as one would hold a club. Mystified, Elizabeth and I watched. Oldham, forcibly held by his escorts, was placed in position at the head of the double row, and then we heard the Captain shout an order which we did not understand. Propelled by a great push from John Alden, the unlucky man started between the guard in a stumbling run, while Myles lifted his musket and administered a staggering blow on Oldham's backside! Each of our men in turn followed suit with the butt end of his gun applied to the butt end of John Oldham, until the howling intruder finally raced through the Lower Gate and disappeared. Never had I seen such a punishment before, and I looked at Elizabeth in astonishment. She, the minx, was laughing until tears streamed down her cheeks.

"Ah, Constant," she gasped. "I wager we have seen the last of Oldham now! If only someone had thought to do that afore!" And wiping her eyes with the corner of her apron, she turned back into the house to serve the supper.

August 1625

Stephen Deane came to Father but a few moments ago and asked his permission to marry me! I can scarce believe it even yet. He strode into the house, as scrubbed and neat as he could make himself, his red hair darkened with the water he had used to try and tame it a little, and no sooner had he set foot in the door than he blurted, "Sir, I would speak with you!"

Father looked at him, surprised at his brusque tone. "Yes, man, what is it? Is there trouble?"

Stephen swallowed hard. I could see the lump in his throat as it moved. "I should like to marry Constance, sir," he said, and in truth he looked like a man about to be hanged!

"Marry her?" Father roared. "Good heavens! She's not old enough to marry!"

Elizabeth went to him, putting her hand on his arm. "Of course she is, Stephen. Constance is twenty now. You must remember."

"Twenty." He repeated the word thoughtfully. "Hmm. Well, Con, what have you to say to this?"

I knew not what to say! I looked at Stephen, so very tall and strong, his blue eyes flaming at me, and tried to imagine living with him, cooking for him, mending his clothes, bearing his babes. He stared back at me, and never did I see such a miserable face! Perhaps I was distraught, I do not know what made me do it, but I began to giggle.

"You look as if marrying me was the last thing in the world you wanted, Stephen," I said. "Is the thought so fearsome to you?"

"Fearsome! I want it more than all else! For what other reason would I come bludgeoning in here, making a fool of myself?" He wiped his forehead where the sweat stood in little beads. "So help me, I'd rather fight every Indian in New England than ask this way for a wench!"

The corners of Father's mouth twitched a little, but he looked thoughtful. " 'Twould seem you are the one to answer, Con," he said finally.

So there it was, back to me. I looked down, not quite daring to face Stephen, knowing there was naught to say but Yes, but unable to bring the word from my mouth. At last I said faintly, "You do me great honor, Stephen."

"Then you *will?*"

Not a sound would come from my throat. At last I bowed my head, and, heaven help me, Stephen took it as assent. In one stride he reached me, grasped my hand and held it against his lips.

"Bless you!" was all he said. Then he whirled on Father and shook him so vigorously by the hand that Father's head waggled up and down. "Thank you, sir! Thank you! I must go now! We will make plans in a day or so. Good evening, Mistress Hopkins, good night, Constance, good night, sir." And backing and shuffling and talking, he was out the door and gone.

"Well!" said Father.

Elizabeth came to me. "I wish you happiness, child. If ever I said aught against Stephen Deane, forgive me. He is a good man."

"Yes," I murmured, "yes, he is." I paused, and then added quickly, "By your leave, I shall go to bed now. A good night to you both."

And I came here to my chamber to think. Now, suddenly, the thought of marriage frights me! Oh, not the babes, nor the work, nor the leaving home; but to spend the rest of my life with a man—with Stephen—whom I scarcely know! I have walked with him, and talked with him, and danced with him—he has held me and kissed me—but I do not know how he *thinks!* Rarely have we talked of anything more than the lightest subjects. Even with Nicholas I have discussed more weighty matters—Nicholas! What will he say? What will he think? Will he mind that I am marrying Stephen? If I had waited, would he have asked me? He has not been in Plymouth as long as Stephen has. Perhaps he is not yet able to wed. Pox on him! It serves him right! Always mocking and teasing me! No, not always. Sometimes serious, as he was that day we walked with the baby on the shore, talking of what was good for Plymouth. But why do I think of Nicholas? It is Stephen I am going to marry. Mistress Stephen Deane. Constance Deane. The name sounds unfamiliar to me. I must sleep—if I can sleep.

Is it always like this when a girl decides to wed?

September 1625

I remember that sleep was long in coming that night, and when it came, brought with it such a dreaming that I would rather have stayed awake. Sometimes it seemed to be Stephen I dreamed of, and sometimes Nicholas, and sometimes I could not tell the one from t'other. When I rose in the morning to a ripe September day I felt as weary as though I

had never been to bed. By the time I dressed and left my
room, Giles was mending the fire. He looked up as I entered.

"So! I hear you're going to marry, Con," he said.

"Stephen asked me."

" 'Twill be strange, not having you about," my brother said
gruffly.

"It will not be for a time yet, Giles, I am sure of that. There
must be a house built, you know—perhaps it will not be until
spring."

"Perhaps," he agreed. He busied himself with blowing
gently on the flames. Between puffs he said, "Are ye happy,
Con?"

"Happy? Yes, I think so," and then, with more force, "Of
course I'm happy! Why should I not be?"

"I only wondered. I had thought—well, there is Nicholas
Snow—"

"So there is. But Master Snow has never asked me to marry
him, and Stephen did. Not, of course, that it would have
mattered if Master Snow *had* asked me—" I stopped, for even
to myself that last remark sounded strangely weak. "Where
are Elizabeth and Father?"

"Father has gone for more wood. Elizabeth took Caleb outdoors. She said he was making so much noise you would not
be able to sleep, and she wanted you to. She thought you might
be tired."

"Oh," I said. I went to where the new baby, three-month-
old Deborah, lay in the cradle, kicking her feet and smiling at
the sunbeams. Kneeling down, I played with her little fingers,
touched her tiny nose, thought for a moment of how it would
be to have a babe of my own, Stephen's babe, lying thus. I

knew not why I should feel in such a turmoil, and wondered whether I might go and talk to Prissy, but I was afraid Nicholas might be there, and somehow I was fearful of seeing him.

I was helping Elizabeth with the morning's chores when Stephen appeared. His face was wreathed in smiles, and he looked as though he had slept well and dreamlessly.

"Step outside with me a moment, Constance. I just want a word with you."

I looked at Elizabeth and she nodded. "Go, child. And do not let her hurry back, Stephen. I can manage."

"I can't stay," he said. "I just wanted to see her for a minute."

We went out the door, and taking my hand, he led me around behind the house, where the little fence, the shrubs and late flowers, made a partial screen.

"I just wanted to look at you this morning, Constant. I had to know that you were as happy as I am."

"Of course I'm happy, Stephen. And proud."

"No, let me be the one to be proud. I have been so afraid that—" He stopped suddenly.

"That what?" I asked.

"It doesn't matter now."

"But tell me. Please."

"Nick Snow. I thought he was after you too, sweetheart."

"As you say, it doesn't matter. Not now."

"We will have to wait a little while, Constance—not long."

"I know. I expected to."

"I'm leaving now with Edward Winslow and some others. We're taking one of the shallops—it's already loaded with corn—we plan to trade it eastward of here, up the Kennebec."

"Oh. How long will you be gone?"

"It's hard to say. Maybe a week, maybe two. It depends on how successful we are, and how the weather is—"

"You will be careful? And take care of yourself? Do not take a chill!"

Stephen grinned at me. "You sound like a wife. And I like it!" Then he put his two arms close about me, holding me tight against him. He felt strong, and sure, and suddenly all my doubts seemed but foolish fussing. Lifting my face to his, I whispered, "Kiss me, Stephen!"

"Did you think I would not?" he murmured, deep in his throat, and then I felt his lips, warm on mine. This time he did not need to tell me to close my eyes. We stood so, close and content, and his lips touched my eyes and my cheek and my nose, and then my lips again.

"Oh, Constance, I love you," I heard him say, though it was little more than a sigh.

"And I you, Stephen."

"I must go, sweeting. Think about me—"

"I will."

" 'Twill not be much longer before we can be together."

"I know."

"Then—good-bye, love."

"Good-bye, Stephen."

He started away from me, then paused and turned, and coming back, snatched me close and kissed me again and again.

"Stephen!" I gasped. "My cap! My hair! Please—"

"All right, I'll go now. But only so I can get back to you the sooner!"

He took my two hands, holding them tight, looking deep into my eyes. Then quickly he turned and was out the gate and started down the Street before I reached the front of the house. Looking back, he saw me and waved. I waved, too, and then he broke into a loping run and disappeared through the big gate at the foot of the Street.

As Elizabeth and I worked that morning I told her about the trading voyage Stephen was going on.

"He said Master Winslow was in charge. I do not know who else is going."

"Richard Warren, I believe, and John Cooke, and Experience Mitchell, and Thomas Prence—yes, I think Nicholas is going also."

"Nicholas Snow?" I said quickly, and could have bitten my tongue out.

Elizabeth looked at me. "Is there another Nicholas in Plymouth?" she asked.

"No, I . . . I think there is not," I muttered, and busied myself in dipping a wild duck into boiling water, the better to clean it of its feathers.

As I worked I thought of how pleasant it had been in Stephen's arms, and of how much I enjoyed being kissed. It will be like that all the time when we are married, I thought. There is nothing to fret about at all!

October 1625

But I was wrong. There was much to fret about, and there still is. The first two days after Stephen left in the shallop were clear and bright, but the third day was dark and heavy-lidded, with ponderous black clouds that covered the sky. During the morning the wind rose, swirling the dust of the Street, lashing against the houses, stripping the great branches of leaves, and laying the shrubs and bushes flat to the ground. I hoped the shallop was in some quiet, protected cove, for I recalled that though a roofing had been built to cover the corn, there was no shelter for the men. When the rain started, driving against the side of the house like a solid thing, I became so on edge that I could scarce control myself.

I tried to grind corn, but my hand shook so I could barely hold the pestle. I started to mend a rent that Giles had put in his old breeks, but the stitching botched miserably. Although the weather was sultry warm, we had to keep the shutters closed on all the windows against the rain, and the house was dark and stifling. I found myself pacing from one window to the next, as though I would be able to see from them, which I certainly could not.

"Child, what ails you?" Elizabeth asked finally. "You look like a cat hunting for a corner to drop her kittens!"

"It's the weather. I keep thinking of those men in the open boat."

"They are not children, Constant. They can care for themselves."

"I know."

And I did know, or told myself I did. They were all experienced and strong. They would put the boat in at some likely place and sit the storm out. Most assuredly they would have more sense than to try and sail in such a wind. They were probably snug in some Indian village, cursing the rain that interrupted their voyage, but not made uncomfortable by it. All these things I told myself—and continued to fret.

All that day it rained, and the wind stayed high and gusty. During the night I could hear the growling of thunder, and once the sharp crack as some tree fell headlong into the woods. The next day the wind died, but the rain continued, falling straight down in silver sheets from a leaden sky. And so it went on for four days, sometimes raining, sometimes blowing, always darkly threatening. That night, the sixth night that the men had been gone, the wind shifted and the weather cleared, bringing with it the sharp sudden promise of frost. Overnight late summer had gone and it was autumn, with a chill bite to the air.

I could think of nothing but the men in the open shallop, for certainly they would not have stayed those four days in any one place. They must have sailed some of the time, and to be soaked to the skin, as they would be even with their canvas suits, and then to sit in that cold wind with no protection at all—it seemed certain they would all have chills or fever. I reached such a state of anxiety that I made poor Elizabeth almost as concerned as I, though she insisted that the men could care for themselves, and I was a ninny to get into such a swivet.

I took to scanning the little bay at intervals all day long, yearning for some sight of the returning boat, accomplishing nothing of purpose about the house. Elizabeth suggested I copy some of her herb tea receipts, that I might take them with me when I married, but I could not sit still. She asked me to pick out flower seeds for my new garden from those we had dried, but I could not even read the names. At last, after nine days of this torment, I sat at the board, unable to eat supper. Father laid down his knife and spoon, pushed back his chair and bellowed at me.

"Girl, you will have us all fit for Bedlam! Either stop this twitching and eat your meal, or leave the table!"

I took one mouthful, knew it was useless, and slid from my stool. Taking my cloak from the peg, I went outside.

It was just beginning to dusken, and the sky was clear and shot with flame from the sunset. I pulled my cloak around me, for the air was indeed chill, and walked idly down the Street. I was almost at the Lower Gate when Edward Bangs, who was on guard duty, shouted:

"Here comes the shallop!"

Unbelieving, I looked. There, just pulling in to the shore, came the boat, mounded high with covered bales. Her little sail sprang taut, carrying her smoothly in, and one of the men—John Cooke—jumped over the side and beached her neatly on the sand. Unable to move, I stood just outside the Gate. There were Edward Winslow and Richard Warren, there was Experience Mitchell, and, beside him, Tom Prence. And there were the two bright heads—the flaxen and the flame.

I can never explain what happened next. My breath caught in my throat, my eyes brimmed with tears, and I started run-

ning. I ran as fast as I could, down the rough path that leads
to the beach, my feet slipping on the loose stones, the hood of
my cloak hanging back on my shoulders, the cloak itself
streaming behind me like a banner. Stumbling, half falling,
but always running, nearly blinded with the tears, sobbing
with relief, across the soft sand to where it was packed hard
by the water. The men were all out of the boat now, lifting
from it the great covered bales, and they turned and watched
in amazement as I came flying toward them. I saw Stephen
drop the bale he held and start quickly toward me, joy plain
on his face—yet I raced right past him, on toward that other
face. I had almost reached Nicholas, my arms stretched wide,
when John Cooke stepped in front of me. He grasped my two
wrists tight in one hand, put his other arm around my shoulders, and turned me about.

I tried desperately to pull away from him. "Let me go!" I
said frantically, and my breath caught in my throat so I could
barely hear my own voice. "Let me go, John! I must get to
Nicholas!"

The name I gasped was covered as John said loudly, "Whoa
there, Con! At that rate you will run halfway across the At-
lantic before you can stop!" He pulled my head against his
shoulder, so my words came muffled.

"It's Nicholas," I whispered. "I must see Nicholas!"

Laughing as though he had heard nary a word I spoke,
John held me tightly to him so I could not break away. "You
passed Stephen close to a league back," he said. "You are
fleeter than an Indian, Con!"

"Not Stephen," I breathed, "not Stephen—Nicholas!"

"I know," he murmured, and his lips were close to my ear.

"I know. But you cannot. Not here. You *cannot*, Constance! Do you understand me?"

Trembling, I leaned against him, my breath still choking me, my heart thudding till I thought it would press through my bodice.

"Do you hear me, Con?" he said softly. "Do you understand? Not here! Not now!"

Unable to speak, I nodded my head, close against his shoulder. I could feel his hold on me loosen. "Smile, Con. Lift your head now and smile. 'Twill be all right. Come, girl, *smile!*"

Somehow I managed to raise my head and look at him, forcing my quivering mouth to smile. John's eyes narrowed as he looked closely at me, then with another bright laugh he swung me around toward where Stephen stood, several paces away where I had passed him. I watched him walk slowly toward us, his face white, his lips parted in the awful mockery of a grin.

John's voice was gay. "Here she is, friend. Had I not stopped her I swear she would have run right off the edge of Plymouth!"

" 'Tis a great blessing I never had to race Constance to catch her," Stephen said, and his words came strained and hollow. "My thanks for your help, John." I felt his arm replace John's as I was shifted firmly from one man to the other. "It is good to see ye, lass," Stephen said. "And wait until you see what we have brought! A good seven hundred pounds of beaver if there's an ounce, and some other furs beside. And all for our worthy corn!"

"I am glad," I said, and my lips felt such stiffness they had trouble forming the simple words.

Over Stephen's shoulder I could see Nicholas standing utterly still, his dark eyes fixed on me, his mouth tight. After a moment he turned and shouldered one of the bales. I could feel myself trembling as if with an ague, and my voice was still unsteady, but I dragged my eyes back to Stephen.

"Did you—did you have a safe trip?"

"We might have asked for better weather, but we are all here and all healthy. Come, girl, you're shivering. Best you get home where it is warm."

He started walking me back toward the Street, and my feet felt like two great heavy rocks. At our gate we paused. His eyes were asking me a thousand questions, but I could not meet them.

"I must sleep tonight," he said at last. "I am more weary than I thought. I will see you tomorrow."

"Very well, Stephen," I said.

He was quiet for the space of a breath, then "I love you, Constant."

"Yes, Stephen," I murmured, and leaving him, went into the house.

November 1625

How can so much be said through silence, or so much be seen through absence? No one mentioned what had happened on the beach. In truth, I think only four of us were aware—Stephen, Nicholas, John, and I. John moved and thought more quickly than I had ever known he could, and if all Plymouth does not know my folly, I have him to thank.

But I cannot thank him. I can barely speak to him of even the most trivial things. Perhaps it would have been better had he *not* stopped me. At the least I would no longer need to dissemble. For Stephen goes on with his planning for our marriage as though naught had changed. Can it be that *he* does not know how I feel? And yet, may be that this is best. For certainly it is plain now that whatever foolhardy notions I had about Nicholas, they are not returned.

I try to avoid him—and yet see him everywhere. And often he is with some other girl. It may be Fear Brewster, or sometimes Christian Penn, another of those who came on the "Little James," and that butter-yellow head will lift and the dark eyes will meet mine with an expression I cannot read. We do not speak. It is clear he wants nothing to do with me, and no doubt considers me as little better than a trollop. A maid, bespoken by one man, showing immodest interest in another—what else am I than a trollop?

Whatever Stephen says, I have agreed to. Surely that is the least I can do for him. He says a house will be started for us soon, and asked which spot I preferred, but it made so little difference that I told him to make the decision. We kiss, and while I do not mind, it seems now that not only are my feet cold, as they were that day so long ago, but my whole body is cold.

Elizabeth asks why I do not eat and urges various decoctions on me, which I would rather take than demur. I feel always on the edge of tears, my sleep is restless, my hands tremble when I pin my hair—never have I been so wretched! And why? I am to marry Stephen, who is a good man, a strong man, a kind man, an honest man, a man who loves me, a

man I once dreamed of all day through. I do *not* care for
Nicholas! How could I, when he so plainly cares nothing for
me? He does not speak to me, he will not come near me; it is
most clear how much he dislikes me!

If only there were somewhere I could go!

December 1625

I woke this morning feeling that I must get away
from the house for a bit. The day was cold but clear, and the
sky arched light blue over the little snow that has fallen. I
could think of no errand that would take me out, since Giles
and the Two Teds do all such things as bringing water from
Town Brook and keeping wood cut for the fire, but at breakfast Father and Ted Dotey agreed it would be wise to increase
the woodpile beside the house, since the next few months will
be the coldest of the winter.

"Bring more of the twigs and small sticks this time," Elizabeth said. "They are best to use in the early morning to rouse
the fire, and you rarely leave me enough of them."

"They are a monstrous nuisance to gather," Ted complained. "They take more time than they are worth!"

"Let *me* go," I said quickly. "I should like to get out of
doors, and I can take Caleb's little sled and the small axe and
bring back enough for weeks."

"But it is bitter cold out, Constance," Elizabeth reminded
me. "And your cloak is beginning to wear thin."

"The exercise will warm me. Truly, I shall be all right. I

will bring back some of the pine cones too; they catch a fire quickest of all."

Before anyone could stop me I tied my cloak firmly, took the smallest axe, and dropped it into Caleb's sled by the door. I picked up the woven grass rope, and pulling the sled after me on the slick, thin covering of snow, I went out the North Gate, taking the beaten track that runs through the cornfields into the wood.

The air smelled clean and cold and fresh, and as the sun rose higher it sent down a little pleasant warmth. I felt better than I had in weeks, and walking quickly away from the village seemed like escape. If only I could keep on walking— away from Stephen—away from everyone and everything!

In the wood hung a beautiful, thick stillness. Even the trees were silent, with no wind to disturb their branches. The pines were green and fragrant, softening the bare outlines of other trees that stood stripped and strong in the winter morning. Hoping that action would stop my poor brain from going round and round in its unhappy circle, I started gathering up small sticks and pine cones from the ground and piling them into the sled. As I moved under the trees, bending and straightening, low branches caught at my hood until I threw it back, feeling warmer the more I moved. My white cap brushed against the rough trunk of a pine and was knocked askew, and I snatched it off, made somehow angry by this interference with my movements. Then a smaller twig caught at my hair, pulling a long strand loose from the pins, until, in a desperate desire for freedom, I pulled the other pins out and folded them into my cap, tucking it under the sticks on the sledge. My hair swung free and I shook it back, breathing quickly.

Picking up the axe, I reached high for a small branch, and holding the end with one hand, chopped it sharply clear of the tree, feeling a fierce pleasure in the action. I hacked at all the low limbs I could reach, cutting them down, kicking them together into a low pile on the ground. The movement, the sound of the axe against wood, the quick rushing of my blood as I reached and chopped and kicked, seemed to grow into some strange emotion inside of me. When I heard the crack of a twig behind me I whirled around, the axe upraised, looking probably like some wild thing with my hair streaming past my waist, tangled with bits of leaf and pine needles and twigs. Nicholas Snow stood not the sled's length away from me.

"Constance," he said.

I looked at him, hating him for intruding. "Go away," I screamed. "Go away and let me be."

"Not yet. I want to talk to you."

"I don't want to talk to you! Why can you not leave me alone?"

"I have left you alone, Constance. I have not been near you nor spoken to you for weeks."

"And I much prefer it that way!" In a blazing anger I turned and caught the end of a branch, raising the axe to cut it clean. My eyes were so filled with sudden hot tears I could barely see the branch I held, and I jumped when Nicholas' hand caught my raised arm.

"You stubborn little idiot," he growled, "do you want to cut your hand off?"

"Let go of me!"

"Give me that axe!"

"I won't!"

"Give it to me, I say!"

"And I say I won't!"

He tightened his hold on my wrist until my fingers fell open, and as the axe dropped he caught it. Driving the blade hard into the trunk of the tree, he grasped me by the shoulders, turning me toward him.

"You can't marry Stephen Deane," he said.

"Why can't I?" I flared at him, the tears stinging my eyes.

"Because you are in love with me."

"I am not in love with you! I hate you!"

"You love me, Constance."

"You are a vain, pompous oaf, and I detest you!" A huge sob caught me, and I stood there in front of him, the tears coursing down my face, my hair sticking to my wet cheeks, crying as though I could never stop, saying over and over, "I hate you! I hate you! I hate you!"

And then his two arms were tight around me until I could scarcely breathe, and I was being kissed as I had never been kissed before. The earth and the sky spun into a roaring circle, and I neither knew nor cared where I was. It seemed as though all life was there in the strong circle of his arms, and when he raised his head and loosened his hold I would have fallen had I not clutched at him.

"I love you, Constance," he said.

"No, you don't. You couldn't." My voice would not keep steady when I tried to talk, but at least the sobbing had ceased.

"Why couldn't I?"

"You have avoided me."

"Believe me, Constant, 'twas only that I thought if you were going to marry Stephen I must keep far away from you."

"I have seen you with Fear Brewster—"

"No doubt. Most likely with Christian Penn as well."

"How did you know?"

"Because I always saw you."

" 'Tis a wonder, since you keep yourself surrounded with other females!"

He kissed me again, very hard. "That is to teach you not to be sharp-spoken!" He held me close against him. "I do not think it wrong to have women for friends as well as men, Con. And if it eases your mind, both do nothing but babble into my ear of their approaching marriages."

I pulled away so I could look up at him, brushing away the tears to see more clearly. "Fear and Christian are to marry? With whom?"

"Fear has accepted Isaac Allerton, and Christian said Yes to Frank Eaton." He smiled at me, a tender mischief in his eyes. "Where have your thoughts been, poppet, that you did not hear these things?"

Confused and miserable, I could not answer, but tried only to move away from his arms. Nicholas took my two hands in one of his big ones, with the other brushing the hair from my face. "Constance," he said, "will you marry me?"

And then I burst into tears again. "I can't," I sobbed. "I'm going to marry Stephen!"

He picked me up in his arms as though I had been baby Deborah, and laying his back against the tree, slid down until he was sitting in the thin snow, holding me in his lap.

"Constance," he sighed, "I vow you are the weepingest wench I ever knew!"

"I can't help it," I gasped. "Everything is so wretched!"

"Tell me you love me, Con."

I looked up at him, his face close above mine, my cheek against his shoulder. "I love you, Nicholas," I said. "I love you, I love you, I love you, I love—" But his lips were on mine again, and it was impossible to speak.

I don't know how long we sat there. Nicholas talked to me, softly, gently, telling me all the things I needed to hear. That I could not marry Stephen when I did not love him, that it would be sinfully wrong. That he, Nicholas, had known from the moment he first saw me that he would someday be my husband.

"Husband," I repeated after him. "What a beautiful word!" And then, pulling away, I said, "But you could not have liked me then! I was impossible to you that first day! I said monstrous things!"

"You did indeed. With your eyes as big as trenchers and as dark as the midnight sea."

"And it was none of my business, really."

"Quite true."

I remembered back to the summer meeting. "You called me a shrew!"

"I called you a *sweet* shrew," he corrected. "Surely that was far better than you deserved."

I burrowed my cheek into his shoulder, delighting in the warmth of his body, and the wonderful male smell of him. "Why did you never tell me before?"

"Tell you what?" Idly his fingers twisted a long strand of my hair.

"That you loved me, that you wanted to marry me."

"I believe a man should be able to support a wife before he asks for one."

"Can you now?"

"I think so. Since Plymouth provides little in the way of costly baubles to entice a wife, we will manage."

"When can we be married?"

"What a brazenly impatient lass I've found! When do you want to be married?"

"Right this very moment," I said, sighing blissfully.

Nicholas pretended shock. "Constance! That is hardly a seemly remark for a modest girl."

"I don't want you ever to leave me."

"Nor will I. Let me build a house for us."

"Yes. A house of our own. I do not want to live with anyone else but you. And as soon as it is built, then will we be married?"

"Just as soon."

"Oh, Nicholas, I *am* so glad you found me!"

"Sweet love," he murmured very softly. Then he shifted uneasily.

"What is it, Nicholas? Am I too heavy to hold?"

"Heavy? No heavier than a featherweight. No, my love, the truth of the matter is that sitting in the snow is making my backside most uncommon cold!"

Startled, I twisted off his lap, coming to my knees on the ground beside him, and then I burst into laughter. Nicholas got to his feet, brushing the light snow from the seat of his breeches, stamping up and down to warm himself, looking at me aggrieved.

"It is surely not that humorous," he said. "It is, in fact, most exceedingly uncomfortable!"

"But it is comical, Nicholas! You sitting there so bravely, making sweet speeches to me—and freezing!" The laughter rolled out of me, while he stood looking down at me. Then he reached down and pulled me to my feet.

"I pray we will laugh often together, Constant," he said, and his voice was husky. "I love you so much, I want so much to make you happy! You are beautiful when you laugh!" He twisted his hands in my hair, pulling my face close to his, and kissed me again until I felt too weak to move. "Now come," he said, releasing me. "We have things to do."

While I tried to coil my hair again, making a poor job of it with no comb but my fingers, Nicholas loaded the wood on the sled, and pulled the axe from the tree, and so, at last, we started home. We walked together, our hands linked, the sled pulled behind us.

"Thank God I came today, Constant," he said.

"Why did you?"

"Because I had to talk to you. I could stay away no longer."

"But how did you know where I was?"

"I saw you go out the gate this morning."

"But you came right to me in the wood. How could you tell where to find me?"

He looked at me, one eyebrow raised. "Look down, my beautiful, witless wench," he said.

I looked and blushed. The tracks I had made were sharply clear in the thin snowcrust, footprints, outlined with the streaks made by the sled.

"Oh," I said, very softly.

When we entered through the palisade's North Gate again and turned left, going directly to my own gate, I was appalled at the length of the afternoon shadows. How long had we been gone? I had no notion. With Nicholas' hand gripping mine tightly, I pushed open our door. Stephen lounged there before the fire, talking with Father. Nicholas followed me into the house.

"I am glad you are both here," he said. "There is something I think we must discuss."

Stephen rose slowly, his eyes on mine. "Yes," he said. "I have known for some time that there was."

January 1626

How beautiful Plymouth is, held tight in winter! It seems as though all the world within my sight is decking itself in wedding finery. The snow glitters under the cold midwinter sun, shafting with a million diamond lights that brighten the house as I sit snugly by the chimney, sewing on my marriage gown. It is of a beautiful rich, deep red, cut from a great length of the linsey-woolsey that Nicholas gave me— the same cloth we talked of that night at the Aldens'. Elizabeth has helped me fit the bodice, which clings warm and close, the skirt falling in soft fullness to my ankles.

If I open the door onto the cold, still air I can hear the clear ring of hammer on nail as the house where Nicholas and I will live grows each day. Father has put the Two Teds to working on it, saying gruffly that with no farming to be done in the dead of winter they may as well be useful as to putter their time away. Since neither one has ever dawdled in the six years they have been with Father, I know perfectly well he is doing extra chores that they may be released to help Nicholas.

The house is tucked in at the foot of the Street, just between the home where Christian and Francis Eaton now live, and the great palisade, across from the Common Storehouse. Each day I walk down to note the progress, and Nicholas and I stand hand in hand while he points out to me the latest achievements. I can scarce believe that we will truly live there together!

Often in the evenings we walk up the Street to see the Aldens, where John is making us a most tremendous cupboard. He has polished the wood until it gleams, and the smooth shelves seem to be waiting for the linens, the coverlets, the trenchers, that I shall keep there. Although Nicholas commissioned John to build the piece, John will not hear of taking payment.

"Surely a friend can give the work of his own hands," he told us.

"But so *much* work, John! 'Tis far too large a gift!"

Priscilla paused from skimming cream off the top of the milk pans to laugh at us. "Truth," she said, "it is worth it just to see you both so happy. Never had I seen two such woebegone faces as you carried before you came to your senses! It seems, Constant, that you and I had great difficulty allowing ourselves to be caught by the proper man!"

One night at the Aldens' we sat and talked with John and Prissy as we often do, discussing Plymouth, and its gradual, steady growth. The house that Nicholas is building for us will be the seventeenth dwelling on the Street, and in addition there are the two Common Houses, where several of the unmarried men live, and the Common Storehouse, filled with the rich harvest from the various fields. The first tiny homes have been enlarged as the years have slipped by, and the raw look of the clapboards has weathered to soft, pleasant gray tones. The little family gardens, snow-covered now, burgeon in spring with flowers and herbs and berries, making of the Street a colorful, fragrant place.

To some of the houses (and Father's among them, of a surety) have been added brewing rooms, since the barley has prospered so that there can be heady, golden beer. Every small yard how boasts its own hencoop filled with chickens, for the "Charity's" last trip saw the town supplied with a great collection of fowl, as well as a few more cattle, and pigs and goats. Such luxuries as fresh milk and butter, cheese and cream and eggs, are divided daily between the households (and if only they could have come in time for baby Oceanus!)—and 'twill not be long before there can be bacon and ham and beef in every Plymouth home.

"I heard today the Governor plans to form the townspeople into groups of twelve or so, giving each group an equal amount of livestock." John was speaking, puffing comfortably on his long pipe. "From there it should not take long for each family to have its own beasts."

Nicholas, sitting beside me on the settle, took my hand in his, touching my fingers absently. "And that will lead in time to other towns," he said. "As we cultivate the acres around Plymouth we must go farther and farther away to find pasture for the animals."

I felt most troubled of a sudden. "But I don't understand," I said. "Do you mean that this . . . this progress for Plymouth, more settlers, and the livestock, and such things, do you mean that these will make an *end* to the town?"

Nicholas tightened his hand on mine. "I am sure not. As I

see it, Plymouth will gain in importance as the central town for many miles around. As other new settlements are formed, I should think that Plymouth will still, for many years to come, be the seat of government and trading and all like activities. Ships will still sail into Plymouth Harbor, newcomers will arrive here—you need not fret, Con. I feel that Plymouth has only begun to grow. And every new village that is born in the miles around here will strengthen her still more."

"It even seems as if a few more years would see the end of the debt to London," John added. "And when we are no longer beholden to anyone but ourselves—"

"It will be heaven, indeed!" Prissy finished for him. "You are sure, John? The debt is truly lessening?"

"Constantly. Our fishing has improved . . ."

Nicholas looked at me and grinned, squeezing my hand. "Indeed it has!" he said softly.

". . . and greater quantities are being sent to England with every ship that sails," John went on. "What is more, this winter's cold has made the furs thicker and better than ever, bringing a greater price in England. With our good supply of corn for trading, Massasoit's men are pleased to devote their time to trapping for us."

"And a good thing it is," I said, "for surely Englishmen are better farmers than trappers!"

Nicholas laughed as he rose to his feet and lifted me to mine. "Oh, I don't know," he said. "I am English, and look what I caught!"

We said good night to the Aldens and went outside. The winter stars hung close and brilliant as Nicholas walked me home. I think I hold all the happiness the world can give.

February 1626

I wakened early, and knew immediately what day it was. My wedding day! For a moment, with my eyes still closed, I lay curled tight, hugging my happiness to me. Then in a fury of impatience I slipped from bed to help Elizabeth with breakfast.

As soon as it was done we shooed the men from the house, and Elizabeth helped me fill our largest wooden tub with water we had been heating. Then, while she scoured the trenchers, refusing my help, I bathed carefully and washed my hair. I was drying it in front of the fire, dressed in my fresh white shift and drawers and petticoats, my new white knitted stockings tied tight above my knees, when there came a tap at the door. Throwing me my cloak to hide my immodesty, Elizabeth opened the door to find Minnetuxet standing there. I jumped up, letting the cloak fall to the floor in my joy at seeing her, and 'twas not until I was holding both her hands in mine that I noticed the babe strapped to her back in the little hooded carrier the Indian women use.

"Minnetuxet! You have a . . . a *papoose!*"

She laughed shyly. "Aye."

"Oh, let me see him! May I hold him? Her?"

"Him." Deftly she slipped her arms from the plaited leather loops, and laying the carrier on the table, lifted the child from his warm nest while Elizabeth and I watched with pleasure. She laid him in my arms, and I looked down at the soft, round, dusky face. The infant's bright black eyes gazed at me wonderingly, and then his mouth opened in the endearing crooked smile of all babies.

"He is beautiful!" I said. "And so strong!" I looked at Minnetuxet, who watched the child with pride. "And you. You are happy?"

"Most happy," she said softly.

Elizabeth took the babe from me and carried him to where little Deborah sat playing on the floor. Whilst the two children inspected each other solemnly I drew Minnetuxet toward the fire where we could sit together.

"I am to be married today," I said, "to Nicholas Snow."

"I know."

I was astonished. "How could you know?"

"The man John Cooke, your friend. He sent word by Samoset, my father. He said you would want Minnetuxet to know."

My mind flashed back to that evening on the beach when my heart had tried to carry my feet straight to Nicholas, and John had stopped me.

"Yes, he is a friend," I said. "And I cannot thank him enough for getting a message to you! You will stay for my wedding?"

"Minnetuxet cannot stay. Snow comes, and baby must be safe at home. But there is small gift for you."

Going to her son's carrier she reached into it, bringing forth something white which she handed to me. As I took it my fingers went deep into fur—a rounded hood, cleverly fashioned, with a thin white leather thong to tie it beneath the chin. I held it against my face to feel its softness.

"Oh, Minnetuxet! It is beautiful! But . . . *white* fur? Surely this is fox, but I have never seen a white one—"

"Minnetuxet's man go on hunting trip far north. Bring this back. It is for you."

My hair was close to dry, and I slipped the hood on my head, where it fitted snugly. "Oh, if only I could *see*," I cried. "Mother, how does it *look*?"

Elizabeth smiled. "Just as you would want it to," she said. It seemed no time at all before Minnetuxet said she must go.

"You will come back?" I begged.

"When Constance have baby, Minnetuxet will come."

I blushed, ridiculously. "But . . . how will you know?"

"Constance have no fear. Minnetuxet will know."

And somehow, I am sure she will.

The rest of the day Elizabeth and I spent preparing the food to be served after the wedding, cleaning the house until it shone, and pushing the long board against the wall to make room for the guests who would be there. Late in the afternoon, when the winter dark crept in and the men were free of their chores, I put on my new deep crimson gown, with a beautiful lace-edged kerchief Elizabeth had made me, and coiled my hair neatly, fitting it under the white fur hood.

Giles, tall and sober, held my cloak for me—which I think he has never done before for anyone—and I took Father's arm, and Giles took Elizabeth who carried Deborah, and little Caleb followed with the Two Teds, and together we walked the short distance to Governor Bradford's house. When the door opened and I saw Nicholas standing there, I wanted so much to run to him that 'twas all I could do to walk across the room in modest manner, speaking to John and Prissy, to Alice Bradford, and to the Governor.

And then Nicholas and I stood hand in hand, and in a daze of happiness I heard Will Bradford's deep and quiet voice say the few simple words of the Plymouth service.

It seemed no more than minutes before we were back in Father's house, and everyone was gathering round the board, and Father was pouring tankards of his beer and fragrant wine, and Elizabeth and Prissy were passing round the food, and Ted Dotey brought out his flute and suddenly there was high sweet music, and the Cookes came in, and the Winslows, and the Brewsters, and then I saw Stephen Deane's red hair above the crowd and looked aghast, till Nicholas, close beside me, said, "I asked him to come, Con. You do not mind?"

I shook my head, and could not even answer with all the toasts, and the talk, and the movement and the merriment around me. And then, just a little later, I saw Stephen dancing with pretty little Jane Cooke, and over her dark head his eyes met mine and he gave me one most devilish wink! I could not help it—I laughed aloud, and across the room Stephen laughed too. How great a cure for many things is shared laughter!

And then Nicholas was slipping my cloak about my shoulders, and Elizabeth was kissing me on the cheek, and Father was coughing the odd little choking cough that emotion gives him, and he too kissed me, and then there was Giles—my brother—and he was holding both my hands.

"I know I need not wish you happiness, Con," he said, "you have it." And then he laid my hands in my husband's, and Nicholas and I went quickly out of the door.

The sudden cold air was filled with white.

"Look!" I cried. "It is snowing!"

" 'Tis a good omen for us," Nicholas said, "for you are a Snow now, also."

He lifted the edge of his heavy cloak and put his arm about me, so that I walked close against him, wrapped warm in my cloak and his. We left Father's gate, and turning left, walked down the Street, past the Howlands' house, and Dr. Fuller's, and then the Warrens' and the Soules', and lastly Francis and Christian Eaton's—and then we entered ours.

A fire burned bright on our hearth, casting flickering shadows on the smooth wooden walls. Some of Nicholas' clothes hung on pegs, and next to them hung some of mine, which looked exciting and strange. There were our pots and skillet and kettles hung on the trammels, there stood our table—the wood white and unstained. There were four stools—we had no chair yet—and there, looming so large it seemed to dominate the room, stood our bed. Against one wall was the chest that Father had asked Francis Eaton, who is an excellent carpenter, to make for us, and there was the handsome tall cupboard that John Alden had given us. I stood in the middle of the room, gazing around me in complete joy, for though I had watched the progress of the house, and had even brought my clothes here and put them away, it was only now that I really saw it as my *home*—mine and Nicholas's!

"I have a surprise for you," Nicholas said.

"There is no room in my heart for new surprises," I told him. "If I know any more happiness, I shall burst!"

"Still, look in the bottom of the cupboard."

His face was so filled with anticipation that I ran to the

cupboard, and kneeling down, opened the doors at the bottom. My few sheets were neatly folded there, scented with some of Elizabeth's dried lavender, and on top of them lay a small flat parcel wrapped in a piece of deerskin. I touched it, looking up over my shoulder at Nicholas.

"Is it this?"

"Aye. Open it."

Lifting the package out, I rose and gently folded the leather back. There, winking brilliantly in the firelight, lay a thin, polished silver disk, nigh as large as my spread hand. As I stood with it flat upon my palm I could see a corner of our tall cupboard reflected on its surface.

"Nicholas!" I breathed. "A mirror!"

"I wanted you to see what a beautiful woman I married," he said, and taking my hand, led me to the fireside. "Look."

He held the mirror in front of me, so that—for the first time in nigh seven years—I saw my own face clearly. In astonishment I stared! The face I saw there—in truth, I *must* say it—was lovely! Long and oval, the eyes very large and darkly blue, the cheekbones high, the nose long and slender, the mouth full and soft and tremulous. I could not imagine it was my own face—it seemed like that of some radiant stranger, someone I had never seen or known before. Then I looked closer, and turned to Nicholas indignantly.

"There is a smudge on my chin," I said, "and you never told me!"

Open-mouthed, Nicholas looked at me for a moment, and then broke into laughter.

"I show her the bonniest bride in the world and she complains of a smudge on her chin," he shouted.

And then he took the mirror from me and laid it on the table and put his arms about me, holding me close. "My wife," he whispered, very softly, suddenly sober.

And his head bent down to me, and just before I closed my eyes under his kiss, a log snapped in the fire and a glittering great explosion of sparks showered up the chimney.

About the Author

While Patricia Clapp Cone, wife of a descendant of Constance Hopkins, was typing a genealogical report for a relative, she became fascinated by a copy of Stephen Hopkins' will. One thing led to another, and soon she was visiting London and Leyden and the site of the Plymouth Plantation in Massachusetts. Somehow, she felt, she must tell the story of this settlement. Although she had written many plays for children, Mrs. Cone sensed that this tale would need a different mode of expression. One night, making her usual diary entry, she realized that an imaginary journal kept by Stephen Hopkins' daughter, Constance, would be the perfect format. After all, in those days, journals were kept by many, many people.

Mrs. Cone grew up in what she terms "formal Brownstone Boston," and later attended the Columbia University School of Journalism. She lives in New Jersey.